A

THE COLONEL'S FAMILY WITHDRAWN

D0167249

Some other books from Norvik Press

Sigbjørn Obstfelder: *A Priest's Diary* (translated by James McFarlane)
Hjalmar Söderberg: *Short stories* (translated by Carl Lofmark)
Annegret Heitmann (ed.): *No Man's Land. An Anthology of Modern Danish Women's Literature*
P C Jersild: *A Living Soul* (translated by Rika Lesser)
Sara Lidman: *Naboth's Stone* (translated by Joan Tate)
Selma Lagerlöf: *The Löwensköld Ring* (translated by Linda Schenck)
Villy Sørensen: *Harmless Tales* (translated by Paula Hostrup-Jessen)
Camilla Collett: *The District Governor's Daughters* (translated by Kirsten Seaver)
Jens Bjørneboe: *The Sharks* (translated by Esther Greenleaf Mürer)
Jørgen-Frantz Jacobsen: *Barbara* (translated by George Johnson)
Janet Garton & Henning Sehmsdorf (eds. and trans.): *New Norwegian Plays* (by Peder W.Cappelen, Edvard Hoem, Cecilie Løveid and Bjørg Vik)
Gunilla Anderman (ed.): *New Swedish Plays* (by Ingmar Bergman, Stig Larsson, Lars Norén and Agneta Pleijel)
Kjell Askildsen: *A Sudden Liberating Thought* (translated by Sverre Lyngstad)
Svend Åge Madsen: *Days with Diam* (translated by W. Glyn Jones)
Christopher Moseley (ed.) *From Baltic Shores*
Agnar Thordarsson: *Called Home* (translated by Robert Kellogg)
Janet Garton (ed.): *Contemporary Norwegian Women's Writing.*

The logo of Norvik Press is based on a drawing by Egil Bakka (University of Bergen) of a Viking ornament in gold, paper thin, with impressed figures (size 16x21mm). It was found in 1897 at Hauge, Klepp, Rogaland, and is now in the collection of the Historisk museum, University of Bergen (inv.no. 5392). It depicts a love scene, possibly (according to Magnus Olsen) between the fertility god Freyr and the maiden Gerðr; the large penannular brooch of the man's cloak dates the work as being most likely 10th century.

Cover illustration: Painting by an unknown artist from the 1830s. National Museum of Finland.

THE COLONEL'S FAMILY

by

FREDRIKA BREMER

Translated and with an Afterword by

Sarah Death

Norvik Press
1995

Original title : *Familjen H**** (1831) by Fredrika Bremer.
© Sarah Death 1995: English translation of Fredrika Bremer, *The Colonel's Family*.

British Library Cataloguing in Publication Data
   Bremer, Fredrika
     Colonel's Family
     I. Title.   Death, Sarah G.
     839.736 [F]
     ISBN 1-870041-31-3

First published in 1995 by Norvik Press, University of East Anglia, Norwich, NR4 7TJ, England
Managing Editors: James McFarlane and Janet Garton

Norvik Press has been established with financial support from the University of East Anglia, the Danish Ministry for Cultural Affairs, The Norwegian Cultural Department, and the Swedish Institute. Publication of this volume has been aided by a grant from the Swedish Institute.

Printed in Great Britain by Page Bros. (Norwich) Ltd., Norwich, UK.

Part One

Arrival – Tea – Portraits.

One evening at the end of February 1829 I found myself at Skanstull Gate in a little open sleigh at the height of a dreadful snowstorm, frozen, exhausted, and wishing I were asleep. I had to wait for the statutory visit of the customs inspector before I could enter the Swedish capital. My dear young reader, your sympathetic soul will appreciate that I was in a most unenviable position.

My poor horse had the strangles and was coughing and snorting. The farmhand who was my driver hugged himself to keep warm. The storm howled and the snow swirled around us. I closed my eyes and waited, as often before. I have always found that to be the best policy in any storm that you happen to be caught in, indoors or out. At last, slow steps were heard crunching through the snow. The inspector approached with his lantern in his hand. He had a red nose and looked unhappy. I had a banknote in my hand which I hoped to slip into his to buy myself some peace and an undisturbed passage. He drew back his hand. 'There is no need,' he said, shortly but politely. 'I shall not trouble you long,' he continued, as he began lifting my pelts and sorting through my packages and boxes. I was mortified at finding myself obliged to get out. In a bad temper and in secret pleasure at his discomfort, I stuffed my banknote back into my reticule and thought: Well then, he need have nothing for his trouble!

My sociable driver meanwhile struck up a conversation with him: 'Terrible old weather tonight, guv'nor!'

'Yes.'

'I'd have thought you'd have been better off sitting at home in your warm cottage taking a drink, than freezing your fingers off holding us up here, which you'll get no thanks for.'

No reply.

'I'd give a lot to be sitting by the warm stove with the wife eating my Sunday porridge. That'd be to my taste, sir.'

'I'm sure it would.'

'Are you married, guv'nor?'

'Yes.'

'Children?'

'Yes.'

'Well, how many then?'

'Four.' And a deep sigh followed the answer.

'Four! You've mouths enough to feed then. Hah! Thought you'd found some contraband there, did you? Cheese, my dear sir, cheese, you see. Yes, you may well lick your lips – I bet you'd rather have a bite of that than of the moon, sir. Now can't you see that's just a tub of butter? Do you have to dip your fingers in that brine?'

Once the inspector had convinced himself that the contents of the sleigh consisted chiefly of a great many cheeses, loaves and ginger biscuits, he gave me his hand to help me back in and wrapped the pelts around me. My irritation had completely vanished meanwhile. It is the poor inspector's duty, I thought, to be the traveller's plague and torment, and this one has been mine, in the politest possible way. And as he continued conscientiously and neatly restoring everything to its former order, a host of ideas surfaced in my mind, which put me in even gentler mood. The nose red with cold, the dejected appearance, the stiff fingers, the four children, the snowstorm, the dreadful dark evening, they all danced before me like shadows in a camera obscura and softened my heart. I fumbled again for my banknote; I thought of a loaf and a cheese for the four children's supper; but as I fumbled, as I thought, the inspector opened the barrier, lifted his hat politely, and I was carried off past the customs post intending to call out 'Stop!', but failing. With heavy heart and ill at ease, as if I had lost something valuable along the way, I was carried through the city, and saw illuminated before me in the swirling white snow the nose red with cold and the sad face which I could so easily have cheered up, however fleetingly.

How many opportunities to do a good deed, great or small, does indecision let us pass by? As we are asking ourselves 'Shall I or shan't I?', the moment is lost and the flower of happiness we could have offered has withered, and can seldom be revived by our tears of remorse.

These were my dejected thoughts as my sleigh went slowly through the deep mud of the streets, often sliding into the gutter and requiring great effort to haul it out again. The storm blew out the street lamps, leaving only the bright candles in the shop

9

windows to light our way. Here I saw a gentleman almost losing his coat and, as he wrapped it more tightly about him, his hat blew off. There I spied a woman gripping the brim of her hat with one hand and her pelisse with the other, walking boldly but blindly right into a fruit stall, bringing a sharp 'Watch your step!' from the pinched woman in charge of it.

Here I heard the howl of a dog, there the oath of a man who had driven his cart into someone else's. A little boy went whistling through the noise of the blizzard, his calm child's mind undisturbed by the din. Now and then a covered sleigh with lamps blazing shot past like a comet on its brilliant path, making both man and beast give way. This was all that I saw and heard that evening of our great and splendid capital. To cheer myself up, I began thinking of the dear family which would soon receive me into its bosom, the happy occasion that brought me there, and any other bright, happy, heart-warming thoughts I could summon to mind. At last my sleigh came to a halt. The driver cried 'This is it!'. 'Here at last!' was my delighted reaction, and soon I heard the sound of many happy voices calling out: 'Hello, hello! Good evening to you! Welcome, welcome!' I was taken to a lovely warm room where I, my loaves, cheeses and ginger biscuits were all given a hearty welcome. Half an hour later I was sitting in a pretty, well-lit drawing room, where Colonel H*** and his family were gathered. It was teatime, and a cloud of steam swirled up from the hot tea urn and hung there above the shining teacups. Baskets piled with cakes, biscuits and wafers covered the broad tea table. Telemachus arriving from Tartar at the Elysian fields could not have felt greater satisfaction than I did, reaching the friendly harbour of the tea table after my stormy journey. The attractive, happy people moving about me, the pleasant room, the bright candles which often help to lighten the heart, the lovely, warming drink I was enjoying – it was all splendid, reviving, refreshing, it was all ... But can you believe it, dear reader, the frozen nose back at the customs post appeared on the rim of my teacup in the midst of my enjoyment, and brought a bitter taste to my nectar? Indeed it did – and I think I would have been less startled if I had seen my own double. To recover my composure, I resolved, 'I will put right my omission tomorrow.' Content with my good intentions for the morrow, I sat quietly in a corner as I usually do, knitting a stocking, taking a sip of tea now and then from the cup on the small table beside me, watching attentively but unnoticed the picture of family life in front of me. Colonel H*** sat at one end of the sofa playing patience, *blocade de Copenhague* I think. He was tall and powerfully built, but worn thin and with an unhealthy look. His features were noble, and the look in his deeply sunken eyes was penetrating but calm, with an expression of almost unworldly goodness, especially when he looked at his children. Though he seldom spoke, and never made speeches, his slow but gently emphatic words commanded great respect. Seriousness and gentleness were his dominant characteristics. He held himself strangely upright, and I have always fancied that this was not so much his military bearing as a reflection of his uncompromisingly upright and honest character.

He took no part in the lively conversation going on between his children that evening, but occasionally let slip some droll comment, accompanied by a look which combined mischievous humour with such tolerant tenderness that the recipient felt both embarrassed and pleased.

His wife (Her Ladyship, as I still feel I must call her), Her Ladyship sat at the other end of the sofa, doing her netting work, distractedly. She could scarcely have been a beauty even in her youth, but there was something kind and lively about her that was a pleasure to look at, especially when she spoke. There was something troubled about her too, and it showed in her eyes. They revealed a heart continually weighed down by that endless list of cares and concerns which is the lot of a wife, mother and housekeeper. It begins with husband and children, extends to every home and household duty down to the smallest detail, and does not even end with that speck of dust which always needs blowing away yet always settles again.

Her Ladyship's tender, troubled look contained both joy and pain that evening as it rested on Emilia, her eldest daughter. A kindly smile was on her lips, her eyes glistened with tears, both smile and tears expressing maternal warmth and devotion.

Emilia seemed oblivious to her mother's gaze, and was completely composed as her pretty white hands served the tea. She adopted her most dignified manner as she tried to stop her brother Carl creating as much havoc among the tea things as he claimed there was in his sweet sister's head. She was of medium height, sturdy but well-proportioned. Blonde, fair-skinned, not beautiful in the usual sense, she had an attractive face with an expression of innocence, goodness and sincerity. She seemed to have inherited her father's calm disposition, but combined it with greater gaiety, and laughter frequently cut through her assumed dignity, laughter so genuine that it infected everyone around her.

Laughter is not becoming to many people; so often they use handkerchiefs to hide the screwed up eyes and wide open mouth caused by this expression of their joy. Emilia would have despised such precautions even had she needed them – even in such small things she was too straightforward and honest ever to play the coquette. But in this case she had absolutely no need to anyway, for her laugh was so infinitely charming, both because it was so naive and genuine, and because it displayed the loveliest white teeth that have ever graced a pretty mouth – not that she gave any thought to all that.

Had I been a man, my first thought on seeing Emilia would have been: That's the wife for me! (If she will consent, of course). And yet, Emilia was not always quite what she seemed, or rather, she possessed her fair share of those inconsistencies which are interwoven with, and part of, even the noblest of human natures, like knots in an otherwise finely and carefully woven cloth. What is more, Emilia was no longer in the first flush of youth and you, my sixteen-year-old reader, may well consider her very, very old. 'How old was she then?', you may ask. She had just passed her twenty-sixth birthday. 'Ooh, how dreadful! She was really, really old then!' Not so very dreadful, not so very old, my rosebud. She was simply a rose in full bloom, and that view was shared by Mr. ..., but more of that later.

I pity the artist with the difficult task of painting Julie's portrait, for she is a *perpetuum mobile* in more than one respect. One moment she would be playing tricks on her brother, who never failed to pay her back, the next she would be busy with her sisters. From time to time, she would trim the candles, putting them out in order to have the pleasure of lighting them again. She would arrange and disarrange the ribbons on her mother's peignoir and would repeatedly creep up behind the Colonel, put her arm around his neck and kiss his forehead. His cry of 'Let me be, child!' would do nothing to deter her from returning a short time later.

A dainty little head with a plaited crown of blonde hair, lively blue eyes, dark eyebrows and lashes, a shapely nose with a distinguished little curve, a somewhat large but pretty mouth, petite, with small hands, and small feet more eager to dance than to walk – here you have Julie at the age of eighteen.

Brother Carl – I do beg his pardon, Cornet Carl – was three cubits tall, well-built and supple, thanks to nature, gymnastics and Julie. He had many unshakeable convictions, but three firm favourites: 1. That the Swedish people are the foremost and finest people in Europe. No one in the family disputes this. 2. That he can never fall in love, as he has reached the age of twenty without once having felt his heart pounding, while many of his lucky comrades have been madly in love. 'Just you wait!' says the Colonel. Julie says that one day he'll be head over heels in love. Emilia sighs and begs God to preserve him. 3. That he is so ugly that he even frightens horses. Julie says that this could prove very helpful in a surprise encounter with hostile cavalry, but she, her sisters and many others consider the open, honest, manly expression in her brother's face to be ample compensation for any lack of beauty in his features. To his secret pleasure, she often says how awfully ugly and unbearable she finds that lifeless, expressionless Apollo Mr. P*. Cornet Carl loves his sisters dearly and does them all the services in his power, particularly that of exercising their patience.

The youngest of the daughters, seventeen-year-old Helena, sat beside her father. Your first instinct would be to pity her, your second to congratulate her. She was plain and hunch-backed, but wisdom and cheerfulness shone in her unusually clear eyes. She seemed to possess a calm and resolute character and a clear-sighted, balanced and optimistic disposition, all greater guarantors of a peaceful, happy life than those dazzling, superficial charms celebrated and adored by the world. She was working busily on a white silken dress , and only looked up from her sewing to give a friendly, meaningful nod to Emilia, or to regard her father with reverent, almost adoring tenderness. It almost seemed that this child, the one least favoured by Mother Nature, was the one the Colonel loved best, for often when Helena leant her head on her father's shoulder and looked up at him so lovingly, he bent forward and kissed her forehead with an expression too tender to describe.

On the other side of the Colonel sat another young lady – his niece. She could have been mistaken for a classical statue: beautiful, marble-white and unmoving. No lovelier dark eyes than hers could be found, yet she certainly deserved our pity. Those beautiful eyes would never again see the light. For four years she had been afflicted with cataracts. It was hard to tell whether storm or calm lay in the depths of her soul, for its mirrors were in darkness and there was something stiff, cold and almost lifeless about her appearance that repelled any questioning gaze. To me it appeared that, in her despair at the moment Fate had dealt its blow: 'You shall no more see the light!', her pride had made her take a solemn vow that no one should see her pain.

One more little group must be included in my picture, and that is the one in the background consisting of Master Pinch, the tutor, and his disciples. Master Pinch was a man of few words, mild-mannered, well-read, short-sighted, snub-nosed and absent-minded. His disciples, little Axel and little Claes, the Colonel's youngest sons, were remarkable for their rude health and extreme clumsiness, which within the family had earned them the title the Puddings.

In spite of having set his wig on fire three times already, Master Pinch still sat undaunted with his nose in his book precariously close to the candle. The Puddings were eating biscuits and playing Beggar My Neighbour, while waiting for a fourth conflagration on their tutor's head, exchanging conspiratorial nudges and whispers of, 'Now look! Just wait and see! It must go now!'

I can't tell you how much I am longing to know if any of my young readers, genuinely curious or just being polite, would like some further description of that person who is sitting in one corner of the drawing room, keeping quiet, knitting, taking an occasional sip of tea and giving you her commentary on the rest of the company.

In order not to disappoint any reader who might be hoping for it, I shall sketch this figure for you too. She belongs to that class of people whose lives, as a rather foolish colleague of mine once remarked, run thus: 'At times you are expected to give the impression of being everywhere, at others you must appear not to exist.' This curious life is usually led by a person who, without belonging to the family, is drawn into it as a companion, a helpmate, a general factotum in sickness and in health. I can give you a brief description of such a person, but so as not to leave her without a position in our title-conscious society, I shall call her the family adviser. Her sphere of activity is wide-ranging, as you will see. She is expected to put her mind, her hand, her nose, her hopes into everything, but no-one must notice. If the master of the house is in a foul mood, she is pushed forward, either in her capacity as lightning conductor, or as a gust of wind whose duty is to blow away the storm. If the mistress has the vapours, she is as indispensable as the eau de cologne bottle. If the daughters have troubles, she is there to share them. If they have any little wishes, plans and projects, then she is the mouthpiece through which they can reach rather deaf ears. If the children are screaming, she is sent to quieten them; if they won't sleep, she must tell them stories. If someone is ill, she sits up; she runs errands for the whole family, and must be ready with good advice for one and all on every occasion. She must keep watch over the kitchen even as she serves the coffee in the drawing room. If fine guests are expected and the whole house is on parade, she – disappears. No-one knows where she is, any more than they know where the smoke goes after it rises from the chimney, but the effects of her invisible presence must continue to be felt. The decorative dinner table is not the place for the saucepan in which the fruit fool has been thickened; that must remain on the kitchen stove, and the family adviser shares its lot, for she too must make things wholesome and pleasant, but do without the credit. If she can do that with Stoic perseverance and resignation, her existence can often be as interesting for her as it is important for the family. It is true that she must be humble and silent, close doors quietly, make less noise than a fly, on no account buzz intimidatingly around people, and yawn as little as is humanly possible. But on the other hand, she is free, with a little care, to use her eyes and ears, and she has many first rate opportunities to use them to her advantage. In contrast to the laws of the physical world, the moral world offers no better place for an observatory than the lowest, least noticed by everyone, and so our family adviser has the best possible vantage point from which to train her searching spyglass on the family. Gradually she will see every movement and shadow on the planet of the heart, follow the path of the smallest orbiting comet, and see eclipses come and go. Watching these phenomena – the changing thoughts and feelings of the human soul, more numerous than the stars in the sky – she will learn each day to decipher and interpret one more piece of life's great and wonderful puzzle. So as you can see, she gradually amasses a good store of that precious but always useful treasure called knowledge of human nature. Before her lies the hope that at some future time, when spectacles adorn her nose and silver hair her ageing head, she will be an oracle telling listening youngsters about things she knows, which they cannot even imagine.

So much for the general duties of the family adviser, now a few words about the person who comes closest to filling that role in Colonel H***'s family. I say 'comes closest', because luckily there she is treated more as a friend, and does not merely wait in the wings or act as prompter, but usually comes

17

on stage and says her lines as openly and confidently as the other actors.

The first word that faltered from those childish lips after a year on this base earth was 'Moon'. Eight years later, she wrote her first verses – to the moon. The dawn of a life that later turned out so dry and prosaic was a sweet, poetic moonlight dream. Her pen dedicated many a sonnet and ode to the delights of nature in those rich, youthful days when her heart beat fiercely, her feelings flowed like the spring torrent, and her sad, sweet tears welled in floods. But in all that she sang, wrote or dreamt, there was always something about moonlight.

Her parents shook their wise heads and said, 'Daughter, if you remain a poet, you will never learn to be a cook, your sauces will burn onto the pan. You must think of learning to support yourself later on, you must be able to spin and to bake cakes. Moonlight satisfies no-one's appetite.' But the girl wrote her poems, minced the meat, did not burn the sauce, worked deftly at her spinning wheel, baked her cakes, yet did not forget her childhood friend, the gentle moon. Later, when its friendly light shone on her parents' grave, she wrote no poetry in its honour, but looked up imploringly into its mild celestial countenance, as if to a motherly comforter offering light to lead and protect the orphan on her lonely path. But alas, that orphan would have almost starved to death in the gentle moonlight, if light of a different kind had not been her salvation. This came from the fireplace of a noble kitchen, where she succeeded in making a good wine jelly – and became a great success. Having discovered her talent for making an exquisite wine jelly, they gradually noticed her other invaluable qualities. A young lady with chapped lips found her home-made lip-salve wonderfully soothing; an old gentleman was comforted to find in her a tireless listener to the tales of his forty-nine aches and pains. A devoted mother of four small and amazingly clever children was much moved to hear from their rosy lips of her rare skill in finding rhymes like love and dove, toy and joy, tease and please, eat and treat. Her yawning Ladyship was suddenly wide awake when the same talented person read her fortune in the cards and predicted that she would shortly receive a present; in no time nine people were singing the praises of her excellent remedies for toothache, pains in the chest and colds in the head. At a wedding, they discovered her amazing ability to arrange everything from her Ladyship's coiffure to the cakes and pastries, from the bride's crown of myrtle to the sandwiches to go with the aquavit. On the more solemn occasion of a funeral, they found she could arrange everything from the sleeping bride's last bed to the refreshments for those who never forget, even on the saddest of days, that we have to eat to live.

By using all these talents industriously, and perfecting various others of the same kind, she rose step by step to the rank, respect and dignity of family adviser. She has almost forgotten how to write verse, except for a few meagre lines now and then for birthdays and name-days, squeezed out from a sense of duty. She rarely looks at the moon, except to see whether it is full, and yet its rays may be the only friends to visit her lonely grave. But this is no time for elegies. Does anyone want to know more about this prosaic friend of the moonlight? Her age? Somewhere between twenty and forty. Her looks? Like most people's, though maybe most people would be rather offended that she considers herself at all like them. Her name? Oh yes! Your most humble servant,

Christina Beata Workaday

Julie's letter – Helena – The blind girl – Emilia – The prospective bridegrooms.

I said that there was a happy reason for my journey to the capital, and I think I can best explain the nature of it by letting my readers see a letter from Julie H***, which reached me a short while ago in my isolated country home.

Dear Beata,

Put down your never-ending half-knitted stocking as soon as you see these lines, and trim the long wick of your candle (you get your post in the evenings at R., do you not?). Shut your door, so you can settle down quietly and comfortably on the sofa without fear of being disturbed, and devote due attention to the great and marvellous news I have to tell you. I can see from here how terribly curious you are, and how wide your eyes have grown, so now I shall tell you ... a story!

Once upon a time there was a man, who was not a king or a prince, although he deserved to be. He had a daughter, and although fate had not let her be born a princess, half a score of fairies gathered around the little one's cradle out of sheer respect and good will to her father. They gave her gifts of beauty, good sense, grace, accomplishments, a noble heart, a sweet temper, patience, everything, in a word, that can make a woman attractive. To crown this collection of lucky gifts, fairy Prudentia stepped forward last of all, saying slowly and deliberately, 'For the sake of her happiness in this life and beyond, she shall be extremely cautious and serious, not to say particular, in her choice of husband!' 'Well said! Wisely said!' echoed all the married fairies with deep sighs.

This richly endowed young lady grew up, became just as charming as you would have expected, and soon suitors were knocking on the door of her heart morning, noon and night, sighing and imploring. Ah, but for most of them that door stayed firmly closed, and if she opened it just a crack for an instant, she shut it again, and double-locked it, the moment after. Luckily this was long after the time of Princess Turandotte, and in Sweden, where the fair Elimia lived, the air must have been cooler than in that country where Prince Caluf sighed, because word never came that the rejected suitors had ended it all. In fact they hardly lost their appetites, and some (can you believe it?) were even known to change lover as casually as one changes a pair of stockings.

The first one to announce his intention to lay claim to fair Elimia's heart, she pronounced too sentimental, because he shuddered at the crime of killing a mosquito and sighed over the fate of the innocent chickens who appeared roast on the dinner table and happened to be his beloved's favourite dish. United with him, she foresaw herself in danger of starving to death on a diet of blancmange and vegetables. The second one did not object to treading on ants, loved fishing and hunting, and was immediately considered too cruel and hard-hearted. She would rather, far rather, have a hare for a husband than a hunter. A hare came along, with frightened eyes and trembling knees, and stammered forth his sighs, wishes and fears. 'Poor little thing,' came the answer, 'Go and hide, or you will be easy prey for the first wild animal that finds you in its path.' The hare hopped away, and the lion stepped forward with proud words of courtship. Now, our fair one was in great fear of being devoured herself, and she hid until the mighty one had passed. He was the fourth suitor. The fifth, cheerful and happy, was

21

considered irresponsible, the sixth seemed inclined to be a gambler, the seventh had a few pimples on his nose, and so might have a taste for strong drink. The eighth looked as though he could be mean, the ninth was thought an egotist, the tenth said 'Damn it!' in every sentence. No good would come of venturing out into life at his side! The eleventh looked at his hands and feet too much – and was therefore a fool. The twelfth came along. He was good, noble, manly, handsome; he seemed sincerely in love, he pleaded his case well; there was great consternation about whether a flaw could be found in him. He appeared to love truly ... but perhaps it was mere appearance or, if he loved, perhaps it was the more unpredictable mortal flesh, than the immortal soul. God preserve us, what a grave sin! If that were the case ... well ... . But the suitor swore it was the soul, the soul alone, that he adored, and in lucky moment he overwhelmed our fair heroine's already softened heart so completely, that finally her trembling lips moved in such a way that he sensed they formed the door through which a 'yes' of capitulation might emerge. He took it for granted, took the word for said, fell on his knees, kissed her on the hand, on the lips, and fair Elimia, on the point of collapse from amazement and astonishment, found herself without knowing how – engaged!

The wedding date was settled by her father and her betrothed for a short time afterwards. Elimia did not give her consent, but nor did she withhold it, and her betrothed thought, 'She who is silent, is willing.' As the time went by, fair Elimia counted, 'Now there are only fourteen, now only twelve, merciful heaven, now only ten and, good grief, now only eight days left!' Her mind was in the grip of growing anxiety and alarm. Fancies and ghostly imaginings, as numerous as the locust plagues of Egypt, intruded into her normally calm and happy thoughts, creating chaos and darkness there. She wanted to put off, not to say break off, her union with noble Almanzor, who certainly, she said, had many more faults than everyone thought, the greatest of these being how clever he was at hiding them. Perfection was not the lot of human nature, and he who appeared the most perfect was perhaps actually the least. What is more, she believed that their natures were not in the least in harmony; furthermore he was too young, she too old, and so on and so on, and the upshot of it all was that she would be unhappy all her life.

A very good friend of Elimia's felt a great desire to break the neck of fairy Prudentia, whose unfortunate gift made Elimia reject the happiness that awaited her in a union with a man who seemed made for her in every respect, and who was devoted to her in the tenderest fashion.

Now I can see you are becoming impatient Beata, and asking, 'What is all this leading up to, and why?' All this, my dear friend, is intended primarily as a little aperitif to stimulate your appetite for the main meal, and after that to show you the wonderful magic powers which have suddenly been bestowed on your little Julie, for with a few strokes of my pen I shall now transform all my characters, turn *then* into *now*, and fairytale into reality.

So Almanzor becomes the young and charming Algernon S., and his betrothed, the fair Elimia, becomes my sister Emilia H***, who at times regrets her promise so bitterly. Fairy Prudentia also undergoes an amazing transformation and becomes none other than the indecision and hesitation which have taken such a firm hold on Emilia's heart on the matter of committing herself to holy wedlock. Unless several of us now push her forward, she will move like a crab – backwards. And that Emilia, whom I love so much, and who so often makes me impatient, is now sitting in the corner of the sofa opposite me, pale and red-eyed, thinking of her wedding day and having an attack of the vapours! Shall we laugh or cry? I do each by turns, and try to coax Emilia into doing the same.

The only thing that can be done now to stop poor Emilia thinking and brooding, worrying and fretting for nothing, is to make sure there is such a wild bustle and commotion all around her right up to the wedding day that she feels quite dizzy – if we can. I know that Papa would never tolerate it if one of us shrank from keeping a promise. Emilia knows it too, and I think that is what is making her so downhearted at times. And yet she does love Algernon, even admires him sometimes, but she would still refuse him if she dared! Tell me, how can this all be explained, how does it all fit together? But once her fate is finally sealed, I know all will be well, and the strange thing is, that Emilia believes it too. However, everything will fall into place next week. Sunday, that is to say, a week on Sunday, is the dreaded wedding day. Emilia is to be married at home, and the only guests will be a few relations. Emilia wishes it to be so, and we are arranging everything as she wants it, within reason. She says that is how the condemned person is always treated. Ridiculous idea! You see, dear Beata, how vital it is for us that you should be here. The truth is that we are in great need of your advice and help. So pack your things at once and come as quickly as you can.

On Monday, Algernon arrives in Stockholm, and with him my betrothed too. I have not been as choosy and timid as Emilia, and yet my choice is no worse. My Arvid is an Adonis and has a heart worth its weight in gold. Papa likes him very much, and that is the most important thing for me. My good, honoured, beloved Papa! I was so firmly resolved never to leave him and Mama. And yet, I hardly understand how, I decided to become engaged to be married ... but it was impossible to resist my Arvid. Papa will still have Helena, who will never marry; Helena is worth three Julies such as I. Papa was very much

24

against my marriage to begin with, and raised so many objections that our plans almost came to nothing … but I fell on my knees and wept, and Arvid's father (Papa's old friend) made such a moving speech, and Arvid himself looked so ready to hang himself, that Papa allowed himself to be persuaded and said, 'Very well; they may have one another!' Arvid and I sang for joy like two larks. You must see him: he has a dark moustache and pointed beard, big blue eyes, the most beautiful … but you will see! He has the most beautiful *son de voix* in the world, and let Emilia say what she will, he sounds really charming when he says 'By Jove!' You may think that sounds odd, but you will see, you will hear! Come, come, and by the evening of the day after tomorrow you can be giving a hug to

Your friend
Julie H.

P.S. I beg you, please bring with you some of those lovely loaves that you know Papa and Mama like so much, some cheeses for Carl and Helena and a few ginger biscuits for me. I know you always have some in the larder. Emilia, poor Emilia, will have quite enough to do ridding herself of the vapours, I think. You can't imagine how anxious I am that all this worry and grief will make her look pale and plain for when Algernon comes. I think Emilia almost hopes she will, probably to test whether it is her immortal soul he loves. I truly believe she would demand that he should love her just as much if she turned into a blind mole. I am really worried because Emilia's appearance can change so much, and she is not the same person when she is sad and anxious, as when she is calm and happy.

Farewell once more.

P.P.S. Do you know who is to conduct the ceremony? It is Professor L., who always looks so awfully earnest and has a limp, a red eye and two warts on his nose. He has just taken over our parish. Papa feels great respect and friendship for him. For my part, I should not much care to be married by a bleary-eyed parson. But I shall not be getting married for a few years, or perhaps this autumn, so there is no point in thinking about it now.

I almost forgot to send the impatient greetings of the whole family.

I heeded Julie's cry for help and arrived at Colonel H***'s, as you have already seen, one evening in late February.

A few words remain to be said about the events of that evening, so I will take up the thread of my story once more. The blind girl, who had sat silent and unmoving for so long, suddenly said, almost fiercely, 'I should like to sing.' Helena rose at once, led her to the piano, and sat down to accompany her. The blind girl remained standing. Helena asked what she wished to sing. 'Ariadne à Naxos' came the short, firm reply, and they began. At first I did not find the singer's voice attractive; it was powerful, deep, almost eerie, but the more carefully I listened, the more aware I became of the feeling in that voice, the fascinating truth it revealed, and the more captivated I became. I shivered involuntarily, felt my heart beat in sympathy with Ariadne, in the grip of growing terror, as she seeks her lover and decides to climb upon a rock in the hope of finding him more easily. The accompaniment expressed the skill of her climb; I could picture her hurrying to the top, panting and full of foreboding. At last she has reached the summit, her eyes scan the sea and she catches sight of a white sail growing ever smaller. The blind girl followed Ariadne with her whole soul, and from the tension in her face one could almost believe that she saw more than – darkness alone. Tears welled up uncontrol-

26

lably in everyone's eyes as with a heart-rending expression of love and pain in her voice and on her face, she cried out with Ariadne, 'Teseo, Teseo!' At the height of her passion and our delight, the Colonel stood up abruptly, went over to the piano, took the singer by the hand without saying a word, and led her away to sit back down on the sofa, then seated himself beside her. I saw how she violently freed her hand from his. She was deathly pale, and beside herself. No-one but me seemed surprised at this scene. Someone then introduced some trivial topic of conversation, and everyone but the blind girl joined in. After a time the Colonel said to her, 'You need to rest,' and immediately got to his feet and led her out of the room, once she had solemnly bowed her head in a gesture of farewell to those remaining. As he went, the Colonel called, 'Helena', and Helena followed them.

Soon afterwards, I too gratefully sought my bed. The image of the blind girl stayed with me and kept me awake for a long time; I could hear her penetrating voice and see her expressive face, and I could not prevent myself speculating about the feelings which so shook her soul.

I was still not asleep when Emilia and Julie quietly crept into their room, which was next to mine. The communicating door stood open, and I could hear the sisters' half-whispered conversation. Julie said, with some annoyance, 'You are yawning and sighing, even though Algernon is coming tomorrow! Emilia, you have no more feeling than a cardboard box!'

Emilia. How do you know that I am not doing it in sympathy with Algernon, who may be doing just the same at this moment?

Julie. I am quite sure he is *not*. In fact, I think he is so full of impatience and delight at the thought of seeing you, that he hardly knows what to do with himself.

Emilia. Is that how you interpret his last letter?

Julie. But that was written in such a hurry. One isn't always in the mood for writing; maybe he had a bad headache ... or a bad cold ... or a chill.

Emilia. Whatever you will, but nothing can excuse the cold, empty way the letter ended.

Julie. But I assure you Emilia, it says, 'With sincere and fond affection.'

Emilia. And I am sure that it just says, 'Respectfully and sincerely yours.' Just as one might put, 'Yours faithfully,' or whatever, when writing to somebody unimportant, because empty compliments must always step in, when other, warmer sentiments are lacking. Where is my nightcap? Ah, there it is. Oh dear me, Julie, you do see everything in a rosy light.

Julie. I see that a lover must beware of mentioning respect ... I am certain though, that Algernon did *not* choose that dreadful word, but a warmer, more heartfelt one. Sweetest Emilia, do fetch the letter. You will see that you have done him an injustice.

Emilia. For your sake, I *shall* fetch the letter. We will see that I am right!

Julie. And we will see that *I* am right.

Emilia fetched the letter. The sisters took it nearer to the candle. Julie tried to trim the wick, and whether by accident or design, put out the candle. For a moment, everything was as quiet as it was dark, until Emilia's hearty laugh was heard. Julie joined in, and I could not stop myself from making it a trio. After much groping around and tumbling over chairs and tables, the sisters found their beds and, still laughing, called out to me, 'Goodnight, goodnight!'

The day after my arrival was a so-called grand cleaning day in the house, of the sort that takes place from time to time in every well-run house, like a stormy day in nature. After the gales and rains, everything emerges with new clarity, order and freshness.

There was scrubbing, airing, dusting and cleaning going on in every corner. Her Ladyship, who wanted to supervise everything herself, was constantly coming and going, and generally left all the doors open, causing a dreadful draught. To save myself from earache and toothache, I fled from room to room and finally, upstairs in Helena's room, found a port in the storm. That little room seemed to me the most pleasant and happy in the whole house. Its windows caught the sun and its walls were decorated with pictures, most of them attractive landscapes. The most outstanding were two by Fahlcrantz, in which the brush of the great artist had recreated the lovely calm that a fine summer evening brings to the countryside, a calm which appeals so strongly to the human heart. Eyes which had gazed on those pictures soon took on a sweet, sad, dreaming expression, sure proof of the pictures' true beauty.

The furniture in the room was elegant and comfortable. A piano, a well-stocked bookcase and a painting easel showed that this small universe lacked none of those things which allow us to forego the pleasures of the outside world and occupy the hours of the day most pleasantly.

Splendid large geraniums stood on the window-sills, their fresh greenery prompting pleasant thoughts of spring, their leaves interrupting, diffusing and softening the dazzling sunlight as it streamed in that day with all the penetrating brightness of the sharp winter frost. A beautiful carpet covered the floor, looking as though it were strewn with flowers.

Helena was seated on the sofa, sewing. On the sewing table in front of her lay the New Testament. She welcomed me with a smile that expressed her contentment and peace of mind. I sat down to my sewing beside her, feeling in very good spirits. We were working on Emilia's wedding dress.

'I see you are looking at my room,' said Helena with a smile, as her eyes followed mine.

'Yes,' I answered. 'Your sisters' rooms are pretty and pleasant, but I have to admit that they cannot compare with this one.'

'It was my father's wish,' she said, 'that Helena should be the only spoilt child in the house.' With tears in her eyes she went on, 'My good Papa did not want me to miss the pleasure and enjoyment which are the lot of my sisters with their health and beauty, and from which I am excluded by my deformity and sickliness. That is why he has taught me to enjoy the richer pleasures that appreciation and practice of the fine arts can bring to those who approach them with a sympathetic and open mind. That is why he is training and improving my intellect by guiding me through an ordered programme of serious studies. That is why he has gathered in this little corner, where I spend the greater part of my life, so much that is pleasing to the eyes, the senses and the mind. But more precious than all this is the devoted fatherly love with which he surrounds me, just to prevent me ever feeling bitter at missing that other love which nature has denied me. He has succeeded completely, and I have no other wish than to live for him, my mother, my sisters and brothers – and my God.'

We sat silent for a time, and I inwardly gave thanks for this father, who took such good care of the happiness of those to whom he had given life. Helena continued, 'When Mama takes my sisters out to dances and other social engagements, he spends most of his time with me. I read to him and play for him, and he has the great goodness to let me believe that my contribution truly does brighten his life. The thought of it makes me so happy. What a wonderful and enviable lot, to mean something to someone like *him*, who brings blessings to everyone around him.'

'Oh!' I thought, mentally addressing myself to the family fathers of this world, 'Why are so few of you like this father? Masters of the home, just think what happiness you could spread around you, and how well-loved you could be!'

Then we talked about Emilia. 'It is strange,' said Helena, 'that someone who is usually so calm, so definite in her judgements, so decided, so *solid* in a word, is so unlike herself in this one thing. She wants to get married, as she believes a happy marriage to be the most blissful state on earth, but she has had the greatest difficulty in ever deciding to do it. The rather unhappy marriages of two of her childhood friends have put her into a sort of panic, and she is so frightened of being unhappily married that she would never have the courage to dare to be happy, if others did not act for her. Now she is sometimes almost ill with anxiety because her union with Algernon S. is approaching so fast, although in fact she is devoted to him, and we are all convinced she will be thoroughly happy with him. In between she has calm periods, like the one you saw her in yesterday evening. But I am afraid it will not last, and in fact I expect her anxiety and uncertainty to grow as the critical moment approaches which – *I* am convinced – will end those feelings for good. As soon as anything is finally decided, Emilia resigns herself to it calmly and makes the best of it. What we have decided to do to stop all her pointless worrying is to try to distract her any way we can from now until the day of the wedding. Each of us has a special role in this little drama we are acting for and with our dear sister. Papa intends to take her out for lots of walks, Mama is going to ask her advice about all the arrangements that are still to be made for the wedding. Julie aims not to leave her in peace for a moment, one way or another. Carl's idea is to start lots of arguments about Napoleon, whom he considers inferior to Charles XII, a view which she cannot abide, and in fact it is the only topic on which I have

31

known my good, quiet sister to have a heated debate. My task will be to keep her busy deciding her wardrobe. As for my little brothers, nature made them learn their roles by heart long ago, so they will be constantly whining for one thing after another. Normally we all share the task of keeping them occupied, but now we will leave it to her. As for you, dear Beata, your role is, whenever appropriate, to drop subtle complimentary remarks about Algernon into the conversation, which will not be difficult. Emilia thinks we are all on his side, but you are above suspicion, so your praise will impress her much more.'

I was quite content with my task. It is always a pleasure to praise people, when it can be done with a clear conscience.

After we had had a long talk about Emilia and her lover, where they would set up house, and so on, I turned the conversation to the blind girl, and tried to find out more about her. Helena wanted to avoid the subject and said merely, 'Elisabeth has been with us for a year. We all hold her very dear, and hope in time to win her confidence and help to make her happier.'

Helena then suggested that we pay her a visit. 'I go in to see her every morning, of course,' she said. 'I would devote more of my time to her, were it not that she prefers to be alone.'

We went together to the blind girl's room. She was sitting on her bed fully dressed and singing quietly to herself. 'How she has suffered! She is a living portrait of pain!', I thought, now that I could see at close quarters and in daylight that pale, beautiful face bearing the marks of hard and still unresolved struggles, and of pain too deep and bitter for tears.

A young girl whose rosy cheeks and cheerful countenance formed a sharp contrast to this picture of suffering sat knitting in one corner of the room. She was there to attend to the needs of the blind girl. Helena addressed Elisabeth with a moving compassion in her voice and words; she answered shortly and coldly. It seemed to me that, now we had come in, she was

32

trying to assume little by little that cold and lifeless expression I had seen on her face the evening before. The conversation continued between Helena and myself, while Elisabeth occupied herself in twisting and untwisting a black silken cord around her strikingly beautiful hands. All at once, she said, 'Shh! Shh!' A dull red flamed in her cheeks and she drew herself up. We were silent, listening, and some seconds later we heard the muffled sound of footsteps slowly approaching. 'He is coming!' said the blind girl, as if to herself. I looked inquiringly at Helena. Helena looked down at the floor. The Colonel came in. The blind girl got up and stood there as still as a statue, but I thought I could see her trembling slightly. The Colonel addressed her in his usual calm way but not, I thought, with his usual kindness, and said that he had come to fetch her because he wished to take a ride in the carriage with her and Emilia. He added, 'The air is fresh and clear, it will do you good.'

'Me good?' she said with a bitter smile, but the Colonel took no notice and asked Helena to help her with her coat. The blind girl made no objection, silently allowed herself to be dressed and, thanking no-one, was led out by the Colonel.

'Poor Elisabeth!' said Helena with a pitying sigh when she had gone.

I did not possess the key to that enigmatic creature's inner soul, but I had seen enough to join Helena in sighing deeply, 'Poor Elisabeth!'

We returned to our work and our pleasant conversation, which we continued until dinner. Then I went in to Emilia, who had come back from her ride, and found her fighting with Julie, who was in a state of high anxiety and trying to pull away a dress, which Emilia seemed to want to put on. Emilia was laughing heartily. Julie, on the other hand, looked close to tears.

'Help! Beata, help!' she called. 'Have you ever seen or heard the like? Listen Beata! Just because Emilia is expecting Alger-

33

non today, she wants to put on her most hideous dress ... yes! a dress which suits her so badly that she looks quite unlike herself in it. And as if that were not enough, she has also chosen a sash like a swaddling band, and in her hair she wants a comb so frightful that old Medusa must have left it behind. I have been struggling and arguing for a quarter of an hour to try to talk her out of this awful outfit ... but all in vain!'

'If in Algernon's eyes,' said Emilia with a dignified air, 'a mere dress or comb can help to make me attractive, then ...'

'So there we have it!' exclaimed Julie in desperation, 'Now it is to be testing time, and I can guess at once how ugly and horrible she would be prepared to make herself, to test whether Algernon can outdo the most famous romantic heroes in heroic fidelity. I beg you for God's sake, at least do not cut off your ears or nose!' Emilia laughed. 'And you could so easily be so pretty and charming!' Julie continued to plead earnestly, as she tried to seize the unfortunate dress and comb.

'I have decided that this is what I shall wear today,' Emilia answered gravely. 'I have my reasons, and if I disgust you and Algernon, then so be it.'

'Emilia can still be pretty enough, you will see,' I told Julie, to try to comfort her. 'You go and dress for dinner. Remember that you have a young man to please as well.'

'Oh,' said Julie, 'that's not difficult. If I wore a sack and put a jug on my head, he would still say it suited me splendidly.'

'So you think,' Emilia began once more, 'that Algernon is less devoted to me than Arvid is to you?'

Julie looked a little surprised.

'Go, go!' I interrupted. 'We shall never be ready. Julie, you go, and I shall help Emilia, and I wager that she will be pretty in spite of herself.' Julie finally went in to Helena, who each day combed and plaited her exquisite hair for her.

Left alone with Emilia, I helped her with the greyish-brown and, in truth, disastrous dress, and said what I hoped were some wise words about her state of mind and her behaviour. She answered, 'I admit that I am not as I should be ... I wish I could be different, but I feel so uneasy and unhappy that sometimes I cannot control myself. I am about to enter into an alliance that it might have been better for me never to have made; and if, in the time that remains beforehand, I come to the conclusion that my fears are well grounded, nothing in the world will prevent me from breaking off the engagement, to avoid being unhappy for the rest of my life. For if it is true that a happy marriage is a heaven, it is just as true that an unhappy one is a hell.'

'If you do not love Mr. S.,' I said, 'I am astonished that you have let things go this far.'

'Do not love?' Emilia repeated in amazement. 'Indeed I do love him, and that is just the problem, for my love makes me blind to his faults.'

'One would hardly think so to judge by what you have been saying,' I answered with a smile.

'And yet ... and yet ...!' said Emilia, 'It is true nonetheless, but some of them are *so* obvious that no-one can be blind to them. For example – he is too young!'

'How disgraceful!' I laughed, 'That really is mean of him!'

'You may laugh! I do not happen to find it at all amusing. I admit it is not exactly his fault, but it is still a fault that he has, when considered in relation to me. I am twenty-six years old and so coming to the end of my youth, he is two years older, which means that as a man he is still quite young. I will be a worthy matron when he is still a young man. He could be irresponsible, and glad to escape from his dull wife to ...'

'Aha, I see!' I interrupted. 'That really is over-cautious. Have you any reason to believe him to be irresponsible?'

'Nothing definite ... but in these irresponsible times, faithfulness and loyalty are such rare virtues. I know I am not Algernon's first love, and who can be sure that I will be his last? I could bear anything but my husband's unfaithfulness ... I believe I could not live to endure it. I have told Algernon ... He has assured me ... but a man in love will say anything. Furthermore, how can I tell whether he loves me with a true and genuine love, the only kind that is strong and enduring? Perhaps he has merely taken a liking to me – and that is a weak and easily-broken thread! It has even occurred to me (and the thought often grieves me deeply) that perhaps my fortune, or the one that is one day likely to be mine, may have influenced ...'

'No! Now you are going too far,' I said. 'You are seeing ghosts in broad daylight. How can you even begin to suspect such things? After all, you have known him ...'

'For only two years,' interrupted Emilia, 'and from almost the first moment of our acquaintance he began courting me, so of course he only showed me his charming side ... And who can see into men's hearts, after all? You see Beata, I cannot say that I *know* the man, with whom I shall go through life. And how indeed could I have got to know him? When you only see one another in polite, refined society, where true character never has a chance to show itself, you only get to know one another's outward appearance, the superficial things. A person can be ill-natured, miserly, inclined to be mean and bad-tempered, and what is worse than all that, can be completely without religion, and yet you can meet him in social circles for several years without in the least suspecting all this. And the one least likely to discover it is, of course, the object of his attentions and charms.'

I did not really know what I should reply; I felt that Emilia's account was accurate, and that her fears were not without some basis. She continued, 'Certainly, if we had known and been meeting one another for ten years, particularly if we had travelled together – because on journeys we are not so much on our guard, and reveal more of our natural character and temperament – then we would have a fair idea of how we really felt.'

'That method,' I said, 'seems likely to be too slow and laborious, excellent though it may be, and no doubt highly practical for lovers at the time of the Crusades. These days we take a stroll along Drottninggatan and venture perhaps as far as Norrtull Gate. We can ask no more. On our way we see the world and are seen by it; we give and receive greetings, we talk and joke and laugh, and find one another so agreeable that at the end of our little journey we feel no hesitation in embarking on the great journey through life together. But to be serious, have you never discussed frankly with Algernon all these subjects on which you consider it so important to know his views?'

'Yes, many times,' answered Emilia, 'especially since our engagement, and I have always found, or thought I found, that his views and feelings were what I wished them to be, and yet ... oh dear! I can so easily have allowed myself to be blind, because I secretly wished it. Perhaps Algernon too, in his eagerness to please me, has deceived himself. I have made up my mind to devote all my attention to discovering the real truth in the short time of freedom I have left, and I will not, if I can help it, make us both unhappy through my self-inflicted blindness. Even assuming that he has splendid qualities, he may still not be suited to me, nor I to him. Our basic temperaments and characters may essentially not be in harmony at all.'

In this miserable condition, Emilia was dressed, and I had to admit that her outfit did not suit her. She ended the conversation by saying, 'Sometimes I wish I were already married, for then I would be spared the painful prospect of getting married.' 'How inconsistent the human mind can be!' I thought.

At dinner, Emilia's toilette was much criticized, especially by Cornet Carl. Julie was silent, but her eyes spoke volumes. The Colonel said nothing, but looked at Emilia with a sarcastic expression which made her blush.

After dinner, Julie said to Emilia, 'Dear Emilia, I did not mean that Algernon would not find you just as charming if you were wearing sackcloth and ashes; I just wanted to say that it would be wrong for a bride-to-be not to want to please her betrothed in every way, I meant that it would be right ... that it would be wrong ... that it would be ... ' Here, Julie lost the thread of her argument and became almost as embarrassed as a certain mayor who found himself in the same predicament. Emilia squeezed her hand kindly and said, 'You have certainly followed your own principle yourself, and very successfully, for I have rarely seen you looking better dressed or prettier than you do today, and I am sure Arvid will think the same.'

Julie blushed, more gratified by her sister's words than she would have been by a compliment from her betrothed.

Towards evening the turmoil of cleaning was over, everything returned to its usual pleasant state of order, and her Ladyship too could relax at last.

At teatime, Algernon and Lieutenant Arvid arrived. Emilia and Julie blushed like roses in June; the one looked down, the other up.

Algernon was in such a state of joy and excitement at seeing Emilia again, was so preoccupied with her, and her alone, took so little notice of her dress, not even glancing at it, and was so visibly delighted, so happy and charming, that the joy shining out from his eyes gradually lit a sympathetic sparkle in Emilia's, and in spite of the dress, the sash and the comb she was so sweet and attractive that Julie forgave her the outfit.

Lieutenant Arvid was no less content at the side of his charming little Julie, although he did not seem inclined to express this in the same way as Algernon, with eager but well-chosen compliments. Not everyone has a way with words, and we all have our way of doing things. He drank tea, three cups, ate a dozen biscuits, frequently kissed his beloved's hand, and looked very happy. I heard him say a few times, 'By Jove!', and decided that an attractive mouth and a pleasing voice can soften the effect of bad language. Lieutenant Arvid truly was an Adonis, or rather, an Adonis with moustaches.

His face expressed goodness and honesty but also (I beg his pardon a thousand times over) a degree of foolishness and conceit. His handsome twenty-year-old head did not appear to have room for many ideas.

Algernon was of extremely noble appearance; it stood out that he was good, manly and shrewd. He was tall, with fine, regular features and the most attractive easy bearing.

When Emilia studies that noble face, I thought, how can all her fears and forebodings fail to melt away?

For that evening at least, they did melt away, or retreated into the dark depths of her mind. The whole family seemed happy, and all was joyful activity.

The blind girl did not make an appearance that evening.

Five days before the wedding.

In spite of the cheerful and good-humoured note on which Monday ended, Emilia awoke on Tuesday morning with the words, 'One day less until the dreaded day!'

Some lovely presents arrived that morning from Algernon. Emilia did not like the custom of a man giving his betrothed presents. 'It is a barbaric practice,' she said. 'It makes the woman into a commodity, which the man can somehow buy. Knowing that it is the custom among brutal and uncivilised peoples should be enough to persuade the civilized ones to give it up.'

Furthermore, she thought some of the presents chosen with more regard to luxury and sparkle than to what is practical.

'What if he is a spendthrift?' she sighed. 'How little he knows me, if he believes that jewels are worth more to me than flowers from him. My love for attractive and elegant things is matched by my dislike of anything showy, ostentatious or frivolous. What is more, it would be quite out of place in our circumstances.'

Emilia's good humour had evaporated; she scarcely looked at the presents, which Julie continued to admire with cries of, 'Delightful! *Charmant!*' She kept the curl papers in her hair all morning, and went around wrapped in a vast shawl, which hung down at a crooked angle. Cornet Carl said she looked like a Hottentot woman, and begged her, although she was surrounded by 'brutal and uncivilised customs', not to imagine she was turning into a savage. As we were going down to dinner I, mindful of my role as truthful, skilful giver of praise, told her how uncommonly handsome and attractive I thought Algernon was.

'Yes,' answered Emilia, 'He is quite handsome, and a much more attractive man than I am a woman, and that seems to me a real misfortune for us.'

'Oh dear!' I thought, 'Now I have run into another sand-bank.'

Emilia went on, 'It is exceptional for very good looks not to make their possessor vain, and the most unbearable thing I know is a man fond of his own appearance. He usually considers it his less attractive wife's duty to adore and pay homage to his beauty and charm. Vanity belittles women, but degrades men. In my opinion, a man's looks are of little or no importance to his wife. I could adore a noble Aesop, I am certain, and I would a thousand times sooner choose him than an Adonis. A Narcissus, who worships his own image, is the most distasteful thing I can think of.'

As Emilia finished what she had to say, she opened the door to the drawing room. Algernon was alone in the room, standing – before the mirror, and apparently studying his reflection intently. You should have seen how Emilia blushed! And seen her expression as she faced her betrothed, who for his part, confused by her embarrassment and her look of annoyance, and perhaps even a little shamefaced at being caught in his *tête-à-tête* with the mirror, was completely nonplussed. It then fell to me to keep the conversation going with remarks about the weather, the state of the roads, and so on. As luck would have it, the other members of the family began to arrive to provide a welcome diversion. Emilia continued to look sullen, and as Algernon watched her, his features darkened too. I thought I detected a stye in his left eye, and supposed that that had been the reason for his *tête-à-tête* with the mirror; but Emilia refused to see it. Several little things made the atmosphere between the

41

two lovers worse. Algernon happened to talk approvingly of things which Emilia did not like, and at table he did not even sample Emilia's favourite dish. No doubt Emilia thought that they were completely out of sympathy with one another. Algernon made some true but not pointed comment about caprices and how annoying they are. On this occasion it would nonetheless have been best left unsaid. Emilia took it personally and assumed a very superior and self-righteous air. Julie grew worried. 'It would be much better,' she said, 'If they had a real quarrel, instead of sitting there keeping quiet and storing all their anger up inside.'

Cornet Carl went up to Emilia and said, 'Good sister, I beg you, do not sit there like the Great Wall of China, repelling all the arrows fired at you by Algernon's amorous eyes. Be, if you can, a little less icy. Look at Algernon! Go to him and give him a kiss!' But, as you might imagine, there was more chance of seeing the Great Wall of China start to move. Emilia did not look even once at Algernon, who seemed to be longing beyond measure for a reconciliation. He suggested that they might sing together a new Italian duet, presumably in the hope that the spirits of harmony would chase away those of harshness and hostility which had disturbed the peace between him and his beloved, the hope that the duet's *Cor mio, mio ben* would soon strike a chord in their hearts' duo. A vain hope! Emilia pleaded a headache. She really did have one, and a bad one too, as I could see by her eyes. She was very prone to them, whenever she was unhappy and anxious. Algernon thought the headache was just an excuse, and without paying any further attention to his betrothed, who sat in one corner of the sofa resting her throbbing head in her hand, he announced that he intended to go to the opera to see Mozart's Figaro, made a hasty bow to them all, and left.

The evening dragged on. No one was in a good or happy mood. Everyone could see that Emilia was suffering, so no one expressed any displeasure at her conduct.

Only the Colonel pretended to notice nothing, and went on with his game of patience.

As we parted for the evening, the Cornet said quietly to me, 'Things are going terribly! Tomorrow we shall have to fire off our whole battery of distractions!'

Wednesday came. Algernon arrived quite early in the morning. His look was so loving, his voice when he spoke to Emilia so tender, that she thawed, and tears appeared in her eyes. Peace was restored between the two lovers, no one knew quite how or why, not even they themselves.

Things went smoothly that day, apart from two shocks to Emilia, but she survived them. The first happened in the morning, when Algernon was in conversation with her Ladyship, and Emilia heard him say things, which for a minute convinced her that he was the worst miser in the world. Luckily she soon discovered that he had merely been quoting the words of a Harpagon he knew, words at which he laughed heartily afterwards. Emilia took a deep breath, and joined in his laughter. The other shock came in the evening, during a serious discussion some of us were having, sitting by a window in the clear moonlight. I said, 'Yet there are noble, good people who are unfortunate enough not to believe in a life hereafter, or in a higher destiny for our being. We should pity them, not blame them.' With an indescribable look of anguish in her beautiful eyes, Emilia looked questioningly at me. She was thinking: are you making excuses for Algernon? I answered by drawing her attention to Algernon, who at my words had gazed up at the starry heavens with a look of wonderful hope and conviction. Then Emilia too looked up with gratitude, and their eyes met, and shone with tenderness and joy.

The day looked set to end so well! Oh why did Algernon have to receive a note during the evening meal? Why did the reading of it have to disconcert him and rob him of his cheerfulness? Why did he leave in such haste and with no explanation?

Yes, why? No one knew, but many of us were simply dying to know.

'Now you must not dare to blame Algernon for that note,' Julie said to Emilia as they went to bed.

'Good night Julie', answered Emilia with a sigh. But for Emilia, there was no good night.

Thursday. A dark cloud over Emilia. Unsuccessful attempts on our part to disperse it. No sooner was it breakfast time than the Cornet took to the field with Napoleon and Charles XII. Emilia did not feel like an argument, and it was in vain that Julie and Helena tried to encourage her. In my role, I did not dare to say a single word. The note, the note, stood in the way of everything.

Algernon arrived at twelve o'clock. He looked rather agitated, and there was a steely glint in his eye. The day before, Emilia had promised to go out for a sleigh ride with him. A beautiful sleigh draped in reindeer skins stood at the front door. Emilia refused flatly and coldly to go. 'Why?' asked Algernon.

'Because of the note' would have been the honest answer, but Emilia said, 'I want to stay at home.'

'Are you ill?'

'No.'

'Then why will you not do me the honour of coming with me, as you promised?'

The note, the note! thought Emilia, but she just blushed and said again, 'I want to stay at home.'

Algernon grew angry and flushed, and his eyes blazed. He went out, almost slamming the door behind him.

The servant who was in charge of the sleigh at the front door had meanwhile left it unattended. The horse, left alone, and frightened by some snow crashing down from the roof, gave a sudden start, knocked down an old woman, and would surely have bolted if Algernon, emerging at that moment into the square, had not thrown himself in front of it and taken a firm grip on the reins. When he had calmed the horse, he called a man to hold it, while he hurried to help up the old woman, who had been too terrified to move, but who as luck would have it did not seem to be the least bit hurt. He talked to her for a while and gave her some money.

When the servant eventually returned, Algernon boxed him round the ears, leapt into the sleigh, took the reins himself, and drove off like a flash of lightning.

A pale Emilia had been watching the whole scene with me from the window, but as it drew to a close she cried, 'He is violent, bad-tempered and wild!' And she burst into tears.

I said, 'He has human weaknesses, that is all. He was already upset and agitated when he arrived; your refusal to keep your promise without giving any good reason was bound to make him angry; his servant's negligence, which could so easily have led to a serious accident, made his temper worse, although he only gave vent to it by a single box on the ears, well deserved by the recipient. It is asking too much of a young man to expect him to stay completely cool and calm, when a sudden series of vexations provokes him so. It is quite enough if he manages in his anger to remain as human and as kind as we just saw Algernon being to the old woman. And incidentally Emilia, I think that if instead of frustrating Algernon with your whims and awkwardness – excuse those two charming words – you would make better use of the strong influence that we can all see you have over him, then you would never have to see him "bad-tempered and wild", as you put it.'

I was very pleased with my little speech when I had finished it, and thought it would make a powerful impression, but Emilia remained silent and unhappy.

Algernon did not return for dinner.

Cornet Carl told us that afternoon how he had heard from a comrade that a duel had taken place that morning. One of the duellists was Algernon's best friend, who had called on him to be his second. He had sent word in a note (the Cornet said, most definitely) which had been delivered here, where Algernon was dining, yesterday evening at a quarter to ten. Algernon had done everything possible to prevent the duel, but in vain. The two sides met, and Algernon's friend badly wounded his opponent. The Cornet had no further details.

Now everything was explained, and Emilia saw Algernon in a much rosier light.

Algernon arrived towards evening; he was completely calm, but grave, and did not go and sit beside his betrothed as he usually did. Emilia was not happy, but seemed afraid to take the first step towards a reconciliation, although her many little attentions to Algernon showed how much she wanted to win him round. She offered him tea, asked whether he found it sweet enough, whether she could pour him another cup, and so on. Algernon's attitude remained cool; he often seemed to become lost in thought and forget where he was. Emilia, hurt, left him to himself, and in rather low spirits sat down to her sewing, keeping her eyes on her work for a long time.

Cornet Carl said to Helena and me, 'This is not going at all well, but what on earth can we do to help matters? I cannot bring up Napoleon and Charles XII again; I tried them only this morning, and anyway it did no good. You have to admit that Emilia is not an amiable lover. If she is no better as a wife, well then ... Should she not go to Algernon now and try to comfort him and cheer him up? Look, she *is* going – no, she was just

46

fetching another skein of thread. Poor Algernon! I begin to think that I am fortunate to be so unsentimental. Lovers seem to have an even harder time of it than ambitious soldiers. If I were engaged to be married – bless you little Claes, what are you whining for now – a biscuit? Go to Emilia, go to Emilia, I have no biscuits! Yes, it will do her Highness good to take a little exercise.'

The Cornet failed to see how humble her Highness was at the bottom of her heart that evening, and that Algernon was the main cause of the coolness between them. Algernon and Emilia did not approach one another all evening, and parted coldly, or so it appeared.

On Friday morning, Emilia decided that they should separate. Algernon was noble and splendid, but he was too severe and he did not love her – that had been plain to see the evening before; she now wished to talk to him in private, etc. Algernon came. He was in a much better mood than he had been the previous day, and seemed to want all the unpleasantness to be forgotten. Emilia began by being very solemn, in view of her important announcement, but Julie, Helena, her Ladyship, Cornet Carl and I were so busy all around her that we gradually drew her into our whirlpool and kept her both from private conversations and from brooding. From time to time, we even heard her hearty laugh, and her thoughtful mood did not turn into melancholy.

That afternoon the marriage contract was signed.

Sir Charles Grandison's bride, Harriet Byron herself (so it is said), dropped the pen which she had taken to sign her marriage contract, and lacked the strength and presence of mind to seal her fate. Millions of young women engaged to be married have trembled at that moment and done as she did. It is hardly surprising, then, that our fearful and irresolute Emilia was beside herself with fright! The pen did not just fall from her fingers, it made a great ink-blot on the important document, which at that moment seemed to her a bad omen, and I doubt whether she would still have signed, if the Colonel had not (just like Sir Charles) taken the pen, put it between her unresponsive fingers, and guided her trembling hand.

That evening, when we were alone in our rooms, Emilia said with a deep sigh, 'I suppose it has to happen then! There is nothing more to be done ... and the day after tomorrow he will take me away from everything I hold so dear!'

'One might almost believe,' said Julie smiling, but with tears in her eyes, 'that you were facing a journey to the end of the world, but only a few streets and squares will separate us from you, and we will be able to see each other every day.'

'Every day, yes,' said Emilia, 'but not, like now, every hour!'

On Saturday, Emilia was kind and affectionate to everybody, but apprehensive and in low spirits, seeming to want to escape from the thoughts which pursued her everywhere.

Algernon looked graver with every passing moment, watching his bride with a worried, questioning look. He was afraid, or so it appeared, that she was not giving him her whole heart along with her hand in marriage. Yet he seemed afraid to seek an explanation, and avoided finding himself alone with Emilia.

I had heard from a cousin of our cook's stepsister's sister--in-law that Algernon had arranged for food and money to be distributed to several poor families, with instructions to them to celebrate with a good meal on Sunday. I told Emilia, who had done the very same thing herself. This sympathy of thought between them pleased her and put her in better spirits.

Meanwhile, sewing and other tasks had been diligently done all over the house, so that everything was ready and in its place by the day before the wedding.

Our parting that evening had an air of solemnity about it. Everyone embraced Emilia, and there were tears in all our eyes.

Emilia held her emotions in check, but could not speak. Everyone's thoughts were on the day that lay ahead.

The wedding day.

The great, long awaited, much feared day finally arrived.

Emilia was hardly out of bed before she was casting an apprehensive look to the sky. It was overcast with grey clouds. The air was cold and misty; everything visible through the window bore the melancholy stamp that a bleak winter's day sets on things both living and inanimate. The smoke rising from the chimneys was forced back down again to descend in a slow arch onto the roofs, blackening their white coverings of snow. A few old women with red noses and blue cheeks were bringing their cartloads of milk to the market square, pulled step after slow step by thin horses, whose matted heads hung even lower than usual. Even the little sparrows did not seem to be in their usual good spirits; they sat still and huddled up along the edges of the roofs, not making a sound, not looking for food. Now and again, one of them stretched a wing and opened its little beak, sorrowfully it seemed. Emilia gave a deep sigh. A clear sky and a little sunshine, would have cheered and refreshed her flagging spirits. Who does not wish for a clear sun to shine brightly on their wedding day? We would feel that Hymen's torch could not burn brightly enough unless it was lit by the pure light of heaven's rays. A secret conviction that Heaven does not look with indifference on our earthly fate always lingers in the depths of our heart, and although we are only dust and atoms, when the vaulted heavens are darkened by clouds or bathed in brightness, we see in their changing mood some sympathy or omen for ourselves, although often, very often, our hopes or fears are mere children of the wind and the clouds!

Emilia, who had spent a sleepless night and was oppressed by the events of the previous day, was thoroughly disheartened at the sight of the bleak morning. She complained of a headache, and after embracing her parents, sisters and brothers at breakfast, she asked to spend the morning alone in her room. This she was allowed to do. The Colonel looked graver than usual. Her Ladyship looked so troubled that it quite broke my heart to see her. Concern and anxiety for Emilia and worries about the wedding feast preoccupied her by turns, and everything she said began with 'Oh dear!' The Cornet was not happy either, and Helena's expressive face was a little sad and pensive. Julie was astonished beyond description to find that a wedding day could begin in such a dismal fashion, and her expression changed constantly from tearfulness to laughter and back again. Only the tutor and the Puddings were in their usual frame of mind. He bit his nails in silence with his nose in the air; they consumed a never-ending breakfast.

I assisted her Ladyship all morning, and there was plenty to discuss or arrange with others, and to prepare or attend to ourselves. We whipped the lemon cream, basted the joint, salted the broth, despaired together at the ruined tartlets, applauded the magnificent wedding cake, and burned our tongues tasting at least seventeen sauces. They are certainly not poetic flames which Hymen's torch kindles in the kitchen hearth!

The Colonel himself prepared punchbowls of Swedish punch and mulled red wine with oranges, and generally made a nuisance of himself; he needed so many people and so much space and was so convinced that this was more important than anything else remaining to be done, that he rather annoyed her Ladyship. She therefore gave her husband a little lecture and he – admitted she was right!

While I was showing the cook the most elegant way to prepare one of the *hors d'oeuvres*, Julie came running into the

51

kitchen with tears in her eyes. 'Give me, oh give me,' she cried, with her usual sense of urgency, 'Something tasty for Emilia! She ate nothing for breakfast, she will be ill, she will swoon from sheer weakness before the day is out! What have you got here? Eggs in broth! Two of those. Glasses of jelly! Two of those! I may, may I not? Ah, a little caper sauce, that will liven her up – and now a little fish or meat to go with it, a couple of bread rolls ... oh yes, and a few pastries as well, that should do. Emilia enjoys sweet things so much. Do you know what she is doing, Beata?' she went on in a whisper. 'She is praying to God! I looked through the keyhole; she is on her knees in prayer. God bless her!', and clear pearls of tears trickled down Julie's cheeks as she rushed out carrying, though I scarcely know how, three laden plates.

At last our arrangements were complete, everything could be left, with the necessary instructions, in the hands of the servants, and the Colonel, her Ladyship and I went to dress for the midday meal.

Later, I went in to Emilia. She stood in front of a mirror, dressed in her bridal gown, contemplating herself with a look that expressed neither pleasure nor that self-satisfaction which an attractive and well-dressed woman nearly always feels at the sight of her charming person. Helena was fastening Emilia's bracelet while Julie knelt to adjust the trimming of the gown.

'Look!' called out Julie as I came into the room, 'Is she not sweet? Is she not beautiful? And yet,' she added in a whisper, 'I would give away half of everything I own to buy her a different expression. She is as gloomy and grey as the weather, to be sure!'

Emilia had heard these last words, and said, 'It is impossible to look pleased when you are not happy. Everything feels so heavy, so unbearable. This is a dreadful day; I wish I might die!'

'Good heavens!' said Julie, clasping her hands. 'Now she is going to cry and make her eyes and nose red and will not be at all pretty any more. What are we to do?'

'Dear Emilia,' said Helena gently, pressing her sister's hand to her lips, 'Are you not being a little foolish? After all, this marriage is your own wish as much as everyone else's. Human reason tells us that you are bound to be happy. Is Algernon not full of the noblest virtues, does he not love you most tenderly? Where could you find a husband who would be a more loving son to your parents, a more devoted brother to us?'

'All that is true Helena, or rather, it all seems true. But, oh! When I think that I am now on the point of changing my whole existence ... , that I will be leaving my parents, abandoning you, my dear, my beloved sisters, this home, where I have been so happy – and all this for a man, whose heart I do not know as I know yours, whose attitude to me could change, who could make me unhappy in so many ways, and this man is to be my all from now on ... my fate will be tied irrevocably to his ... o sisters, when I think of it all, I feel my knees tremble – and when I think, that it is today ... today ... in a few hours, that my fate is to be sealed ... and that I still have my freedom, can still draw back ... then I feel an agony of indecision, of uncertainty, which no one can imagine. Beata, sisters, never marry!'

'But dearest Emilia,' responded Helena, 'You always find it so easy to resign yourself to the inevitable, so consider the fact that your fate already is sealed, that it is already too late to step back from the brink of happiness.'

'Too late!' cried Emilia, paying no heed to the final words. 'It is not too late, until the parson has united us ... even at the foot of the altar, I still have the right to ... and can ...'

'And you would have the heart to?' Julie burst out in tragic tone. 'You would want to plunge Algernon into despair? You would bring yourself to do ...'

'What a scene!' said a voice from the doorway, and there stood the Colonel with his arms folded and an amused expression, looking at Julie, whose pose was not unlike those for which the famous actress Mademoiselle George was applauded in Semiramis and Mary Stuart. Julie blushed, and Emilia even more so.

The Cornet, who followed his father into the room, presented Emilia on Algernon's behalf with some exquisitely beautiful fresh flowers and a note, which contained only a few lines, but they were anything but cold and formal. Emilia's face brightened, and she squeezed her brother's hand. Indulging in a sudden fit of chivalrous passion, he fell to his knees and begged leave to kiss the toe of her shoe. She graciously extended her little foot, and as he bent down, not as I thought to kiss the toe of her shoe, but to bite it, she put her arms around his neck and kissed him warmly. The Colonel took her hand, stood her in the middle of the floor, and we made a ring around her. When she saw his affectionate, fatherly look and our faces full of delight and love, a pleasant sensation came over her, and she blushed and looked as pretty as Julie could ever have wished. Her attire was simple, but very tasteful and elegant. For those of my young readers who wish to know more about her toilette, here you have it: she wore a dress of white silk trimmed with lace, in her light, beautifully done hair was the crown of myrtle, over which a veil (Helena's magnificent work) was prettily arranged, giving her mild and innocent face the look of a Veronese madonna. All that was lacking to make her lovely was that expression of joy, hope and love which is a bride's greatest adornment.

Her heart meanwhile seemed to have grown a little lighter and, as if to be in harmony with her sentiments, the sun broke through the clouds and sent a few pale rays into the room. But neither this external brightening, nor that within Emilia, lasted more than a few moments. It grew dark once more. When we were going down to dinner, Julie pulled a sorry face as she showed me how all the food that she had taken to Emilia had been left untouched. Only a glass of jelly had been eaten.

At table Emilia looked around at all the people she was soon to leave, and her heart swelled as tears rose in her eyes. We dined without our customary cheerfulness, and no one seemed to have much appetite, except of course the tutor and the Puddings. Emilia, who seemed more weighed down by her crown of myrtle than ever a king was by his crown, ate nothing and did not laugh once during the meal, in spite of the many excellent opportunities afforded her by the tutor's various strange antics. First he confused his snuffbox with the salt cellar, which were both standing near him on the table, sprinkled a portion of snuff into his soup and sniffed a hearty pinch of salt, which all resulted in a great many tears and facial contortions. Secondly, in an attempt to dry his eyes, he mistook one end of her ladyship's shawl for his handkerchief, but found it whisked out of his hand with great haste and consternation. Thirdly, he paid flattering compliments to the servant who was offering him the roast, and asked the young lady next to him to be so good as to hurry up and help herself. Julie looked anxiously at her sister. 'She is neither eating nor laughing,' she whispered to me. 'It really is too bad!'

It went from bad to worse during the afternoon as the few invited guests assembled, and Algernon, who had been expected to arrive early, did not appear. Her Ladyship glanced continually and with the most troubled look in the world towards the door, and came up to me three or four times just to say, 'I cannot imagine why Algernon is taking so long.' The new arrivals also enquired after him; Emilia said nothing, nor did she look at the door, but it was plain to see that she was growing paler and graver with every passing moment. Julie sat down beside me and told me the names of the guests as they arrived, adding a few comments of her own. 'That beautiful and stately woman who is introducing herself so graciously is Baroness S*** . Who would believe that every time she enters a drawing room, she is so self-conscious that she trembles? See her soulful eyes? Do not be deceived by them: she can speak about nothing but the weather, and at home she yawns her way through her days. Who is coming now, holding his hat in front of him like a beggar to precede him as he enters the room? Aha! Uncle P.; he is a good old fellow, but prone to sleeping sickness. I shall give him a kiss instead of a coin. God preserve him from starting to snore during the ceremony. Look at my Arvid, Beata, over there by the stove. Is he not an Apollo? And yet, I think he stands there warming himself with too much regard for his own comfort ... he seems entirely to forget that there are others in the room. That's my cousin, Mrs M., who just came in. She is an angel. And that fragile little body contains a great soul.'

'Look how Emilia is receiving everyone ... for all the world as though she were saying: It is good of you, ladies and gentlemen, to be present at my funeral! I cannot imagine what Algernon is thinking of, being so late. Dear God, how unhappy Emilia looks!'

'There is the parson! In spite of his warts and his red eye, he still looks kind. I feel a sort of respect for him.'

'Look how Carl is trying to cheer up Emilia and distract her. A good try, brother of mine! But now it is too late to help.'

'Well thank goodness, here is Algernon at last! But how grave and pale he looks! Yet still attractive. Much more attractive than Emilia at this moment, at any rate. He is going up to her, just see her proud look! He is apologizing, I think ... What! He has had raging toothache, had to have a tooth pulled! Poor Algernon! Toothache on his wedding day! What a fate! Look, now they are all sitting round in a circle. People sitting in a circle can give even me the vapours. What are they talking about? I do believe they are discussing the weather. Most interesting topic, to be sure. But really not a cheerful one: just listen to the snow and rain rattling the windows. It is dreadfully warm in here ... and Emilia is making the atmosphere even more unbearable. I must go and talk to her.'

After a time, word was sent in that a crowd of townsfolk was blocking the steps and the entrance hall, asking to see the bride. New torments for the unassuming Emilia. She stood up, but quickly sat down again, the colour draining from her face.

'Eau de cologne! Eau de cologne!' cried Julie to me. 'She has gone so pale, she is going to faint!'

'Water!' thundered the Colonel. The tutor grabbed hold of the little tea urn and came rushing forward. I do not know whether it was the sight of him, or an inward effort to quell her agitation, which helped Emilia to master her weakness. She quickly recovered and went out, followed by her sisters, and casting an anxious and unhappy glance at Algernon, who stood motionless some distance away, watching her with an unusually serious, almost stern expression.

'Are you mad?' hissed Uncle P., shaking the tutor's arm as he stood there with the tea urn in his hand and confusion in his eyes, The tutor turned round in a panic and collided with the Puddings, who tumbled over one another like a pair of skittles knocked down by a ball. The tea urn wobbled in the tutor's hand, burning his fingers – and he let it go with a yelp of pain onto the unfortunate Puddings, over whose unmoving bodies a cloud of smoke billowed up. If the moon had fallen from the sky, there could hardly have been a greater commotion than in the first moments of this catastrophe with the tea urn. Axel and Claes made no sound – and her Ladyship was quite ready to believe that this was the end for her little Puddings. But once Algernon and the Colonel had picked them up and shaken them, it was clear that they were very much alive. They were just so surprised, so terrified, so beside themselves with shock, that at first they were able neither to move nor to speak. Luckily, the hot water which had been tipped on them had mostly been soaked up by their clothes; it had also probably cooled down a little, as they had all finished drinking tea half an hour before. Only a scald-mark on Axel's forehead and Claes's left hand required treatment. The tutor was in despair; the little boys were in tears. They were put to bed in another room, where I promised to spend as much time with them as I possibly could. Her Ladyship's kindness and goodness, which meant that she could never relax while there was a sad face to be seen, led her next to try to comfort the tutor. She managed to do so mainly by pointing out how the boys had borne the shock in a truly Spartan spirit, and by saying that she considered this an excellent indication of the splendid education he had given them. The tutor began to look happy and flushed, threw out his chest and said that he 'hoped to make real little Spartans out of her Ladyship's promising sons!' Her Ladyship hoped that this would not be by means of renewed dousings with boiling water, but she kept this hope to herself.

The viewing of the bride was meanwhile at an end, and an exhausted Emilia left the room where she had been forced, in keeping with the strange but long-observed tradition in Sweden, to display herself to a sea of inquisitive and coolly appraising eyes.

'They did not think she was beautiful,' Julie lamented to me, 'And that is no surprise, for she was as gloomy and chilly as an autumn sky!'

We had taken Emilia to a quiet room to let her rest a while. She sank down onto a chair, buried her face in her handkerchief and made no sound.

In the drawing room, everything was ready for the ceremony. They were only waiting for Emilia.

'Smell some *eau de cologne*, Emilia! Sweet Emilia, drink a glass of water!' begged Julie, who was now beginning to tremble.

'They are waiting for you, dear Emilia!', said Cornet Carl, entering the room to offer to accompany her.

'I cannot – I really cannot come,' said Emilia in a voice that betrayed deep anguish.

'You cannot!' exclaimed the Cornet in amazement. 'Why ever not?' And he looked at us all questioningly. Julie stood in a tragic attitude, her hands clasped above her head. Helena sat with a look of disapproval on her calm face, and I – I find it impossible to recall what I was doing, but in my heart I was sympathizing with Emilia. Not one of us answered.

'No, I cannot come,' continued Emilia with a depth of emotion quite unusual for her. 'I cannot swear this oath that will bind me for ever. I feel quite sure ... we would be unhappy together ... we do not suit one another. I may be wrong ... but I am nonetheless convinced. At this moment he is no doubt dissatisfied with me, thinks me a creature of whims ... loathes the thought of sharing his fate with such a person ... I could read all that in his stern look just now ... he may be right, wholly right ... and so it is best for him, and for me, that we now part.'

'But Emilia!' exclaimed her brother, 'Do you realize what you are saying? It is too late, you must see that ... the parson is here ... the wedding guests ... Algernon ...'

'Go to him, dearest Carl!' cried Emilia in rising panic. 'Ask him to come here. I shall talk to him myself, tell him everything ... it cannot be too late, when it is a question of salvaging a lifetime's peace and happiness; go, I beg you, go!'

'Dear God, dear God! Where will it all end?' said Julie, looking as though she wanted to call on Heaven and Earth for assistance.

'Emilia, think of Papa!'

'I shall throw myself at his feet; he cannot want his child to be unhappy for ever!'

'If we could only distract her somehow ... fix her attention on something else for a moment!' whispered Helena to her brother.

Cornet Carl opened a door as if to go out, and at the same instant we heard a loud thump; the Cornet cried: 'Oh, my eye!' There was general consternation, for this little deception was done so naturally that none of us stopped to consider that it might be a trick. Emilia, always ready to be the first to assist anyone in distress, remained so now in spite of her great anxiety, and hurried up to her brother with a handkerchief soaked in cold water. She drew his hand from the eye and began to bathe it energetically but carefully, asking anxiously, 'Does it hurt very much? Do you think the eye is damaged? At least there is no blood ...'

'That could be all the more dangerous!' said the Cornet in a mournful voice, but by then he could not hold back a treacherous grin, which destroyed the whole illusion.

Emilia took a closer look at him and was at once assured that the blow was very far from real. 'Ah,' she said, 'I see what this is. It is one of your pranks, but it does not deceive me. I beg, I implore you Carl, if you feel the least affection for me, then go to Algernon, tell him that I ask for a few minutes to talk to him!'

'Why did none of you have the presence of mind to blow out the candle!' complained the Cornet, looking in annoyance at us, and principally at me. Helena whispered something to him, and he went out of the room, followed by Julie.

Helena and I stayed still and quiet, while Emilia, clearly in a state of mental torment, walked up and down the room and appeared to be talking to herself. 'What should I do? How should I act?' she muttered several times. Then steps were heard in the adjoining room. 'He is coming!' said Emilia, and her whole body trembled.

The door opened and Algern... no, the Colonel entered with a look of grave authority. Emilia caught her breath, sat down, stood up, sat down again, went pale and then flushed. 'You have kept us waiting too long,' he said, calmly but a little sternly, 'And now I have come to fetch you.'

Emilia clasped her hands, looked imploringly up at her father, opened her mouth and closed it again, intimidated by the stern, grave look on his face, and when he took her hand, all power of resistance seemed to desert her. With a kind of despairing submissiveness she got up and allowed him to lead her out. Helena and I followed them.

The drawing room was brightly lit, and everyone gathered there had their eyes fixed on the door through which Emilia, led by her father, entered.

She has told me since that when she came in she could not clearly distinguish a single object, everything seemed black before her eyes. 'It was hardly surprising then,' said her brother, 'That you looked as though you were sleepwalking.'

Algernon watched Emilia with a gravity that did little to encourage her at that moment. Neither of them spoke. The ceremony began. The young couple stood before the parson. Emilia was deathly pale and trembling. Julie completely lost heart. 'This is awful!' she said, and went almost as pale as her sister.

Now the voice was heard that was to set forth for the young husband and wife their holy duties. That voice was deep and sonorous and seemed inspired by a divine spirit. It spoke of the sanctity of marriage, of the mutual obligation of man and wife to love one another, lighten life's burdens for one another, cushioning the blow of any troubles they might meet, and set one another an example of true piety. It spoke of that prayer for one another which unites them in spirit and brings them nearer to the eternal truth of how the highest form of happiness can be fostered by a union, thus begun and continued according to God's will. It called down the blessings of the Almighty on the young couple. These words, so sweet to the ears, so beautiful, so serene, awoke still and holy sentiments in all our breasts. It was so quiet in the room that one might almost have believed everyone was holding their breath. I could see clearly that Emilia was becoming calmer with every passing moment. The few words that she had to speak were said clearly and with a steady voice. As they knelt there, she seemed to me to be praying with hope and reverence. I, meanwhile, cast an observant glance around me. The Colonel was paler than usual, but was watching the young couple with a wholly calm and tender expression. Her Ladyship was crying and kept her face hidden in her handkerchief. Julie was beside herself, although she moved neither hand nor foot. Helena had her clear eyes raised to Heaven in supplication. The Cornet was trying valiantly to pretend that it was something other than tears making his eyes so red. The blind girl was smiling quietly. The other people present displayed varying degrees of emotion; the most visibly moved was the tutor, who as the ceremony neared its end was alone in disturbing the silence as he repeatedly blew his nose. Fortunately, he had managed to find his handkerchief. The blessing was pronounced over the bridal couple in a voice so mellow and majestic that it might have come from Heaven. The wedding was over. Emilia and Algernon were united for all time. Emilia turned to embrace her parents. To me she looked a completely different person. A soft radiance glowed on her brow and smiled out of her eyes. A warm, clear colour lit her cheeks. All at once she was transformed into the ideal picture of a young and happy bride. 'Thank God! Thank God!' whispered Julie with eyes full of tears and hands clasped. 'Now all is well.'

'Yes, there is no helping it now,' said the Colonel, trying to overcome his emotion by adopting his comical look. 'Now you are caught; now you can no longer refuse!'

'Nor would I wish to, now,' answered Emilia with a sweet smile, and looked up at Algernon with an expression that brought pure and eager joy to his face. A contented and cheerful mood spread among the guests. They all looked as though they felt like singing or dancing. Even Uncle P. was wide awake, arranged a quadrille and was soon stamping cheerfully at the side of the elegant Baroness S***, who glided like a zephyr to and fro across the floor. Arvid and Julie made a charming impression on the dance floor; no-one could take their eyes off such an attractive couple. I danced with the tutor, whose invitation was not, I hope, made in a fit of absent-mindedness. We made an impression too, but in an extraordinary manner. It felt to me as if we were a couple of billiard balls perpetually at the ready for the others to cannon into. It is quite true that at times we were pushed, but at others *we* were doing all the pushing, a fact which I ascribe principally to my partner's constant confusion of left and right, not to mention all the steps of the quadrille. We laughed, however, as heartily and loudly as everyone else at our antics, and the tutor said that he had never danced such a merry *waltz*!

Helena played the piano for the dancing. Emilia had not wished to dance. She sat with Algernon at her side in a small inner room with its doors open onto the dancing area. They talked quietly, with animated but affectionate looks, and I believe that at that moment the Gordian knot of misunderstanding, hesitation, anxiety and doubt which had previously kept

63

them apart was untied for ever. The soft rays of a lamp, shining through an alabaster shade, cast an enchanting light on the young husband and wife, who now seemed as happy as they were beautiful.

They seemed to have forgotten the world around them, but none of the company had forgotten them. Each and every one cast sidelong glances into that little room and smiled contentedly to themselves. Julie came up to me several times and delightedly indicated the lovers' tableau, saying 'Look, look!'

Later in the evening some of the guests gathered in the little room, and a more general conversation began. Some newly published books which were lying on a table there prompted various comments on their merits, and on reading in general.

'I simply cannot fathom,' said Uncle P. with his slight Finnish accent, 'what the devil is the matter with me these days. After all, I am usually as lively and wide awake as a jumping fish, but as soon as I start reading these d.. books, there they are resting on my nose, and I am oblivious to the world.'

'Does my dear Aunt like reading?' Emilia asked Baroness S***.

'Alas, my God!' she answered, and raised her beautiful eyes to the ceiling, 'I never have time for it; I am so busy.' And she draped her fine shawl carefully around her.

'If I ever marry,' said a man of about sixty, 'it will be on condition that my wife never reads any books, with the possible exception of the psalter and her cookery book.'

'My late wife never read books other than those ... but even so she was a splendid housekeeper!' exclaimed Uncle P., drying his eyes and taking a pinch of snuff.

'Yes by Jove, I cannot understand why womenfolk these days spend so much time reading, by Jove I cannot!' said Lieutenant Arvid, reaching out to take a handful of sweets from a plate.

Julie gave her betrothed a hard stare, and I think that on this occasion she found the 'By Jove' very little to her liking. Flushed with vexation, she said 'I should rather go without food and drink than be deprived of reading. Is there anything more improving for the soul than reading good books? Anything which better raises the spir... I mean to say raises our thoughts and feelings to ... about ... to ...'

My poor little Julie was never a great success when she tried to discuss high-flown topics. Her thoughts were rather like rockets, which suddenly shoot up like brilliant tongues of fire, but die almost at once and are reduced to ashes.

Cornet Carl hurriedly poured a glass of wine and water over Lieutenant Arvid and pretended that he had made his sister lose the thread of her argument with his exclamation: 'I just knew it would never work! I was trying to balance the glass on the end of my thumb. I beg your pardon, brother-in--law! But I believe you were somehow sitting in my way ... my arm was obstructed.'

'I shall certainly take care not to get in your way another time', said Lieutenant Arvid half humorously, half indignantly, as he rose to dry off his dinner jacket with his pocket handkerchief, caution prompting him to seek a seat on the far side of the room.

But Julie was not to be freed from her predicament so easily. The old gentleman who was so hostile to books turned to her with great gravity and said, 'I presume cousin Julie reads mostly books of morality and sermons?'

'N-o ... no ... not, not sermons exactly,' answered Julie in embarrassment, and at that moment she became aware of Professor L.'s penetrating gaze resting on her, which caused her to blush deeply.

'Presumably then my cousin reads history – certainly a very worthy subject to study.'

'Not exactly history,' said Julie, happy and bold once more. 'But histori*es* I like very much. In short, if Uncle wishes to know which reading matter it is that will make me willingly go without food and drink, then it is ... novels.'

The old man raised his eyebrows and hands with an expression of horror. His expression tempted one to believe that Rousseau's statement 'Jamais fille sage n'a lu de romans' had led him wholly to shun such dangerous reading matter.

There was something disapproving in almost everyone's eyes at Julie's frank admission. The Baroness seemed completely taken aback by her niece. Only the Professor smiled kindly, and the Cornet leapt in with 'My word! It is no wonder people read novels, the way they are written these days. Madame de Staël's heroine Corinne cost me a sleepless night, and Walter Scott's Rebecca made me lose my appetite completely for three days.'

Julie looked at her brother in astonishment. Even Emilia's gentle, light blue eyes were raised questioningly towards him. But he found it prudent to avoid them.

'My Euphemia shall never read novels', said Baroness S***, whereupon she clasped her hands tightly together, sat back in the corner of the sofa, and looked down at her beautiful shawl.

'Oh, but Aunt!' said Mrs M., smiling and shaking her head. 'Whatever *shall* she read then?'

'She shall read nothing at all!'

'An excellent idea!' said the old man.

'I truly believe,' said Algernon, 'That it is better to read nothing at all, than to read only novels. Novel reading is to the soul as opium is to the body: continuous use of it weakens and harms us. Begging your pardon Julie, but I believe a young lady can make better use of her time than spending it on that kind of reading.'

Julie looked as though she had no inclination to pardon this remark.

66

Emilia said 'I think like Algernon that – particularly for young ladies – that sort of reading does more harm than good.'

Tears came into Julie's eyes and she looked at Emilia as if to say, 'Are you against me too?'

'I admit,' said Mrs M., 'That it can be very harmful, if ...'

'Harmful!' interrupted the old gentleman, 'Say depraved, poisonous, destructive through and through!'

Julie laughed. 'My dear Professor,' she cried. 'Help, help! I am starting to think myself a lost and sinful creature. Say something, I beg you, in defence of novel reading, and then I will give you something tasty.' With a mischievous smile she held up a garland of sweets.

'It certainly has it good points,' answered the Professor, 'When it is done discriminatingly and in moderation. For my part, I consider good novels both the most useful and the most pleasant reading for young people.'

'Do you hear, do you hear!' cried Julie, and clapped her hands.

'But you must justify that comment, my good Sir, justify it!' exclaimed Uncle P.

'Yes, yes, justify it!' bellowed the old gentleman.

'Good novels,' the Professor went on, 'That is, those which like good paintings reproduce nature in a true and beautiful way, have advantages which no other kind of book can combine to the same degree. They relate the story of the human heart; and is that not the most valuable and interesting subject for all young people, so anxious to find out about themselves and their fellows? The world is depicted in its many complex, ever-changing guises, in the liveliest possible way, and young people can see mapped out before their eyes the country in which they will shortly begin their long journey through life. The fine and appealing aspects of virtue are presented in the novel in a poetic and fascinating light. Hot young senses are inspired here by

67

what is right and good, things which if presented in a sterner and more serious form could have seemed repellent to them.

'In the same way, vices and base actions are revealed as abominations, and one learns to despise them, dressed by the great and splendid trappings of this world though they may be, and instead is seized by enthusiasm for virtue, albeit weighed down by all the miseries on earth.

'The true depiction of how goodness is rewarded and evil is punished in a person, however little his or her outward fate reflects it, is brought out in the novel with all the clarity, energy and power that one could wish to attach to every moral truth so that it is easy for everyone to understand, and can bear fruit.

'It is also natural that high-minded young people should love novels as their best friends, when they find in them the great, noble, passionate feelings which they nourish in their own hearts and which have there awakened the first heavenly intimations of happiness and immortality.'

Julie got quickly to her feet with a look of great delight on her pretty face, went over to the Professor and gave him, not the garland of sweets, but a childishly affectionate hug, saying 'A thousand thanks, a thousand thanks, I am content, completely content!'

The old gentleman raised his eyes heavenwards, and sighed.

Lieutenant Arvid did not look 'completely content', but continued his endless consumption of sweets.

Uncle P. closed his eyes and nodded; but not in agreement, according to the Cornet.

The Professor, on the other hand, looked quite content, and with an expression of paternal kindness kissed first the vivacious girl's hand and then her forehead.

Lieutenant Arvid pushed back his chair with a great clatter; at that moment the doors to the dining room were opened, and the wedding feast was served.

68

A meal is always of special interest to those who have helped to arrange and prepare it. Each dish, child of our cares, contributes to our interest and sense of satisfaction now that it stands on the table, dainty and tempting, and soon to disappear for ever. But on such occasions, one develops a heart of stone, and I am sure her Ladyship was as pleased as I was to see how all our delicious *hors d'oeuvres, entremets* and desserts disappeared into the mouths of the wedding guests, apparently with great relish and enjoyment on their part. Her Ladyship, her mind at rest about Emilia, and seeing how splendidly the serving of the meal was going, did the honours with a charming cheerfulness tempered only by the occasional anxious thought for the Puddings. The bride was gentle and radiant. Algernon seemed the happiest of mortals. Cornet Carl, seated next to me at the table, said, every ten minutes, 'Look at Emilia, look at Emilia! Can you believe she is the same person as the one who tormented herself and us half the day?'

Julie adopted a superior and haughty expression, whenever her beloved addressed her. He eventually made up his mind that he would sulk as well, although his mouth was always full.

Uncle P. fell asleep with a blob of blancmange on his nose, and his snores could occasionally be heard above the chatter and laughter of the company, like the sound of a double bass joining in with the higher notes of the smaller fiddles.

Towards the end of the meal, toasts were proposed, not the tiresome ceremonial kind, but happy, heartfelt ones. The tutor, carried away by the occasion and the wine, stood glass in hand and improvised the following toast in honour of the bridal couple:

> Fill our glasses to the brim
> Drain the punchbowl too
> Let bubbles overflow the rim

Dear couple, the toast is – you!

To the sound of chinking glasses
May we with assembled cheer
Find each happy year soon passes
Until your gold wedding is here!

The toast was drunk to the accompaniment of general laughter and the chinking of glasses. Another was drunk to the tutor himself who, I am sure, now considered himself as good a poet as Bellman.

After the meal, Emilia had a very pleasant surprise. On a large table in the drawing room, portraits of her parents, sisters and brothers were laid out. They were painted in oils and almost all were very good likenesses. 'In this way we can all follow you to your new home,' said the Colonel with his arms around her. 'So you see, you will not be rid of us!' Tears of happiness ran down Emilia's cheeks; she embraced her father, her mother, her sisters and brother, and for a long time could not find words to thank them. Then they all began to study each portrait in detail, and comments of every description were to be heard. Here was something a bit wrong with a nose, here the eyes were too small, here the mouth was too large; moreover, the artist had made no attempt to be flattering, in fact quite the reverse, and so on and so on.

Poor artists! This is the review to which a fondness for finding faults, that most common of complaints, subjects your work: poor artists! It is indeed fortunate for you that you so often turn a deaf ear, and are satisfied with the feel of money in your pocket and the knowledge of your talent in your own soul!

Emilia alone found no faults. That was precisely her father's look, her mother's smile, sister Julie's mischievous expression, brother Carl's impatient charm, Helena's aura of goodness and calm. And the little Puddings – oh! What an amazing likeness. You could almost be tempted to offer them sweets.

Poor little Puddings! Scalded and agitated, they had been forced to leave the party which they had been looking forward to for three weeks. But throughout the evening there was always someone creeping upstairs with apples, sugar buns and other things for them. The tutor was the most eager to run up and downstairs to begin with, but having knocked himself down three times on the unfamiliar route, he was content to stay in the drawing room.

Her Ladyship meanwhile had said to me at least six times and in an extremely anxious tone, 'My poor little boys! I shall certainly have to sit up with them tonight!' and each time I had answered, 'Your Ladyship shall not, for I shall sit up with them.'

'But you are sure to fall asleep!'

'I shall not fall asleep, your Ladyship.'

'Parole d'honneur?'

'Parole d'honneur, your Ladyship.' And, haunted by her Ladyship's anxiety, I went up to them even before the company had departed, armed with sticking plaster, bottles of drops, and nice things to eat.

The little boys were very pleased with the last of these, and delighted that I would be burning the midnight oil on their account. Their evening's adventure was very much on their minds, and they never stopped telling me how the tutor had bumped into them, how they had fallen, and what they had thought and felt when the tutor spilt the contents of the tea urn on them. Axel had thought of the Great Flood, Claes of the Last Judgement. In the middle of their story, they fell asleep.

At half past eleven I heard the noise of harness bells, coaches and horses outside the Colonel's house. By twelve, all was quiet and still both indoors and out.

71

Soon everyone will be sleeping peacefully, I thought, and I too gradually began to feel too sleepy for words.

There is no greater torment than being alone, being sleepy, and being obliged to stay awake, especially when those one is keeping watch over are snoring for all they are worth, and if I had not given my *parole d'honneur* not to shut my eyes, I am sure I should soon have done as they did. I took out the stocking I was knitting, but had to abandon it as I was in danger of poking out my eye at any moment. I read, and took in not one word of what I was reading. I went over to the window, looked up at the moon, and thought – nothing. The wick of my candle grew as tall as an iris. I tried to trim it – and most unfortunately put it out. My watching role was now even harder to carry out. I tried to frighten myself awake and to imagine that the vague shimmer of the white-tiled stove was the ghost of the White Lady. I thought of a cold hand suddenly grasping mine, a voice whispering horrible secrets in my ear, a bloody figure rising up through the floor, when suddenly – a cock's crow was heard from a neighbouring courtyard, and combined with the light of dawn to make all my imagined spectres evaporate.

The melancholy song of two small chimney-sweeps, greeting the morning from the tops of their smoky pavilions, formed the overture to the general awakening of life. In kitchen regions, friendly fires were soon blazing, fragrant coffee spread its Arabian aroma through the house, people appeared in the streets, and through the clear winter air came the melodious pealing of church bells with their summons to morning prayer. Clouds of purple smoke arched upwards into the pale blue sky, and with joy I saw at last the rays of the sun, which first greeted the weathercocks and stars atop the church towers, then spread their mantle of light over the roofs of ordinary people's dwellings.

The world around me was opening its clear eyes, I was thinking about shutting mine, and as happy voices greeted me with a 'Good morning!' I answered with a sleepy 'Good night!'

Part Two

Midday meal.
A little of everything, all stewed together.

The wedding day – and the morning after! A dull day in the wedding house. The only thing we have left of all yesterday's festivities is what you get when a candle has gone out, the lingering *smell*. And when the familiar home circle has lost, along with all the festive sounds and costumes, a friendly face (a star that shone in its sky), it is not surprising that the horizon darkens. Yes, my little Julie, I found it quite natural for you to get up and wander around all day like a raincloud, since your brother was not unlike a thundercloud as he walked from room to room, tootling away at the Star Song, which did not make pleasant listening.

It had been agreed that the newly-weds would spend the day with Algernon's elderly grandmother, who lived shut away from the world with her maid, her cat, her bleary eyes and her philanthropy, which led her to wish that people should never marry, a pious hope that she had even expressed to her grandson and Emilia, but in vain. Even in the midst of her annoyance, however, she had asked the young couple to visit her and had, so the rumour went, herself peeled the apples for the apple cake, which was to be the crowning glory of the frugal midday meal. The next day, they would come to us, and the day after that, we were invited to their house.

Meanwhile, we got through the day after the wedding in a kind of numb silence. Her Ladyship ate nothing all day but thin gruel.

Once the heavy day was over, and each and every one of us had gone to our rooms, Julie felt a pressing need to cheer herself up, so she sent for some walnuts, came in to me, and sat down to crack them and to heap praise on her betrothed.

'He was exceptionally well-behaved! So neat, so wise, so even-tempered, so calm, so pleasant, so proper (what a tasty nut!), so considerate, so careful, so methodical in what he had to do ... not mean either ... so good ... but not too good ... so ... so absolutely just right!'

I nodded in agreement with all this, wished Julie great happiness and – yawned a great yawn. There are things so perfect that they *send you to sleep.*

The next day, a slightly fresher breeze was blowing. The newly-weds came to dinner. The matron's cap suited Emilia very well; she was mild, calm, charming – but just not happy, whereas Algernon was unusually cheerful, lively and talkative. This surprised and vexed Julie, who looked from one to the other, and did not know quite where she stood. All the family servants were extremely anxious to be allowed to call Emilia 'Your Ladyship'. Her new title did not seem to please her, and when a faithful old maidservant said for the seventh time, 'Miss ... oh Lord Jesus ... Your Ladyship,' Emilia finally said, in a slightly sad and weary tone, 'Please do not worry! It really does not matter.' The manservant waiting at table did not offer her a single dish without asking obsequiously 'Would your Ladyship care for ...' 'Yes indeed, that man knows what is what,' remarked the Colonel. Emilia looked as though she found this not at all to her taste. Julie, anxious at heart, took her sister aside that afternoon, knelt before her and wrapped her arms around her, crying tearfully, 'Emilia, what is wrong? Dear Emilia! ... Good God ... you are not pleased, you look dejected. Are you not content? Are you not happy?' Emilia embraced her sister warmly and said comfortingly, but with tears in her gentle eyes, 'I am sure I will be, dear Julie. Algernon is so good, so noble, I cannot fail to be happy with him.'

But Julie, like all those of a lively disposition, was not content with this 'I will be'; she wanted an 'I am', and thought it a tragedy, quite unheard of and unnatural, that a young wife should not be indescribably happy. *She had read novels.* She was very short with Algernon for the rest of the day, although this did not particularly seem to trouble him.

Once Emilia, with tears in her eyes, had again taken leave of her home, Julie gave vent to her disapproval, and expressed out loud her indignation that Algernon could be so indifferent and cheerful when Emilia was so downhearted. He was 'an icicle, a barbarian, a heathen, a ...' N.B. The Colonel and her Ladyship were not present at this outburst. The Cornet had his own view on the matter and was dissatisfied with Emilia who, he thought, had expected her husband to wait on her too much. 'Did he not, poor fellow, run to look for her sewing basket? Did he not put her boots, her scarf and her coat on for her? – And did she even thank him?' Julie took her sister's part, the Cornet Algernon's; the spirit of argument soon began to cast its bitter grains of truth into the dispute, and the good brother and sister might easily have fallen out with one another, had they not both bent down to pick up Helena's needle and cracked their heads together, a shock which caused the quarrel to dissolve into gales of laughter. The question of the rights of man and woman, the sea on whose waves they were doing battle, quite unaware that they were cast afloat, was quickly abandoned.

The following day was a great consolation for Julie. Emilia was happier, and so pleased to be able to receive her family in her own home that she set about entertaining them well, with natural grace, sincerity and warmth. All the Colonel's favourite dishes were on the menu at dinner, and Emilia's eyes sparkled with joy when her father asked for a second helping of turtle soup, adding that it was 'damned good'. Her Ladyship was not a little impressed by the quality and orderliness of the meal, and the arrangements in general. She peered a little suspiciously at a pudding, one side of which was something of a *ruin*, but Julie, unobserved, deftly turned the plate round and her Ladyship, who was a little short-sighted, thought her eyes had deceived her and calmed herself.

Emilia seemed very much at home in her role as *Mistress of the House*, and it was extremely becoming. The Cornet was delighted with his sister and everything around her in her new home; everything was so Swedish, he thought, sofas and chairs, tables and curtains and china and so on. There was nothing foreign, and it was precisely that, he felt, that made one feel so comfortable and at home.

Julie was highly approving of Algernon who, while not exactly fussing over his young wife, nonetheless followed her with loving eyes from near and far; one could see clearly how his heart and soul enfolded her, and hers flew in many a clear and friendly look to join them.

How good coffee tastes, when there is a storm outside and a summer breeze within! All we ladies thought so, as we gathered round the fire that afternoon, enjoying the taste of the Arabian bean, and had a long and cheerful conversation. Emilia told us about all the domestic devices and contrivances she planned to adopt to create order and comfort in her home, some of which she had already discussed with, and others which she planned to discuss with her – her *husband* (this little word still seemed rather difficult for Emilia to say); and it was all very sensible, very good, very practical, I can tell you! Between the coffee cups and the fire we talked it all over in a thorough and adult way; we added things and took things away, but still did not come up with anything much better than what Emilia had already thought of.

The family is like both a poem and a machine. Its poetry, or song of feelings, which flows through and unites all its members, which winds garlands of flowers into life's crowns of thorns and helps hope to flower on 'the bare rocks of reality', is familiar to every human heart. But its machinery (without whose well-oiled movements *l'opera della vita* has nothing to support it) is considered insignificant and treated carelessly by many. And yet, this part of the institution of home life is not without importance for its harmonious functioning. This machinery is like the clock's. If all the wheels, springs and so on are well adjusted, the pendulum just needs a swing, and everything is set in purposeful motion, everything continues of its own accord in a calm and orderly way, and the golden hands of peace and well-being point to each hour on the bright clock face.

Emilia was well aware of this, and she was eager to organize her home and household from the outset in such a way that in spite of fate's occasional little knocks and nudges, its whole sense of order and well-being could last to the end – until the clock ran down.

One precious and important component in achieving this aim is the sensible and careful management of the household's financial affairs. These were on a good sound footing in Emilia's case. From the one large balance, several smaller allowances were paid, sub-divided and allocated, which, like streams all flowing from a single source and providentially channelled to different parts, made the home plantation bear fruit.

Emilia was to receive a set sum for her own personal annual allowance, which she could use for her clothes and for the settling of other little bills not provided for in the household accounts. And since her dress would always be simple and tasteful, as it had been up to now, she would be able to spend the larger part of her allowance in bringing joy to her heart; do guess – or do *say* how, dear readers. I am sure you know.

A wife should have her own funds, be they small or large. Ten, fifty, a hundred or a thousand crowns, all according to means, but her own, which she accounts for – herself. Do you want to know why, you good gentlemen who think your wives are there to account for buttonholes and pennies? In fact it is especially and above all for the sake of your own high and mighty peace and comfort. You do not understand? Well then: a maid breaks a teacup, a manservant smashes a glass, or perhaps suddenly the teapot, cups and glasses come to pieces, although *no-one* has broken them, least of all the Mistress of the House, who has no ready money but must have cups and glasses, so comes to her husband, tells him about the accident and asks for a little money to replace the broken ones. He grumbles about the servants, about his wife, whose job it is to keep the servants in order: 'Money, yes ... a little money ... money does not grow on trees, nor does it rain down from heaven ... many little streams make a great river,' and so on and so on. And the sum of it is, he hands over a little money and is often in a bad mood.

If, on the other hand, the wife has her own little bit of ready money, such little vexations need never come near him. Children, servants and accidents will always be the same, but nothing untoward will be noticed, everything will be in its usual place, as it should be, and the head of the house, who might quite calmly hand over a thousand crowns all at once, will be spared losing his even temper, as invaluable to the whole house as to himself, for the sake of a few coppers, extorted five times over.

Do they count for nothing, you unfeeling nabob, these little surprises, little birthday and name-day delights, which your wife can afford herself the pleasure of giving you? A thousand little treats which sparkle as unexpectedly as falling stars in the skies of the home could be yours, prompted by your wife's tender feelings towards you, with the aid of – *a little money*, which you could pay her in gross, and then receive back little by little with a rich interest of comfort and pleasure.

Well, is that clear now? Algernon had long realized it, and that did much for Emilia's future happiness.

For every truly female heart it is such an indescribable enjoyment to *give*, – to feel yourself come alive in the pleasure and good cheer of others. That is the sunshine of the heart, and it is needed here in the bleak North perhaps more than elsewhere. And besides, a little freedom is so invigorating!

Where was I? ... Oh yes, drinking coffee at Emilia's. From there we take quite a long journey on the wings of time.

Anyone who decides to use their pen for telling stories must take great care to be economical with the reader's patience. At times he can certainly give an account of today, tomorrow and the day after; but in between he will need to dispense with time and events, if he does not want the reader to dispense with his book and turn straight from chapter five to chapter eight. Being very anxious to avoid any such thing with my worthy family, I make haste to skip with them over about three months, and only to give you a neatly-parcelled summary of how my H*** friends passed that time.

Julie and her betrothed strolled through it. Every day, weather permitting, they walked all the way up Drottninggatan, greeted and chatted to acquaintances, and gazed at people's figures and clothes in the pleasant awareness of how splendidly attractive their own were. Now and then they went into a shop and bought some little thing, or ate a tartlet at Berndts, which was also 'frightfully pleasant'. In the evenings there would be some supper party, entertainment, ball or other – and this always provided a source of conversation for the following day, so that – thank goodness! – the couple were never short of things to talk about. In addition Lieutenant Arvid, who was involved in everything in the *big* wide world, always had some *small* item to relate, some anecdote for the day ... something said by someone or other about someone or other ... and there you are! That was all great fun, thought Julie.

The Cornet was in the grip of a strange passion. He had decided to study. He studied the Science of War, Mathematics, History etc. and found increasingly that just as the eyes in his head were created to see in all directions, over the Earth and up to Heaven, so were the eyes of his soul created to look on the kingdoms of nature and science and see the light of Heaven there. The peculiar thing was, that the more he learnt to see, the more afraid of the dark he became. He was even afraid of ghosts! Yes gentlemen, it really is true, and the ghosts he was afraid of have been known in the world from time immemorial by the names *Ignorance*, a monstrously fat woman, dressed in some shiny white fabric; *Conceit*, her long-necked daughter, who always follows behind, treading on the train of her mother's garment; and *Boastfulness*, said to be the ghost of an old French schoolmaster, who when alive was supposedly related to these ladies and was often seen in their company.

Otherwise the Cornet liked to seek out the company of older, wiser men; he was often at home with his father and Helena, and often left his young men friends rattling and pounding vainly at his closed door – albeit sometimes in two minds whether or not to open it, for he thought, 'Perhaps my good friend is coming to pay me the money he owes.' But then he reflected for a moment and thought, 'But then he would not be rattling the door so wildly,' and stayed peacefully at his work. The Cornet had two young friends to whom the door was always opened when they gave the word. These young men made a noble triumvirate. Their motto in both wartime and peacetime was 'Forward march!'

————

At the beginning of April, Emilia and Algernon travelled to the province of Blekinge, where an old aunt and godmother of Emilia's lived in a large country house. Soon after the wedding, Emilia had received a letter from her asking Emilia and her husband to visit at their earliest convenience. She had just lost her only child, a son, and now, at the age of sixty, she still wished to gladden, or rather breathe new life into, her heart by giving it something new to love and live for. She asked the newly-wed couple to spend the spring and summer with her, she spoke of neighbours and all manner of good and happy things which would make their summer stay pleasant. She mentioned that she wanted to make her will, and that her fortune would be theirs after her death, if they would treat her as a mother.

'Well, what d'you say! A handsome letter!' said Uncle P. 'Off you go, nephew, chop chop, with your wife ... call for the carriage at once. I wish I were in your shoes, you child of fortune! Wait until the beginning of April? Madness! Well, what if the old woman dies in the meantime! Now that is what I call sleeping through good fortune. Upon my soul, I would not let it happen to me! ... Dear Julie, wake me when the coffee comes.' When the carriage stood at the door and Emilia sat crying at Algernon's side, exchanging tearful and heartfelt looks and sad farewells with her family, who were gathered round her, Algernon took her hand and asked, '*Now* would you rather stay with *them* or come with me?'

'With you,' Emilia answered softly.

'With all your heart?'

'With all my heart.'

'Drive on,' shouted Algernon in delight. 'Emilia, let us travel together – through life!'

The carriage moved off smoothly. O that every marriage were as well sprung!

Silently and sadly, the blind girl crept through her dark days. Her health deteriorated visibly. Her soul was like the fire in the charcoal pile; its flames are not visible, they do not break through, but quietly and surely consume their dwelling place. Only in song could she occasionally express her feelings when she thought she was alone. She invented words and music; they bore the stamp of an unhappy heart which could find no peace. In company she hardly ever said a word, and only the way she endlessly twisted a ribbon or a cord around her hands and fingers betrayed the restless anxiety within her.

There can be in woman a state of mind which means that whatever she does in the domestic sphere is done well, that wherever she goes, a quiet joy goes with her, like that of a still spring day, that wherever she lingers, a sense of comfort and well-being is also found, and communicates itself to anyone who approaches her. This state of mind is the result of a pure, pious and humble heart. How lucky she is! Happy above all others (even if not as richly endowed as them in other respects) is she who possesses it. And Helena was happy, for she was one of those so beautifully gifted. In a letter to a friend written at this time, she herself described her happy state:

'You ask what I do. I enjoy every hour life brings. My parents, my sisters and brothers, my work, my books, my plants, the sun, the stars, Heaven and Earth; everything brings me joy; everything makes it an indescribable delight for me to experience the happiness of living. You ask me what I do when dark thoughts and doubts invade my soul. My dear friend, I have no doubts, no dark thoughts – I can have none – for I believe in God, I love Him, my hopes are invested in Him; I have no sorrows or anxieties, for I know that He will make all well ... that one day all will be made good, all will be explained. Thinking as I do, feeling as I do, I cannot but be happy, you see ...'

'*Curro, curri, currum, currere,*' chanted the young Puddings.

'*Cucurri, cursum, currere,* you wicked Puddings!' corrected the tutor; and they honestly went on like that (I never exaggerate) for nearly three months.

'It is going slowly – but it is going well!' said the tutor comfortingly and confidently to her Ladyship.

Her Ladyship – God bless her obliging Ladyship, but I am certain that our removal to the country could have been achieved without so many worries and so many boxes, so many 'Oh!'s and so many trunks. The Colonel half jokingly said a few words

85

to that effect. 'That is easily said,' answered her Ladyship earnestly.

The Cornet, who could never tolerate the slightest criticism of his mother, in whose doings he could never see the slightest thing wrong, agreed with all her worries and contradicted us when we found them a trifle unnecessary; and when things all became a little too upsetting, he went around singing 'God save the King' (the only English he knew) to divert our attention from her Ladyship.

For a whole month before our move and another month after it she caused a commotion – working in our best interests of course – and the day of the move itself – O heavens

<blockquote>

We are packing! What more
From cellar and store?
In parlour and hall
Chairs and chests hold a ball.
Stool, table and bed
All are turned on their head.
At her Ladyship's summons
The servants come running.
Visits and breakfast and luggage to view
What a great crush, they all want to get through
We all talk of friendship and beefsteak and goose
Mouths open, bags closed, and nothing left loose
A smile of relief from the lady of the house!
'The time has now come
So beat on the drum
So hurry, so hurry ... run hither and yon!
Drive forward, drive back! And put your coats on!'
So noisy, so fraught,
I can scarce bear the thought,

</blockquote>

and so escape to

the estate of the Colonel's father, where we arrived in the
middle of May.

If I had a drop from that vein which flows from Walter Scott's
inkwell, which has spread to 'every land' and primed a hundred
authors' pens with historical-antiquarian ink – then I would give
you a melodramatic description of stately Torsborg castle, built
during the Thirty Years War by a high-minded lady of noble
birth over a period of nine months, with walls as solid as
people's senses were then, and leaded panes as small as the
dawning of enlightenment in the cloisters of that age. I would
tell you of how Lady Barbro Åkesdotter of Göholm and Hedesö,
wife of Admiral Stjernbjelk (and whose portrait, which still
hangs at Torsborg, shows us a proud, stern woman), as a
surprise for her husband who was away fighting for the cause of
freedom in Germany, erected this noble building, on a hill
where it stands to this day in princely grandeur, dominating
countless fields and meadows for miles around. I would tell how
when her hero returned to his ancestral home she had candles lit
in every window of the castle to delight and enchant his eyes. I
might also whisper that her surprise does not seem to have been
a success, for tradition tells that he was sorely vexed by Lady
Barbro's deed. I would go on to tell something of the fate of
their descendants, who lived on the estate after them, including
one with a gift for poetry, who for his or her own commemoration and our edification scratched on a pane still to be seen in
the main hall in Colonel H***'s time:

> 'Miss Sigrid and her Soop together
> The greatest fools that there were ever.'

87

And once the tide of time had carried me on to our present resting place on the burnt-out volcanoes of the Middle Ages, I would wander around looking for remains in the lava flow, gathering in the urns of memory the ash of those extinguished fires to scatter on these pages and – that is, to put it bluntly, I would describe all the old harnesses, helmets and spears which were still kept at Torsborg and in which Cornet Carl took a particularly close interest, bloodstained clothes, rapiers, murderers' bullets and more. Among the more peaceful relics I would mention the door to King Gustaf II Adolf's bedroom with its thousand inlaid wooden figures, moved there from the old castle; the huge hall with its oak floorboards and oak-beamed roof; Lady Barbro's portrait, in which she is sitting with a trowel in her hand; her spinning wheel, and more. To provide the finishing touch I would describe all the ghostly goings-on in the castle, to which no-one seemed as susceptible as the tutor. He would often hear horrible noises – a mixture of the sound of trumpets and the howling of wolves; he would hear something padding about in the billiard room at night, the balls rolling around, little bells ringing, and more besides. I would explain that the people who worked in the castle were very familiar with a headless ghost who walked the great oak hall on moonlit nights, and that quite often in the darkness of the night candles would suddenly shine brightly from every window, and that there was no-one who had not heard sofas, tables and chairs dragged up and down making an awful noise in rooms where no soul was, ... and that even her Ladyship ... ugh! But I am beginning to feel quite ghastly myself ... and now I see clearly that I have only been given the gift of depicting ordinary, everyday things with ordinary ink – so I find it safer and more agreeable to tell you about how the little Puddings, happy beyond words to be in the country, ran around and tumbled about in the hollows and piles of stones left behind from the old manor house, looked for treasure and found – cowslips. How Julie, like a summer bird herself, ran after her winged brothers and sisters daring her betrothed to catch her, until she noticed that it was just not worth the bother, as he never really tried. 'It is too hot.'

He loved above all things sitting on a soft sofa with his little wife-to-be, resting comfortably against the delightfully plumped-up cushions, in a kind of inward contemplation of – the comfortable side of life. In between he went hunting, sometimes on Colonel H***'s land, sometimes on his father's. His father was a cheerful, kind-hearted old man, who valued five things on this earth, namely his noble old family name, his son, Colonel H***'s friendship, his team of white horses known as 'The Swans', and his tobacco pipe, which he lit from a fire kept burning summer and winter in his stove for the purpose. He was delighted with his little future daughter-in--law, although she played many a trick on him, and he grew cross as easily as he was soothed again. He liked telling stories, had a gift for exaggeration, swore like a trooper, and all in all was what we call a *decent old sort*.

At Torsborg, the family soon found itself in a peaceful and pleasant routine. True, her Ladyship did still go around for a long time with her keys and her worries, but no-one let that disturb them, and she was so extremely kind that she never made a fuss or disturbed anyone but herself.

The evenings were particularly agreeable. We would all gather in a little green room, full of pictures and flowers, where Professor L. would read from the works of Franzén, Tegnér, Stagnelius, Sjöberg, Nicander and other Swedish poets, his excellent and expressive delivery heightening our appreciation, so that day by day we grew richer in fine, healthy feelings and thoughts. Often the choice would be more serious reading matter, of the kind intended to give insight into those most important subjects for the human heart, God and immortality. I soon noticed that this was done particularly with the blind girl in mind. The Colonel's gaze always rested on her marble-white face during the reading of those passages where the divine light shone through most clearly and warmly, albeit veiled in human weakness. Often the evening would pass in discussions of these same ideas. Professor L., the Colonel and Helena were the principal contributors. The measures the Colonel had taken, in consultation with Professor L., for the moral improvement of his tenants by provision of good schools and various other amenities for their use and enjoyment, naturally gave rise to discussions of this sort. Humankind – its organism, its education, its destiny, its strength and weakness, the power of God, the ever increasing refinement of humanity by the Gospel properly preached and properly understood, this life and its relationship with a life hereafter: these were the subjects Professor L. discussed with such warmth, beauty, clarity and intensity. His fiery, powerful lectures, interpreting the full depth of his feelings so very well; the fortunate ability, which he possessed to an admirable degree, to provide insights into even the most abstract ideas by using examples taken from history, morality and nature; the calm and lovely wisdom that resulted from his teaching; its benevolent power reaching without fail the hearts of all his listeners; the harmonious sound of his manly voice; his dignified and expressive gestures; all these contributed to our delight in listening to him for hours on end. And when he became more deeply absorbed in his subject and expressed loftier and ever more daring ideas with growing warmth in an increasingly powerful language, we felt as though we were being lifted up from the Earth, nearer to Heaven. It was an apotheosis of thought and feeling, yet after that ascent to Heaven we were always left with a living spark of the eternal fire in our hearts.

In the course of these evenings, I noticed the stirrings of higher and nobler feelings in our hitherto rather childish and flighty Julie. I saw her breast rise, her cheeks flush, as she listened to the talk of truth and virtue with her expressive eyes fixed on the lips of our noble interpreter as if to absorb every word. She would often answer her betrothed in a very short and distracted way when he from time to time asked her opinion of pretty little paper figures and silhouettes, for which he had quite an artistic talent.

The blind girl remained silent throughout our conversations, and only rarely did any movement of her sculptured face indicate that some feeling had inwardly roused her.

In the evenings we also had a variety of discussions of a lighter but nonetheless informative nature; her Ladyship and Cornet Carl excelled here. One evening in the absence of Professor L. and the Colonel, Lieutenant Arvid gave us a long lecture on the best way of 'marinating reindeer meat', and on the sauce to serve with it. Julie asked whether Arvid's speech had not given us all an uncommonly great appetite for eating an early supper and going straight to bed. General approval.

One day, when Julie and I were sitting at an open window working, a bunch of briar roses in a jar on the table between us, and we had been sitting silent for some time, Julie suddenly blurted out, 'Don't you think ...?' and then stopped dead.

I looked at her and asked, 'Think what?'

'Well ... , that ... that Professor L. has a very noble look to his face, particularly his forehead?'

'Yes,' I answered, 'It is a sign of his noble soul and gentle wisdom.'

Julie moved to smell a rose – its pink buds seemed at that moment to be opening on her cheeks too.

91

'Aha!' I thought. Julie said again, 'Don't you think …?' Another pause.

'That Pro…' I said helpfully.

'Yes, … that … that Professor L. has a most wonderful tone to his voice and speaks quite excellently? He makes everything so clear … so rich and beautiful. You can feel yourself improving as you listen to him.'

'That is true. – But don't you think that Lieutenant Arvid has most attractive moustaches, most attractive teeth and a particularly attractive voice, especially when he says "By Jo.."'?'

'Now you are being cruel, Beata!' said Julie, and blushed furiously as she got to her feet and ran out. On the way she woke up Lieutenant Arvid, who was taking his after-dinner nap on a sofa in the next room. This made him grumble a little and, as he lazily stretched his arms and legs, demand a kiss as compensation.

He got – 'Certainly not!'

Julie, meanwhile, grew more earnest with every passing day, and her previously happy and amenable temper started to grow unpredictable and sometimes unfriendly; her mood became quieter and more serious, and sometimes a hint of melancholy would linger on her pretty face. But no-one in the family noticed this change for a long time. They were all so busy with their own interests. Her Ladyship, whose lively nature and energetic goodness kept her constantly on the move, never had a spare moment when she was in the country. She was her tenants' comforter, adviser and teacher in matters large and small, and doctor to the whole district besides. All this she did in a relaxed and sensible way which one would hardly have believed her capable of, in view of her anxiety at the slightest thing within her own home and household. She would go round to the people in person with medicinal drops and encouragement, soups and good advice, and the former gave savour and strength to the

92

latter. She was the darling of the neighbourhood. Old and young, rich and poor, all praised her for being 'just too good, too approachable.'

The Colonel was occupied in an apparently more passive way, but was in fact just as busy working for the welfare of those given into his charge. To his tenants, as to his servants, he was a good, just, but strict master. He was in general more feared that loved, but everyone admitted that during the time he had been in charge of the estate, moral corruption, drunkenness and indeed vice in general had decreased with every passing year. Conversely, orderliness, honesty, clean living, neighbour-liness and a consequent well-being and contentment had spread, even to other places nearby, and the admirable arrangements he had made, the good schools he had started and was now developing year by year, brought hopes for even greater improvement and happiness for the younger generation. Professor L. was at his side as an energetic assistant.

This is the moment to tell you more about Professor L. I shall make it short and sweet.

Professor L. was the son of a wealthy man, and was himself quite well-to-do. He had become a clergyman because that seemed to him to be the most effective way of helping others. He was also, in the best sense of the word, the father of his flock.

The strange thing was, that he took as much notice as I did, and perhaps even more, of Julie. His eyes would often follow her with an expression that was so friendly and earnest, so searching.

Helena supervised the girls' school in the parish, an important task which she carried out admirably, and was as happy as she was conscientious.

The Cornet had to ... supervise the boys' school, perhaps some may think? No, God preserve us! And it was just as well, for his sake as well as the school's. *He* was in the grip of a sudden violent passion for botany, and would go out early in the morning, be away all day, and come home in the evening tired out, his pockets full of weed... of plants I mean. He talked a great deal about how interesting, valuable and useful botany was, and never tired of showing Julie the difference between flowers with five stamens and those with eight, and so on. In particular, he was obsessed with finding a specimen of *Linnœa borealis*, which was supposed to grow in the area, he had heard, although he had not managed to find one as yet. That was what he went out hunting for from morning till night.

'Carl is behaving so strangely,' said Julie. 'When he comes back from his botanical expeditions, he is either so happy that he embraces us all, or he looks angry enough to bite our heads off.'

'He is being quite ridiculous about this botany!' said the Colonel.

Helena smiled and shook her head – and so did I – and I am sure that you do too, my dear young reader. I can guess, that you can guess, that he ... but hush, hush for now ... let us not give away the secret, it is sure to come to light all in good time. Meanwhile, let us take the family carriage and go

Visiting.

The Colonel, her Ladyship, Julie, the Cornet and I. Her Ladyship, who sometimes had ideas that seemed to have fallen down from the moon, had recently decided that I was growing melancholy, which she blamed on my brooding over the Book of Revelations, having found me a couple of times with my Bible open at the last page, where the creation of the new Jerusalem is described. Now her Ladyship feared nothing so much as brooding over books; she half believed I might lose my reason, and so to divert me and get me away from 'all that' for a while, she was determined that I should accompany her on some visits she planned to make in the neighbourhood.

We drove out one fine afternoon, all of us in a good mood.

We took coffee with Mrs Mellander, who with her husband (a mere appendage) leased a small property from the Colonel. Mrs Mellander was dreadfully ugly and pock-marked, with a beard growing on her chin, and thought herself very superior to her silent husband, who wholly accepted her merits and might. All day long she would lecture on good breeding and morals to her two pretty, rather wishy-washy daughters, who the Cornet thought of as weeping birches. Other than that, she was neat, frugal and domesticated, kept her house, her husband, her daughters, a maid and three cats in order – and consequently believed herself possessed of great ministerial qualities.

'Yes, yes!' she said one day with a sigh. 'Now they are saying, "Our great politician Count Platen is dead!" Next year they may be saying, "Mrs Mellander is dead!" '

'The devil they will!' said the Colonel, who happened to be there. While Mr Mellander, who was an actuary, took the Colonel down to the little garden to show him what he called his 'new ploughing' (an extension to an old potato patch), we heard all the latest gossip from Mrs Mellander. Firstly, that she had been reading a very entertaining book about a young man called Fritz.

'Is it a novel?' asked her Ladyship.

'Yes, it is a novel. It is *so* entertaining. The girl Fritz likes is called Ingeborg.'

'Who wrote it?' her Ladyship asked again.

'I do not rightly recall. They say he is a clergyman. And it is all so beautifully written, how they sail across the water, and how she claps her small white hands ...'

'Can it be Frithiof?' cried the Cornet, his voice quite shrill with incredulity.

'Frithiof ... yes, Fritz or Frithiof, that is his name.'

'Frithiof's Saga, by our great poet Tegnér!' cried her Ladyship in turn.

'Ten... yes, yes, I believe I have heard some such name.'

Julie raised her eyes to heaven.

Her Ladyship, who was becoming aware for the first time that one might wish for a change from such a topic of conversation, asked Mrs Mellander if she had heard that Countess B*** had moved out to her country estate.

'No!' answered Mrs Mellander shortly and firmly,'I know nothing of her. We have nothing to do with one another these days. What would you say, your Ladyship my dear, if I told you that she and I were brought up together? Yes – when we were young, we were together every day, and she had a straw hat with yellow ribbons, and I had a straw hat with red ribbons. And I would say to her, "Well then Jeannette!", and she would say to me, "Well then Lisette!", and we were the best friends in the world. Then she went her way and I went mine – to my Uncle, Judge Stridsberg in Norrtälje. Your Ladyship has surely heard of ...?'

'No!' her Ladyship replied.

'Good heavens!' – not knowing a rich man like Stridsberg – he was the one who got married to Miss Bredström, daughter of Bredström who kept a general draper's in Stockholm – I'm sure you know, your Ladyship. Son-in-law of Lönnquist who lived at Packartorget? ...'

'I'm afraid I don't ...' answered her Ladyship with a half-embarrassed smile ... .

'I see ... I see' said Mrs Mellander, somewhat displeased, and perhaps with her respect for her Ladyship's acquaintances rather diminished.

'Well anyway' she continued, 'It happened that we did not see each other for several years. But when I was married to Mellander, I happened to see my childhood friend, now Countess B***, at a concert in Stockholm. And I addressed her several times ... but what do you think? She looked straight at me and said nothing, and pretended not to know me at all. "Aha!", I thought, "When she comes driving along the country road here, past my house, then perhaps she will put her head out of the carriage window and nod and greet me. But I ... will just carry on with my knitting." What do you think, your Ladyship my dear?'

What her dear Ladyship thought remained a mystery to Mrs Mellander on this occasion, for at that moment her better half came in with the Colonel, who was anxious to be off, as it was already five in the afternoon, and it was a journey of quite a few miles to Lövstaholm, where they were due to visit the family of Mr D*** the foundry owner. In the meantime, each member of the company had been obliged to drink two cups of coffee, except the Cornet, who blessed Mrs Mellander, her good intentions *and* her coffee, but firmly declined to drink it. He and Julie meanwhile had done their best to entertain and put some spirit into Miss Eva and Miss Amalia. The Cornet in his outspoken and merry way paid them many little compliments, Julie admired their houseplants and offered to lend them books, sewing patterns and so on, which all had the effect of making the pretty weeping birches gradually raise their branches and flutter their leaves, as if tossed about by a fresh wind or invigorated by a refreshing shower of rain. That is to say, Amalia and Eva cheered up enormously, and their eyes moved both to the east and to the west.

At Lövstaholm, the Colonel and his family were received with noisy enthusiasm. A great fuss was made of the Cornet in particular, whose frank and cheerful disposition and amusing pranks made him generally loved and liked by the neighbours, and put him in great favour at light-hearted Lövstaholm, where balls and spectacular entertainments and other amusements were always going on. It was here he had danced twenty-four dances on one night with twelve different ladies, and had appeared to general acclaim in the comic roles of Captain Puff, cousin Pastoreau, and the Lord Mayor in *Carolus Magnus*. He had always declined any of the lovers' roles because, of course, he *could never fall in love*, and naturally could not feign something that was so much at odds with his nature.

To celebrate Mr D***'s name-day, his three talented daughters and four talented sons were giving a little concert that evening, to which quite a large audience had been invited, their numbers now swelled by the arrival of the five warmly welcome members of the H*** family.

Mrs D*** was said to be a very educated woman, who could talk about Weber and Rossini, education and culture, poetry, timbre, taste, tempo, et cetera. She took it upon herself to entertain her Ladyship with fine speeches about her views on education, and about the plan on which that of her own children was based, and in which both Weber and Rossini, culture, taste and tempo all whirled around one another, without the least sense of timing.

The concert began. Eleonora D***, flushed and fearful, took her seat at the pianoforte and played 'con tutta la forza della desperazione'; with every chord she struck, she treated the listener's ear to two or three other notes besides, and the roulades, thanks to the forte pedal and to her impatience, went across the keyboard like a hard rubber squeaking across a sheet of paper. The finale made a tremendous impact. The whole piano shook. Then the blue-eyed Thérèse sang an aria from *The Barber of Seville*. Splendidly staccato notes, powerful roulades broken off as if by the firm twist of a hand, and shrill cries, all brought lively expressions of gratitude from the audience for so much – effort.

Mr D*** was a plump and cheerful little man, delighted with his children, whom he compared in his fatherly heart to the seven wonders of the world. He would go up to Colonel H*** at every opportunity and, rubbing his hands, would ask with a glint in his eye, 'Well, what do you think, my friend? What do you say, my friend? Eh? Eh?'

The Colonel, who for one thing had too much natural good taste, and for another had heard too much good music in his time, to be quite sure how to respond, took refuge in his good-natured and mischievous grin and the ambiguous compliment, 'She plays like the devil!', or 'Damn me, what a singer!' His forceful remarks were accepted by the happy father with the greatest joy.

In the duet that followed, performed by Adolf D*** and one of his sisters, things went rather (as the Colonel put it) 'to pieces'. And a duet of black looks ensued between brother and sister, whilst the song gradually pieced itself back together again.

The finale was a chorus, sung by all seven virtuosos in unison, and full of rhymes like 'long life without strife', and 'host' and 'toast'. These, together with the rest of the words of the song, had been written by Adolf D*** himself, and I thought they would bring the house down.

Her Ladyship, who had sat through the whole performance with a reverent and slightly sanctimonious air, as if she were at evensong, now did her best to satisfy the musical family's thirst for praise. The Colonel repeated his strong words, and the audience gave a whole chorus of bravo! and *charmant*!, although the message was belied by the looks on many faces. The Cornet deplored such hypocrisy – which was easy enough for him to say, since he could claim, and freely admitted, that he knew nothing about music, and therefore could not pass judgement. Other people, who happen to have musical senses (or for their sins), and are asked to give a verdict, find themselves in a dilemma at concerts like these. We can criticize professional performers, for we have bought the right to do so, but amateurs we can only praise; we seem to see it as our duty, but if we do it with a bad conscience, then the truth takes a back seat, and with bad grace.

We could not think of taking our leave before the evening meal. It was eleven o'clock before we were seated in the carriage once more. It was a mild and unusually beautiful spring night. Her Ladyship soon fell asleep, gently rocked by the swaying of the carriage, and lulled by the sound of our conversation. Gradually, we all fell silent. The Colonel's look remained grave. The Cornet sat looking at the moon, which stood pale and soft above the green and peaceful earth. There was a dreamy look in his eyes that I had never noticed there before. Julie too looked pensive. The coachman and horses must have been lost in thought as well, for we made slow progress through the woods and across the flat countryside. It was about midnight by the time we drove past the parsonage, where Professor L. lived, but light was shining from one of the windows. The Colonel saw it and said, with the light of friendship in his eyes, 'There is L., sitting up late, working for the good of his fellows. He allows himself no rest – and yet it will be fifty years or more before his work will be truly understood and appreciated. And these nights come after days in which every hour has been devoted to carrying out the many duties of his calling.'

'He is like a candle,' said the Cornet, 'Consuming himself to bring light to others.'

'He must be a most noble man!' said Julie with a tear in her eye.

'Indeed', replied the Colonel, 'I know of none nobler. But he cannot live long if he neglects himself in this way.'

'Has he not' Julie asked, 'A sister or mother or someone else at home who attends to his needs, is fond of him, and takes care of him?'

'No, he is alone.'

'Alone!' repeated Julie softly and sadly. As we circled the parsonage, she leant out of the carriage window and kept her head still, her eye fixed on one point.

'What are you looking at, my child?' asked the Colonel.

'The light, Papa ... It shines out so beautifully through the night.'

————

The next day, too, we were to pay several calls in the neighbourhood, but this time it was quite impossible for the Cornet to come with us. He had somehow found out that *Linnæa borealis* was said to grow in a wooded area a few miles east of Torsborg, and in order to find out if it was true, he would have to leave us before dinner.

'I just cannot fathom,' said Julie, 'what Carl lives on some days. However hard I beg him, he never takes any food with him on his botanical pilgrimages. And I think he is getting quite thin.'

'There he goes, running off to the woods again!' said the Colonel, seeing his son stride off across the courtyard. 'I fear that this *Linnæa borealis* has put his head in a whirl.'

Our visits that day were less of a success. At the L***s at Vik, the children had measles, and for the sake of the little Puddings, we departed at a gallop on hearing the news.

At M***, the Countess was not at home. In a little pavilion in the garden, her canaries sang hungrily in their fine cages and with their songs, which varied from laments to joyful trillings, seemed to be trying with all the means at their disposal to alert someone to their plight.

Her Ladyship gave them grain, water, sugar and some grasses, and called them a thousand pretty names.

'What with all this,' remarked the Colonel, 'We seem unlikely to get our cup of tea this evening!'

Not to have tea between six and seven in the evening was a real hardship for the Colonel, and her Ladyship, who knew this, sat in the carriage with a worried and anxious expression as we began our homeward journey, which could easily take more than an hour and a half. The coachman, thinking he was taking a shortcut, took us on a new road, which gave us some new scenery to look at. We paused in a wild and thickly wooded place to let the horses get their breath back. To the right, at some distance from the road, we could see a thin column of smoke rising above the tree-tops and being blown our way by the light breeze.

'Well well!' said the Colonel, 'I do believe they are making some tea for us over there! Look Julie, is that a white wall I can spy through the trees?'

'Yes, I can see something greyish-white ... there really is a house over there ... the smoke seems to be coming from there. Plainly there must be some fairy waiting there to receive us. A fairy fay to offer us tay, that rhymes quite well.'

'I think,' said the Colonel, 'that even if there is no fairy, there will certainly be people, and they would surely provide us with some tea, if we – what do you think, Charlotte? Shall we pay a visit to that charming little woodland palace over there? We will say to the good people there, that we wish to make their acquaintance and that we ... in a word, that we are thirsty.'

Julie laughed heartily. Her Ladyship looked absolutely appalled.

'My dear friend,' she said, 'It would not be proper!'

'It would be dashed proper for me,' said the Colonel, 'To get a cup of tea.'

'And what is more, dear Mama' said Julie, 'We might make some rather interesting new acquaintances. Just think if Don Quixote had not died of being bled, as the story goes, but had come up here to the north, settled down with his beautiful Toboso, and was about to receive us ... Or we could meet a hermit, who told us of all his adventures, or a prince in disguise ...'

'Whatever and whoever you will,' said the Colonel, 'As long as he is Christian enough to give us a cup of tea.'

In spite of the Colonel dropping this fourth hint about his cup of tea, her Ladyship still had such serious reservations about this visit 'à la Don Quixote', as she called it, that the idea was abandoned, and we resumed our journey.

As the carriage began to move – crack! One of the back wheels came off, the carriage toppled slowly over, and amidst a chorus of cries we were tossed one over another down onto the road.

Her Ladyship was lying on top of me. But before trying to get up, she was struggling to free her reticule, which had ended up trapped underneath me. I assured her that this would be quite impossible for as long as I was unable to move from the spot.

At last we were all on our feet again. Her Ladyship was pale and we all gathered round her, concerned and anxious, asking a thousand questions, whether she had hurt herself, or had a great shock, and so on. But when she answered no to all this and we too, in answer to her own anxious enquiries, had admitted we felt neither shocked, grazed nor bruised (I did not mention being squashed), Julie burst into such loud and hearty laughter that we followed suit. The coachman and the footman, also unscathed, were scratching their heads and looking per plexed.

With their help, the Colonel then tried to right the heavy old carriage. But the road consisted of deep, sandy soil, the carriage had as good as fallen into a pit, the coachman was an invalid, the footman an antique. They grunted, 'Oomph ... umph!' – only the Colonel was really trying – and the carriage did not move an inch.

A visit to the grey house, the only visible sign of human habitation, now became a necessity, and the Colonel, who was so intent on the visit and his cup of tea that he was quite glad about the accident, exclaimed, 'Now we must all go together, for better or worse!' He gave his wife his arm, and led her with unusual cheerfulness, joking as he went, along the narrow track which wound its way through a thick forest of spruce and pine, and seemed to lead towards the celebrated grey house.

'It is going to rain!' said her Ladyship, looking anxiously up at the sky. 'My hat ..., could we not wait here under the trees while Grönvall runs to fetch someone to help with the carriage?'

'It is not going to rain' said the Colonel.

'It *is* raining!' cried her Ladyship.

'Let us hurry and get a roof over our heads!' called the Colonel, hurrying cheerfully on, and holding his hat over her Ladyship's head.

At last we reached the little grey house. It had a dreary and dilapidated look, and apart from a small kitchen garden, the area around it was wild and uncultivated. The silvery surface of a lake could be seen some way off, glittering through the dark pine forest.

The rain began in earnest just as we entered the house. A door to the right of the hallway stood ajar. It led to the temple of the kitchen. As the Colonel stepped inside, a maid came running out from a corner like a hare from its hiding place, fixed her startled grey eyes on us, and stammered, 'Do please go up ... they do be at home.'

We went up some dark and narrow wooden stairs, at the top of which the Colonel opened a door, allowing us to see into a small room, covered on all sides in washing. Tables and chairs, as well as some baskets, were draped with clothes, some ironed, some not. The hot, steamy air came billowing out at us as if from an oven.

'Go in, go in!' said the Colonel encouragingly to her Ladyship, who had stopped short on the threshold.

'My dear friend, I cannot go trampling through the clothes baskets,' she answered somewhat indignantly. The Colonel and I moved these aside and we filed through the land of linen to another door. As it was opened, we froze for a moment in astonishment and surprise.

A perfectly beautiful and majestic woman, splendidly dressed in black silk and lace, stood in the middle of a room tastefully decorated with lovely crystal, flower urns, mirrors, and other shimmering impracticalities.

Slightly behind her stood – although to me she seemed to float – a young ... yes, really just a young girl, but so radiant, so angelically beautiful, that one might readily doubt her earthly existence. She must have been sixteen at most, had her fair hair fastened up with a golden arrow, and was wearing a thin dress of white gauze which enveloped the ideally lovely proportions of the sweet, lily-white angel creature like a pale cloud.

The elder woman came towards us, her dark blue eyes fixed on the uninvited guests with a proud and questioning look. Her Ladyship took a step backwards and trod on my toes. The Colonel, whose noble bearing and open, courteous approach always made a good impression, soon brought a charming smile to the lips of the beautiful lady of the woods by giving an engaging and comical account of the reason, or rather reasons, for our unexpected visit. He apologized for this, gave his name (which seemed to make an extraordinary impression on the beautiful stranger) and introduced his wife and daughter. He forgot me. I forgive him. Who mentions the sauce that is served with the goose? It comes as a matter of course, as an appendix. The beautiful lady of the woods answered in broken Swedish, but in a voice that was pure music, 'Most welcome! The carriage shall have help, and you shall have tea ... as well as I am able. – My daughter, my Hermina,' she added, tenderly brushing back the curls which had fallen over the forehead of the sylph.

On her way over to the sofa, her Ladyship paused to nod to a gentleman who until now had been sitting half-hidden by the window curtain, but now stepped forward, took the hand of that dismayed lady, shook it and kissed it, saying with a laugh but not without embarrassment, 'Sweet Mama!' It was – the Cornet!

Her Ladyship said only, 'Good God!' and sat down quickly on the sofa, quite overcome, with her hands clasped and her gaze fixed on her son. The Colonel raised his eyebrows, gave a most comical grimace, but said nothing. A sort of embarrassed and uneasy tension made itself felt among the company. The Cornet, who seemed particularly ill at ease, soon went out to supervise the righting of the carriage.

The beautiful lady of the woods also went out, and we were left alone with the sylph, whom the Colonel was regarding with obvious delight. He, her Ladyship and Julie tried by means of questions and remarks on various subjects to encourage her to talk, but without success; she said but little, and avoided answering their questions. Childish innocence, inner grace and an almost unearthly tranquillity pervaded her and expressed itself in all she said. She spoke Swedish quite well, but her accent betrayed the melodious tones of the Italian language. Julie was in raptures, and kept whispering to me, 'She is an angel, an angel! Look at her mouth! ... no, look at her little hand ... no, look at her foot ... no, look at her eyes ... ! Oh, brother Carl! ... now you are surely caught! ... she is truly an angel!'

In the tastefully decorated room stood also a harp and a lyre. Julie asked Hermina whether she played either of the instruments, and in answer she went over to the harp and played and sang a *canzonetta* by Azioli with such charm and in so meltingly sweet a voice that it brought tears to everyone's eyes.

She had no sooner finished than her mother entered; the Cornet and the tea soon followed. The latter gave everyone something to do, and made their failure to sustain a conversation less noticeable. I could not help but notice (an old family adviser may perhaps be forgiven) the poor state of the tea-things. The cups were Rörstrand's thickest china, three had been mended, the sugar was ordinary loaf-sugar and downright grey; of cakes or biscuits there was no sign.

I fear our beautiful hostess noticed me looking round for them, and her Ladyship looking round for them too, and exchanging looks with me, because her expression betrayed a painful confusion as she stammered something about the difficulty of getting white flour. Her Ladyship in her usual kind and helpful way at once offered to send some from her own store, but was answered with a cold and firm 'No thank you!' which left her feeling diffident and a little offended at the same time.

The Colonel was enjoying his second cup of tea, when all at once we heard a lot of noise, and the sound of footsteps coming up the stairs. Our hostess flushed, went pale, got up and took a few steps towards the door as it was thrown open. A man with a wild expression of suppressed anger on his pale, stern, threatening face came bursting into the room, greeted the assembled company with haughty indifference and went to sit at the window. There he remained silent, but frequently directed wild, angry, penetrating looks at our hostess who, trembling visibly, silently returned to her place at her Ladyship's side. She gradually regained her composure, however, and several times even answered the angry stares directed at her with a supercilious, even contemptuous look.

The Colonel, who was sizing up the newcomer with searching glances, addressed him with a question about the weather. At the sound of this voice, the stranger turned round abruptly, looked sharply at his questioner, and with his sunken cheeks flushing a dull red, answered without seeming to be aware of what he was saying, 'Yes, yes ... it is not raining now ... the road is passable.'

He looked out of the window again and repeated, 'It has quite stopped – you can set off quite safely.'

The Colonel, who seemed possessed by the spirit of provocation and contradiction that day, said, improbably enough, as the sky was visibly brightening, 'Oh, but the wind keeps changing direction – it is clouding over and is doubtless about to rain even harder.'

Her Ladyship gave him a friendly but imploring little look, and at this silent plea he rose, and finally did see that it had almost stopped raining, and that they could now 'be going'.

With thanks and apologies we bade farewell to the lady of the woods and her daughter, who had large tears in her lovely eyes as we left the room, nodding silently to Mr Zernebock (as Julie called him), whose eyes seemed to wish us out and on our way.

'I expect you will come with us Carl?' said the Colonel to his son, 'Or are you thinking of continuing your search for *Linnœa bor*... ?'

'I shall run on ahead to see that the carriage is in good order,' called the Cornet, and was off like a whirlwind.

Once we were back in the carriage, the Cornet was besieged with questions. He declared that he knew no more about the beautiful strangers than we did; he had made their acquaintance on one of his expeditions in the district; he knew that they were beautiful and charming, lived cut off from the world, and seemed poor ... and beyond that he knew nothing more ... nothing at all.

'Poor!' exclaimed her Ladyship, 'And dressed like that ... such lace!'

The Cornet blushed, and said lamely, 'They always seem very well dressed.'

'But who in all the world was the nasty gentleman?' cried Julie.

'The master of the house' answered the Cornet. 'He seems very unhappy and short-tempered ... beyond that, I do not know the family.'

The Colonel looked sharply at his son, who grew very uncomfortable. It fell quiet in the carriage. Her Ladyship was nodding her head as if in accompaniment to her own thoughts.

Once, the Colonel broke the silence to say with a benevolent smile, 'I still have her tinkle tinkle in my ears.'

'Tinkle tinkle?' repeated the Cornet, blushing.

'Yes indeed!' the Colonel replied curtly, and silence descended once more.

Julie no doubt had her heart and eyes full of lively impressions of the two beautiful strangers, but she could not really tell how she stood, in view of her brother's acquaintance with them, and what is more she dared not express her delight in her father's presence, for fear of his sarcastic look, which always made her panic with fright.

'It is strange,' resumed the Colonel, 'that this particular stretch of forest east of Torsborg is the home of the rare *Linnœa bor* ...'

'Do you think, Father,' the Cornet interrupted hurriedly, 'That I might draw up the window ... or perhaps for the present you should not talk – so much ... the cold mist is swirling in.'

'Thank you for your consideration, my boy – I am in no danger. I fear more for you ... that you will contract some sickness on your botanical expeditions, catch a cold ... or get the shivers ...'

'The shivers!' said the Cornet, laughing yet blushing, 'I think it is more likely to be some kind of fever ...'

'I will be your doctor,' said the Colonel, 'And since I can already detect some worrying symptoms, I prescribe ...'

'My humblest thanks, dearest father! But there really is no danger as yet – I assure you. Besides, I have a great – respect for medicaments.'

The Colonel said nothing. Her Ladyship sighed. Julie peered mischievously at me. The carriage stopped. We were home. It was already quite late in the evening.

During the evening, the Colonel said to his son, 'Well Carl, when were you fortunate enough to come across your *Linnæa borealis*?'

The Cornet answered briskly, 'Why, just today, Father,' and taking out his wallet, he removed from it a little plant, saying, 'This little northern flower, which outside Sweden and Norway grows only in Switzerland and on one mountain in America, has an exquisite scent, especially at night. This one has already started to dry out, but it still smells nice – try it, Julie ...'

'Good gracious, Carl!' Julie exclaimed, 'It does have a strong smell of wormwood! ... Or rather ... what am I saying ... it smells of ...'

'Wormwood!' said the Cornet, taken aback, and looked at his sprig of wormwood in dismay. 'I mistook ... I have lost, I had ...'

The Colonel gave a sarcastic smile. 'You have to admit,' he said, 'That *Linnæa borealis* is a most curious plant!'

There was, however, one person who would probably soon discover more about *Linnæa borealis*, and that was her Ladyship. Such loving tenderness prevailed between mother and son, that questions from one of them inevitably drew confidences from the other, if these had not already been offered spontaneously. Her Ladyship loved her eldest son best of all her children, although she would not admit that her heart made any distinction between them. Of them all, he was the most like her, both in looks and in profound goodness of heart. What is more, the care she had devoted to him as a very weak and sickly child had cost her much of her own strength and energy, and this, perhaps above all else, had attached her motherly heart to a child whose survival had only been made possible by many sacrifices. Things which cost us that much, we do hold very dear. In return, she was rewarded with deep filial affection.

If her Ladyship had been let into some secret, it did nothing to enlighten the rest of us. The Colonel seemed to know no more than we did, for he would often joke lightheartedly about botany and *Linnæa borealis*, words which the Cornet had come to dread, and always tried to silence by changing the subject of the conversation to whatever came into his head.

Meanwhile, he continued his expeditions uninterrupted, and even went off on a little walking tour of the surrounding districts, which took nearly a week; then ... but more about that later.

The Colonel remarked in his usual phlegmatic way, 'Our young gentleman will be back with his regiment in a fortnight, then they will be off to Roslagen on the coast for the summer; his fascination with botany and *Linnæa borealis* will no doubt have evaporated by the time he gets back.'

Julie meanwhile was, in a sense, in a rather miserable predicament. Lieutenant Arvid, finding himself out in the country and rather short of the topics of conversation which only life in town can provide, began to find that he had nothing to say *tête-à-tête* with his betrothed but 'My little Julie!', which he would always follow with a kiss to fill in time. Little Julie, however, was not always prepared to co-operate. The lovers, having sat silently and attentively beside one another for a long time, would begin to yawn. Then Arvid would say, 'You are sleepy, little Julie!'

She would reply, 'Yes,' and think, 'Thanks to you!'

'Lean up against me, my angel, and have a little nap,' her future support on this earth would say in a soft voice, 'Lean on me, and on the sofa cushion, if I arrange it just so; I shall lean on the other cushion and take a nap as well ... it will be quite heavenly!' Julie would follow his advice with a miserable look on her face, and soon the couple could be seen both morning and evening, sitting dozing together. Julie, to be sure, often said it was both a shame and a sin to sleep away one's life like that, but her betrothed thought that was the best way to enjoy it, and since a good little wife does as her beloved wishes, even when she is still only a wife-to-be, Julie accustomed herself for a time to morning and afternoon naps. On one occasion she was heard to remark, half in jest, half in vexation at Lieutenant Arvid's plea for her to consider him a pillow, 'I assure you that I am beginning to do so in earnest.'

The Blind Girl.

'I see – nothing but the darkness.'

Her Ladyship, who was now convinced that she had discovered the cause of my alleged melancholy to be the first sign of consumption, prescribed for me a milk diet and lots of gentle early morning walks in the fresh air.

Her motive in doing so may also have been to find a good excuse for me to act as companion to Elisabeth, for whom the doctors had prescribed the same regime. Be that as it may, four facts remained: I was melancholy – I had consumption – I was to be cured – I must take walks.

So I began to drink milk and to walk out on those lovely spring mornings, taking the arm of the silent Elisabeth, into the lovely park where the birds, particularly at that time of day, struck up choruses, undisturbed by the soft steps of the two walkers and the few words they spoke.

To begin with, Elisabeth's mood was cold and unfriendly. She was virtually always silent, and those few words she did speak betrayed a sick and irritable disposition. Her usual question was, 'What time is it?' And in response to my answer she would always sigh impatiently, 'Is that all?'

I kept quiet, because I – I really did not know what to say – because I was afraid a careless word from me would offend her restless, sensitive, unhappy soul. I saw her suffering – would so much have liked to try to comfort her, but did not know the right tone to adopt for my charity to reach her heart. It also seemed to me that human words could not do more to ease any creature's pain than this mild, fresh, invigorating spring air which was gently fanning us; than the tuneful choruses swelling from the murmuring meadows; than the rich and wonderful scent that seemed to be the breath of youthful nature, which we breathed in with the spring, and which flowed in to invigorate our innermost being. Ah, whatever could I have said that would be more eloquent, more tender, more soothing, than nature's wonderful and lovely poetry?

Gradually, Elisabeth's mood softened. My silent but constant attention was no longer rejected coldly. She spoke more often and with greater self-control.

One day she said to me, 'You are as silent and friendly as nature; it does me good to be with you.' As I never asked a single question to try to penetrate to the core of her being, she gradually seemed completely to forget that she was in the company of anything but that natural world, in whose bosom the most unhappy of beings does not fear pouring out its suffering, and which is often its best and most consoling friend. She would often utter short, disconnected sounds, filled at times with a silent misery, at others with awful, wild moanings. Sometimes she would sing, monotonously but sweetly, a kind of lullaby, as though trying to send her heart's stormy emotions to sleep. This sad, pleasing song often induced in me that very melancholy her Ladyship was trying to cure.

Elisabeth's gestures revealed the same release of hitherto pent-up feeling. She often threw out her arms violently, or made movements with them as if trying to ward off something frightening. Sometimes she would press her hands tightly to her breast, or clasp them over her brow with a look of unspeakable suffering. Often her movements were so wild and violent that they seemed almost like fits of madness. But as soon as our morning walk was over and we drew near to the house, she resumed her reserved, cold, almost unnaturally stiff demeanour.

One morning, when we were sitting on a bench, she suddenly said to me, 'We are sitting in the sun – is it not so? I can

114

feel its warmth. Let us seek the shade. I do not like the sun, and it has no part in me.'

I led her to a bench shielded from the sun's rays by a thick lilac hedge.

'It must be very beautiful today,' Elisabeth said. 'I do not think I have ever known such sweet air.' And she began to ask me questions about the colours of the flowers, about the trees and birds, about everything around us, beautiful, but invisible to her. She did this in a tone so sad and gentle, so filled with quiet privation, that I felt moved to the very bottom of my heart, and a few tears, which I did not try to hold back, fell from my eyes down onto her hand, which was resting in mine. She pulled it away sharply, saying, 'You are crying for me, you feel sorry for me! No-one must do that – no-one shall pity me – no-one feel compassion for me; I do not deserve it! You must not be deceived about me any longer; learn to know me, learn to despise me! – This heart desired the crime – this hand has committed murder! I am moving now – I know it, I feel it – towards death, but a quiet, almost painless death, free from shame and dishonour. And yet, I deserved to end my days at the hands of the hangman on the scaffold.'

I felt that at these words, the day darkened around me. Quietly horrified, I sat silent. The blind girl remained silent too, at first with a look of wild despair, then with a contemptuous smile on her pale lips, which finally changed into a look of dismal depression, as she asked, quietly and slowly, 'Is there still someone near me?' – 'I am here,' I answered, as calmly and gently as I could, for I felt that the unhappy criminal needs the goodness of her fellow creatures even more than the innocent sufferer does.

'Soon,' said Elisabeth, putting her hand to her breast, 'Soon the infernal flames which are consuming me here will – burn themselves out. Quiet death, I sense your friendly approach! The breeze from your cooling wing sometimes brings me a moment of relief ... Soon this cool heart will rest, stiffen in the cold earth ... Motherly Earth, you will fold in your arms the tired child, who no mother's heart, no father's arms, no friend's supporting hand has known and blessed through life's long, long day! ... But why do I complain? Beg alms of disdainful pity? And I do not even deserve those! I am a worthless creature.'

She fell silent, but after a time she spoke again, 'It is strange! Today – today – after so many hundreds of days of life's miseries silently borne, my heart wants to speak ... wants, like a long-fettered prisoner, to breathe a freer air, to step into the daylight, indifferent to the feelings of horror and disgust which the sight of the wretched wrongdoer may awaken in others ... The flame wants to burn up once more, and spread its light, however terrible, before it is extinguished forever.'

'Turn your face away from me, Beata! ... Follow the sun's example – it is all the same – or rather, it is better so; I still have something to lose – your sympathy. So be it, I have brought this punishment on myself ...'

She fell silent once more; intense and painful emotions seemed to shake her very soul, and an indescribable expression of passion and melancholy was written on her face, as she yearningly stretched out her arms in front of her and burst out:

'Fatherland, freedom, honour! – I could have lived, fought and died for you ... I would not have become the wretched, fallen creature I now am. If I had been a man, my heart would not have beaten in vain for you, worthy goals of the soul's eagle-flight. This flame that is now consuming my criminal breast could then, burning on your altars, have sent a clear and holy fire of sacrifice blazing upwards. But now! ... how unhappy the woman, who sees in the limited sphere where she is called upon to live and act, silently and monotonously, nothing but a joyless existence, a prison, a living grave.

'I was this unhappy woman. O, how I have suffered in my battle with Fate! *That* was the dragon I fought – believed myself chosen to vanquish – and it has thrown me into the dust, crushed me – trampled me like a worm.

'With the arrogance of youthful emotions, I was proud of my fire, the depth and resilience of my feelings; I despised the idea of moderation ... of acknowledging the authority of any power other than my own will. I felt as though I had wings – I wanted to fly, to rise above all the rest; I have fallen!

'O that my dying voice could be heard by every female creature, who passionately believes herself created to become something great, brilliant and amazing, believes that the breadth and resilience of emotion with which she has been endowed gives her the right to despise the quiet world which the rules of society allot to her, the modest, approved suppression of emotion which laws both human and divine demand of her. O that she could see me, fallen because I breached those laws, and hear my warning: "Confused and pitiable creature, struggle with yourself! Your own impassioned soul – that is the dragon you must fight – whose fire will consume you and be fatal to others, if it is not suffocated. Submit to fate and the laws of society ... resist yourself ... or you will suffer and be crushed like me!"

'For me it is too late to struggle – the strength has gone, the will has gone! The fire has taken hold – the temple is burning, burning, burning – and it will burn until the winds no longer find anything but its ashes. I have lit my own funeral pyre – I am being consumed, and I am suffering!

'You world around me, full of harmony, beauty and song, putting your caressing arms around me now, like a smiling child that has just woken up ... you smile in vain, you caress in vain ... I do not understand you – I am suffering!

'When I was young ... a century ago ... Heaven and Hell filled my breast in turn ... although I was nearer to Heaven then ... now I see it no longer. When I was young – still very young – I already loved with the full force of passion. My first love was my fatherland.. perhaps you smile, and find that an absurd feeling in a girl's breast ... others have. And yet – my fatherland! Sweden's noble and beloved soil! If all your sons had had my heart – the heart of a young girl – then you would still be what you once were – the home of heroes ... Europe's lion.

'You have read and heard about martyrs, about the dreadful torments, the almost unthinkable cruelties suffered by the defenders of freedom and fatherland through the ages, and you have averted your eyes in terror, shut your mind. I too read and heard of their fates, but longed to share them – dwelt on all the sufferings, all the infernal torment ... to me it seemed heavenly happiness, if endured for you, O fatherland! – I prayed to Heaven to share in their glory, their sensual pleasure.

'As the flower of my youth unfurled, and my emotions swelled like the spring tide, the murderous wagon of war went clattering through Europe. Only an echo of the clash of weapons resounding among the fighting masses reached our peaceable country. But it reached my heart, and awakened there the wildest transports of emotion! Alas, I was only a woman! ... They laughed at my infatuation, mocked it. I cried tears of bitter indignation, and hid my fire in my breast.

'Peace was made, and the names *fatherland* and *freedom*, which shine so dazzling and clear in the light of the fires of war, lost many of their entrancing rays in the shade of the olive. In my breast too, the wonderful names lost their magical suspense once they were no longer associated with danger, battle and glorious death. Peace was made, and the excitement of my senses was stilled. The world around me was even more mundane and monotonous than before. But my heart remained as ever, wishing to live and act; I was as before, and more than that, full of desire to conquer the brilliant peaks of life – but people, the rules of society, convention and circumstance consigned me eternally to my non-life. There was never a galley slave as unhappy as I. Restless as the spirit of the storm wind my soul moved, encompassing the world, trying to reach for the stars, fighting its way through what covered all feelings and veiled all knowledge; yet my body and my attention remained tied to life's most petty and trivial things. I lived as two beings in one – and each was the tormentor of the other.

'One single passion the world allows the female heart … in our upbringing we are usually encouraged to develop it by reading novels, sentimental poetry and the like. That is love. I learnt to know it. They say that it ennobles woman, that it is the maker of her happiness … it has led me into crime, and now it is leading me to my grave.

'My father died. He had never understood, never loved me, never made me happy! Why did he give me life? – If my mother had lived, how she would have understood and loved me! I have heard so much about her, she had suffered so much … struggled so much. I was born as she gave her last sigh, I took it in with my first breath … in the first and last kiss of a mother. Perhaps that is why my whole life has been like a death-struggle – a fight, a constant battle. At least it should be over soon!

'My father's brother, who had always lived far away from us until then, took me in. You know him … but no, you do not! You think him a God on Earth – and he is a hard, unrelenting man – a severe, implacable judge. How hard he has been towards me! How I loved him! I had nothing and no-one on Earth. He became my everything. I saw nothing and no-one but him. I told him so. If only he had had some gentleness, some compassion for me. But he was all severity. His look was cold, his words punishing. I despaired, yet still worshipped him.

119

'I was beautiful, I was brilliant, full of youth and life and feeling. Just as waves break in vain against the rock, which resists them and throws them back, so all my feelings, all my natural gifts came flooding forth in vain like sacrifices on his altar. The waves may at least bathe with tears the hard breast which breaks and rejects them; I was not allowed to cry on the hand which thrust me aside, which handed me the poisoned chalice. The one I revered and loved above all things called my feelings for him criminal. I do not know if they were, then. They were not usual and perhaps not fitting for this Earth. In those days I had no fear of the angels' looks in my heart ... they would have understood. The angels in Heaven love too, after all! And must love in a higher and purer form than Earth's children, for they love the highest good – they love God! O, and he was a God to me! Why was he only an angry, punishing avenger? His judgement on me made me despise myself – and worship him all the more.

'For a moment, worldly pride asserted itself in my breast. I wanted to conquer my passion – punish its object's implacable sternness.

'I became betrothed to a young man ... good and kind, I believe ... who loved me; I remember little about him – I wanted to punish, and believed this was a way of doing it ... yes – for at times I still believed that – I was loved by the one who meant everything to me. Could love be the only fire that lacked the power to warm its object, the focus of all its burning rays? – And I was so beautiful too – and he had, I knew and saw it, a weakness for feminine beauty. But what am I saying! Surely he was never weak? When did I see *him* falter, that proud, strong, noble man? And I – oh, I was the weak one, the confused, infatuated, wretched one!

'They made ready for my wedding, the wedding clothes were all prepared, they surrounded me with gifts, caresses and flattery ... I looked at the one I loved ... he was very pale.

'The wedding day came, the marriage hour came ... I looked at him – he was pale, a dark flame smouldered in his eyes – but he said – nothing. At that last critical moment – I was still looking at him – he turned his face away from me; his beautiful, noble, beloved countenance turned away from me – with a look – oh, the memory of it! I said *Yes*! My heart was a bottomless pit.

'The same evening, I went away and hid ... hid away from everyone. There was a strange feeling inside my head and my breast. How they searched for me! ... Hahaha! It was quite a sight!

'I had taken some money with me, and under an assumed name I managed to reach one of the Swedish ports. I saw the sea ... a storm was whipping it up ... the sunrise topped it with red flames. I can still remember it ... Ah, it was beautiful! I sat on a rock and looked out to sea. The vast expanse opened its arms to me; wave came arching after wave ... surging, foaming ... away ... away ... into infinity, into the boundless distance where sea and sky embraced each other. It roared and whispered – Oh, it was dreadful and magnificent! Something like a breath of fresh air swept through my tormented breast. I felt refreshed and strengthened. The waves were speaking a language that did me good. They whispered, they beckoned to me: ''Come away, come away!'' Half the day I sat on the rocks in silence, looking out to sea and listening; I saw the sun rise above the waves, saw the sails with white doves' wings upon the blue sea, beneath the blue sky, glide away towards some coast of distant peace. I heard the voice of the waves urging me on and decided to follow their call.

'I wanted to go to America. Far, far away from the ground he trod, from the air he breathed, from the language and morals that were his.

'The day had arrived for my departure, the time had come. I was to board the ship of salvation; its pennants were fluttering merrily in the following wind; soon I would be rocking on the cool waves, they were singing so sweetly. All at once, their song was penetrated by the sound of a voice ... I felt a hand take hold of me and drag me violently away. Terrible words were spoken to me by a beloved voice ... I scarcely understood them ... everything seemed strange, incomprehensible. I was taken back to my husband like a prisoner. Then I felt again that strangeness in my head and breast, it was a dance, a whirlwind – and also a gnawing pain. It grew more and more intense, I became what they call – mad.

'The same hand that had wrenched me from salvation's strand now grasped my hands. *He*, the one I loved so infinitely, for whom I would have given my life a thousand times over – *he* – put me in chains, and took me to – the madhouse ...

'A time without time passed for me there – day, night, morning, evening, they were all the same, it was all a blank. I remember nothing of that time – only that I once heard a well-known voice say my name; and also that once someone near me said, ''If only she could cry.'' I wondered so much what that meant – and often repeated it with a kind of muddled anxiety: ''Cry?''

'One day ... I do not know where they had taken me ... or who I was with. Everything seemed to be floating in a wild mass of confusion before my eyes. Then I suddenly heard a roaring, like a stormy sea – but the roaring took on a note, a tone, swelled in wonderful and mighty harmony, then sank back into a sweet, grave melody. It was joined by a voice which sang clearly and calmly:

"Behold the Lamb of God, which taketh away the sins of the world."

'Like a cloud of moisture descending from Heaven onto hard, parched earth, the holy harmonies descended into my numbed soul and dissolved its petrified lava.

'Driven by a wonderful force, I began to join in, singing out loud – remembering the words and music perfectly. They were the ones I had heard at my first communion, as I knelt reverently and saw Heaven open above me ... . At the words

"Grant us thy peace!"

my tears began to fall, and from that moment my consciousness returned. Yes, that.. but *peace*, alas, did not return ... and still, always and perhaps for all eternity, the dove of Heaven remains far away from me.

'Oh, I did not deserve its coming to my breast! There was no submission there, no sanctification ... no desire for it to come!

'My husband was dead. I was glad of it. I came back to my uncle's house – I wished it; my heart had undergone a transformation and I now believed myself to hate as much as I had loved before. I wanted to see again the one for whom I had suffered so much – to see him – to defy him – to let him see and, if possible, feel, that I too could be proud, cold – disdainful. I wanted to humiliate him. I saw him, adored by wife and children, loving them tenderly in return, calm and happy in the bosom of a family. To everyone, even the very humblest, he showed goodness, to me he only gave a look even colder, haughtier, and sterner than before.

'I felt the very strings of my soul tremble. An awful sensation overcame me. His true coldness taunted the one I feigned, his strength my weakness, his composure my constant disquiet. He had treated me harshly. I felt that he in his arrogant good fortune trampled me like a worm in the dust. His image haunted me – asleep or awake, I saw nothing but that. It stood before me like a giant – it was suffocating – it robbed me of air. If he were not ... then *I* would breathe! If he were not ... then *I* would be. If he no longer existed – he would cease to be the torment of my life. Struck from the list of the living, he would surely soon cease to exist in the memory of the living ... I could ... get some air ... take revenge ... punish him ... take revenge! Today, today his calm looks still defied me ... but tomorrow!

'A crime is like a word – born of a thought, it leaps out and at first seems quite harmless – but its consequences extend through all eternity.

'One evening I put powder of arsenic in a glass of almond cordial intended for my uncle.

'I also kept some of the powder hidden away for myself – for I had a feeling that I might possibly feel ... remorse.

'Have you known remorse?'

I had not the heart to answer.

Elisabeth continued, 'That innocent action taken, I went up to my room. I felt calm and cold ... my body was as cold as marble – my heart seemed so too ... its pulse dampened. I was standing before the fire warming my icy hands when I heard a great commotion in the house, and the sound of anxious voices.

'Then an uneasiness came over me ... I went down and saw my victim lying back deathly pale and almost unconscious on the sofa, surrounded by his wife and children, who had been plunged into the pain of despair.

'As I entered, my uncle fixed me with a look ... I shall never forget it! Then a vengeful infernal spirit came to me and gripped my heart with sharp, bloody claws. *It was remorse.*

'I confessed my crime out loud – called on those I had made so wretched to curse me. I crawled across the floor and let my forehead kiss the dust ... . No-one raised an accusing voice against me – but no hand helped me up. I dragged myself over to the feet of the man I had murdered – I wanted to kiss them ...

but another foot pushed me away – it was his wife's – I kissed that and mercifully lost consciousness.

'I remained for a long time in a state of complete mental confusion. When I regained consciousness, I saw my uncle standing beside my bed, heard him telling me he had been saved – granting me his forgiveness.

'So low had I sunk that I would rather have heard his curses. It seemed to me that they would have made my unworthiness less deep, and would not have diminished him.

'The wildest storm of all the passions raged in my heart. I cursed the light – and the light withdrew its rays from my unworthy eyes – and perpetual night enfolded me body and soul.

'The storms of nature are short-lived, and followed by calm, clear days. In the human breast, the hurricanes of passion rage long and have only moments of calm. I experienced one of them, but it was the calm of the night – the numbing of life – a trance – the lullaby of the darkness. That came to an end, and a new and all-consuming fire flared up, which even ever-flowing wells of tears could not put out. I came to know a never-ending, yearning, burning desire to be *reconciled*.

'Death on the cross – pain, blood and sweat, never-ending torment – to suffer you, and through you to be reconciled – that, that would have been a sensual pleasure! But blind ... like a mummy among living beings – a criminal wreck of a person – a nought in achievement, a nothing ... I stood, despicable, despised – o misery, misery, misery!

'So that I still might at least punish myself, I decided to live – to live, an object of scorn for those I loved and honoured; to reject every sympathetic hand – and torture myself as much as I could.

'Once more I left the family whose happiness I had almost destroyed, and for several years dragged myself through a wretched existence. I returned, once death had put its hand to my breast. My uncle wished it so. He will rule my being until its final breath. I can no longer help it ... Fate has ordained it. I have no strength left – for me it is all over – all over!'

She fell silent. Softly I began to say a few calming and encouraging words. I spoke of patience, of resignation; I mentioned – prayer.

'Prayer!' repeated Elisabeth with a bitter smile. 'Listen, Beata! For years I prayed ... night and day, every hour, every moment: I knelt until the cold froze my limbs, and prayed – "O Father, take this bitter chalice from me!" Prayer has been for me like a stone which is thrown upwards and falls back down to hurt the sufferer's breast ... I shall pray – no more!'

'O do pray, do pray!' I said in tears, 'Just pray with a meek heart ... God is merciful – gives strength to a pure will.'

'God?' said the blind girl in a mournful voice. 'Oh world – which I no longer see – sun, which no longer lights my eye, you speak of a God! Heart, everlasting anxiety! His name resounds in your beating! Conscience, my punisher! – you herald the avenger. Fire of love, you life of my life! In your flames I detect your eternal origins. But you, bright angel – *Faith* – who should show me my God – I know you not. I have descended into the chasm of doubt too soon. I deny nothing – but I believe nothing. I see – nothing but the darkness!'

'And the light of the Redeemer? And the radiant halo of Christ crucified? – and Jesus?' I asked, amazed and terrified.

The blind girl remained silent for a moment with an expression of bitter melancholy, and then said:

'I once read about a vision or dream[1], and many a time its ghostly figure has risen up to frighten and horrify me.

'In the middle of the night, the doors of a church flew open, shaken by invisible hands. A crowd of ghastly shadows flocked

---

[1] See Madame Staël, *De l'Allemagne*, Part 2, p.276, Jean Paul's dream.

around the altar, the only movement the rise and fall of their panting breasts. The children still lay peacefully in their graves.

'Then, from higher regions, there descended to the altar a radiant figure, noble, sublime, and bearing the mark of indelible suffering. The dead called out: "O Christ! Is there no God?" He answered: "There is none." The shadowy figures all began to tremble violently, and Christ continued, "I have travelled through worlds, I have looked down upon suns and even there, there is no God. I have stepped forward to the very edge of the universe, I have looked down into the abyss and called: Father, where are you? But I heard nothing but the rain, falling drop by drop into the depths, and the everlasting storm, which is beyond all control, gave me my only answer. Then I lifted up my eyes to the arching heavens – and found there nothing but a space, dark, empty, boundless. Eternity rested on chaos and gnawed at it, and slowly consumed itself. Renew your bitter, heart-rending laments and disperse, for it is all over." The inconsolable shadows disappeared. Soon the church was empty, but all at once – terrible sight – the dead children, who had awoken in the churchyard in their turn, came hurrying forward and threw themselves down before the majestic vision above the altar, crying, "Jesus, have we no Father?" and he answered in tears, "We are all fatherless, you and I, we have no-one ..." '

Here the blind girl broke off, as if in horror of this sick, feverish, wild fantasy, was silent for a moment, then clasped together her hands and, slowly stretching out her arms, gave a wild, penetrating cry, filled with the most dreadful despair.

At that moment, rapid steps approached us and the Colonel suddenly stood before us, fixing me with an uneasy, questioning look. The blind girl, who recognized his step, let her trembling hands fall, but quickly raised them again towards him in heart-rending supplication. 'Be lenient, be good to me! I am so unhappy. If I lose my mind again – do not take me to the

127

madhouse. My end will come soon enough. At least let loved hands close my eyes!'

Compassion and deep suffering were written on the Colonel's face. He looked at Elisabeth for a long time, then sat down beside her, put a supporting arm around her waist and let her hand rest on his chest.

It was the first time I had seen him show her any tenderness. Tears ran slowly down her pale cheeks. She was beautiful, but it was the beauty of a fallen angel, whose expression of despair and diffidence shows how unworthy she feels of the compassion she is shown.

Then I saw her Ladyship approaching us from a distance. When she became aware of Elisabeth in the Colonel's arms she gave a sudden start, but then continued to come towards us, although with an expression of surprise on her face. The Colonel remained still. Elisabeth seemed oblivious to everything around her. As her Ladyship drew nearer, the eyes of man and wife met and – melted together in a look of clear friendship. Shared emotion caused them to take each other by the hand.

Her Ladyship stroked Elisabeth and spoke tenderly to her – her only reply was a series of sobs. After a while, the Colonel rose and took one of Elisabeth's arms, his wife took the other, and together they gently guided her back to the house with tender care.

I remained alone in the park. Alarmed and agonized, I stared up into the pale blue spring sky, longing so much for its clarity to stream down into my soul.

On my own untroubled path through the world, spared the tremors which afflict so many of life's pilgrims, and bearing within my peaceful breast a living faith and a healing hope, the unhappiness, suffering and desperation of my fellow creatures have been the only clouds which have occasionally obscured my beautiful sun and my life's joy, and which have sometimes

128

caused me to look up to the heights and cry out a painful, 'Why?'

But the answer was never long in coming, when summoned by the sincere voice of prayer. Calming breezes brushed my agitated soul and whispered:

'The clouds blow away, the sun remains. Humanity's crimes, pains and errors cannot obscure the Creator's goodness. We see only a little part. People die – are transformed. God is unchangeable.'

It is pointless to doubt, grumble or worry. All life's mazes do have a way out. At the moment when the darkness seems most dense, we may be nearest to finding the light. After the midnight hour strikes the morning hour, and even if it were the chimes of death, announcing the hour of our salvation, what could be more consoling to us when life's labyrinth seems cramped and dark than to say, 'A door shall be opened and we shall come out – into the light.' However cramped, however dark it appears, we know that 'a door shall be opened for us'! Well then, let us wait, let us hope!

From that day, Elisabeth's mood became even more volatile. She even had periods of actual madness, and we had to redouble our vigilance and care for her.

The suffering and restlessness of her life transmitted a feeling of depression to the rest of the family. The Colonel's health and temper in particular seemed adversely affected.

So as not to try my reader's patience by letting their eyes dwell on such a dismal scene, I will now take them on to another. It is light, it is happy; in it the youthful earth and the youthful human heart show themselves in unison. We shall call it

Springtime and Love

'I, I too was in Arcadia'

Innocent joys, innocent sorrows, friends of my young years, angels who with smiles and tears opened the gates of life for me, I call on you today! And you too, thoughts as pure as the blue sky, feelings as warm as the May sun, hope as fresh as a breeze on a spring morning, I call on you to come, come to put new life into my dull senses!

I want to sing springtime and love, youth and joy. Sweet, fresh memories, nightingales of youthful moments, raise up your voices, I want to set down your melodies and be charmed by their song once again.

On the twenty-second of May, a clear spring sun rose and dubbed Cornet Carl's eyelids with its golden yellow rays. The stars of the Order of the Sword at once shimmered in their dozens before his dreaming eyes. Eagerly he tried to see them more clearly, struggled to open his eyes, but as he awoke he saw the stars giving way to glorious shafts of daylight on whose prisms a million atoms danced.

A quarter of an hour later he was to be seen with his hunting rifle on his shoulder, strolling off through the fresh morning air. It was a spring morning as lovely as the one Böttiger describes:

> Nature lay so glad and still,
> Each turf so green and fair,
> Each lark sent forth its own sweet trill,
> Each flower its silent prayer.
> The brook went flowing calmly on,
> To quiet lakeside shore,
> Where in the reeds the silent swan,
> Its song and sheen did store.

Up to the sun the eagle flew,
Of light to drink its fill,
The bee sucked its sweet honeydew,
The ant its load did pull.
Within the rose the butterfly,
Hath hid its purple wing,
To the maple branch two doves do fly,
Of tender love to sing.

A bold young man in hopeful mood,
The shady wood-path took,
The Spring was sparkling in his blood,
And longing in his look.'

. . . .

In this young man we can now see Cornet Carl, who with that great sense of sweetness and freshness which only the combination of life's and nature's early morning hour can bring, looked around him, up to the clear blue sky, down to the grass sparkling with the diamonds of morning dew, away into the distance, where the faint rose-coloured mist was slowly dispersing.

A sweet, aromatic breeze, borne on caressing zephyr's wings

. . .

Up to this point I had been writing in a rising fever of emotions, when suddenly I smelt such a strong scent of essence of roses that I felt quite dizzy; at the same time, I also became aware of a loud humming and buzzing around me. I lifted my pen (which seemed poised to run away with me at any moment) from the paper and looked round.

What a vision! The room was filled with small, luminous cherubs with garlands of roses in their hands, garlands of roses on their heads, and constantly quivering wings, which were the source of the strange buzzing. The longer I watched these strange creatures, the more dazzling and bewildering I found the colours which gleamed in their eyes, on their cheeks, on their wings. And when I turned my eyes away from them to other things – imagine! My ink looked white, my paper black, my yellow wall was green, and my reflection in the mirror *couleur de rose*. No wonder the scent of roses went to my head.

Now I recognized those little rascals; I had seen them before, and indeed who has not seen them, who does not know them? They are the ones who tease the seventeen-year-old girl and turn her head. They are the ones who mislead the young man into seeing his future as *pleasure and usefulness* instead of *usefulness and pleasure*. They are the ones who make us take great trouble for nothing and run sixty miles after a will o' the wisp, but at other times render us unable to see clearly enough to raise a hand and grasp our happiness as it passes close by. They are the ones who behave like the April weather, fooling the whole world and making the whole world a fool. They see to it that P. marries and B. stays single, and both do the wrong thing; they make A*** say 'Yes' and J*** say 'No', which was the wrong answer for both of them. They are the ones who force their way into the office of Banker *Calculation* and make him muddled so he writes seven instead of two. And finally, they are the ones who hum and buzz and shimmer so mercilessly around the poet and often make him produce anything but common sense, paint reality in false colours, and mislead himself and others. Charming phantasmagoria of the imagination, little rose-tinted rascals! Who does not know you? But who does not avoid you, who does not want to chase you away, once they have experienced your tricks and deceptions? In particular, should not those who live and weave on the *rez-de-chausée* of everyday life, trying to send their shuttle sensibly and neatly through its homely threads, be more wary than most of allowing their brain to be addled, their thoughts confused by your rose-scented pranks? I saw what danger I was in, what a dangerous path my runaway pen was heading for. I put it down, stood up, drank two glasses of water, opened the window, breathed in the April air still cold as snow, looked up into the clear sky, looked down into the courtyard, where they were beating clothes, and then turned my attention to three cats, who were sitting most decorously in an attic window opposite me, watching the world about them with a philosophical gaze and little shakes of the head. In a word, I let my eyes perceive the everyday world about me, to escape from that fantasy world which was spreading out around me on the wings of my youthful memories. One of the pretty little rascals had whispered in my ear: 'One can allow oneself a little untruth, as long as it creates a pleasing effect,' and if I had not looked about me in time and come to my senses, then my reader might perhaps have seen a springtime and a love, the like of which has never been found – except perhaps in Arcadia.

When I came back from the window, the air in the room was clear and fresh. The little rose-tinted confusions had gone, and I could see everything in its true and natural colour once more.

A picture of reality should be like a clear brook, which as it flows reproduces clearly and faithfully those objects reflected in its rippling surface, revealing through its crystal the sight of its bed and the objects resting there. All that the painter and author should allow their imagination in its depiction is to play the role of a ray of sunlight, which without altering the characteristics of any object nevertheless lends all its colours a more vivid gloss, lends the crests of the waves a more diamond-like sparkle, and illuminates with purifying clarity the sandy bed of the brook itself.

Armed with this newly-won insight, I can calmly proceed with all humility to take the role of a ray of sunlight and let it shed its light on a faithful account of springtime and love. But sunlight can be as tiring as anything else, when it is too all-pervading and persistent (the way it is in Egypt, for example); so I will only let my ray peep out here and there on our stroll through the Elysium of youth, and only shed light on those places, where I think my readers most wish to linger or – where I feel like sitting down to rest and warm myself. So let us now come out of the woods into

The First Glimpse of the Sun

It shines through the gloomy pine forest and gives us a view of a clearing. In the background we see the little grey house which decorated the stage in the previous chapter. In the foreground we see the green shore washed by the clear waves of a lake. The irregular shapes of granite rocks protrude here and there, standing like sentries around the azure palace of the lady of the lake; young birches peep out beside them with their green crowns and wave their sweet-smelling branches in the westerly winds which play there, full of life and desire, full, in a word, of *springtime*.

By the lakeside, in the green birch grove, we become aware of a young man and a young lady, sitting beside one another on the flower-speckled grass. They look happy, they seem to be delighting in nature, in themselves, in everything. He is telling her about something, his eyes are gleaming; now he turns them skywards, now he looks straight ahead with a conscious look of pride and bliss, now he lets them linger on her as if wanting to read her soul.

He beats his breast, he stretches out his arms as if trying to encompass the whole world; he speaks with all the warmth of a deep and heartfelt conviction and therefore cannot fail to be convincing. She listens amiably to his words, they seem to please her; she smiles, sometimes through tears, sometimes with an expression of surprise and admiration, clasping her hands or raising them with an animated exclamation of joy, and looks altogether more and more convinced. Convinced of what? Of the young man's love?

'No such thing!
Love will come later!'

No – convinced that Gustav Vasa was the greatest king, Gustavus Adolphus the greatest gentleman who had ever lived, that Charles XII was a far greater hero than Napoleon, and that *'The Swedish people was of all peoples the first and finest on earth'*.

She among my readers who has a particularly good memory or is unusually skilled at guesswork may be launching the rocket of sudden realization: 'This must be Cornet Carl and his *Linnæa borealis*, or beautiful Hermina!'

So it was.

'But how did they become acquainted?' someone may ask.

To which I reply: see the Old Testament, Genesis chapter 24, Eleazar's meeting with Rebecca. The modifications which may be caused by differences in custom and speech between an idyllic scene in Mesopotamia in the age of the Patriarch and one in nineteenth-century Sweden are not important enough for me to need to give a new account of a scene which would only give you all cause to repeat Solomon's tedious but true saying: 'There is nothing new under the sun!', and which moreover would give me the unfortunate feeling of making a poor copy of a lovely original. Suffice it to say that here too we had a tired traveller, a well, and a young girl who came out with a pitcher to fetch water, and gave the traveller a drink. To be sure, he had no camels, but a gentle, grateful heart impervious to all love but the Christian variety. And this lovely weakness, and this noble strength, caused him to accompany the kindly maiden home, carrying her pitcher.

Now that we have taken one drink of light (so as not to offend the temperance societies I shall not call it an *aperitif*), let us move on to which will give us some Conception of the forest family and Conjecture about the Condition of Cornet Carl's heart, which could lead us to a Conviction of what fate's Conclusion for him might be, and cause some moral reflections on the benign Control over our hearts which is so graciously granted us in life's game of chance.

We may have good reason to liken Hermina to Rebecca, but Baron K***, Hermina's stepfather, was not in the least like the hospitable Bethuel. He was extremely cold and unfriendly, almost hostile to the young traveller. His wife, the beautiful Lady of the Woods previously mentioned, was not much kinder. They behaved as if frightened and vexed at being discovered in their hiding place. But it was hard to be frightened or cold and unfriendly for long with a young man like Cornet Carl. His frankness, his amiable and refreshing cheerfulness, the goodness that shone out of him, his lack of pretension combined with a certain nobility of bearing that he had inherited from his father, his carefree, open, gentle look, always meeting others' eyes clearly and calmly, all this made people of the most diverse temperament, character and mood like him and feel at ease with him. People invariably felt they wanted to take him into their confidence, to be in his company as they might wish to be in the open air – because it makes life seem easier, makes them feel happier and better; for when we ... but what is the point of writing a memorandum about something we all know in our own hearts?

Cornet Carl wanted to, and duly did, impress Baroness K*** and her husband to such an extent that they agreed to his request to be allowed to visit them again, as long (and this was their express condition) as he promised not to reveal, even to his family, his acquaintance with them, or where they lived.

The Cornet promised this because – because he felt a quite incomprehensible urge to come back.

It took only a few days for him to become aware of the strange and unhappy state of affairs in that family; but it took a long time for him to understand the cause of it. Baron K*** was Swedish, his wife and stepdaughter Italian; he had brought them to Sweden some two months previously. Their clothes were opulent and extremely elegant; their bearing and speech, their education and accomplishments revealed that they came from elevated and refined social circles, yet they were living without many of life's barest essentials, that is, things which have become essential to the spoilt children of this world. Apart from a single room, where they had, so to speak, heaped up all the baubles that had been saved from some shipwreck of fortune, everything in the house betrayed real poverty. The daily diet of the two beautiful Italians was no better than that available to every poor crofter's family in Sweden. The Cornet's response was to maintain that there was no better food than herring and potatoes.

The atmosphere between Baron K*** and his wife was nearly always stormy. What they seemed to feel for one another was sometimes the fiercest love, sometimes downright hatred, which in the Baroness' case meant that she assumed an expression of proud disdain, whilst he gave vent to his anger in outbursts of rage. There were often scenes between the unhappy couple in which they would address the bitterest reproaches to one another; the most insignificant trifle could set them off. These scenes mostly ended in an almost frantic raging on his part, and anguished cries and tears on hers. The Baroness's character seemed to be essentially noble, yet she was unbending, proud and passionate in the extreme. Her husband, both weak and despotic, was given to wild outbursts of temper; only in moments of remorseful calm, which descended on him periodically, could one detect that here too was a nobler nature, worthy of love.

Patient, kind and gentle, like a suffering angel, stood Hermina with the snow-white wings of her innocence spread in reconciliation over those two natures made wild and bitter by their battle of the passions.

She had what is called a *beautiful soul*. But unlike her beautiful body, she had not been born with it. It had been fashioned by early obedience, early experience of domestic cares and troubles, and particularly by a feeling for religion, developed at an early age, which made her endure patiently, go without things cheerfully, offer her suffering up to heaven and act lovingly and tirelessly on earth. To ease her mother's suffering and make things a little more comfortable for her, she would take on even the heaviest household tasks, which were really meant to be done by the family's only maidservant. And it was touching to see that lovely creature, educated to fine ideals, working like a hired servant, bearing burdens which made her stagger – or rather, would have done, if Cornet Carl had not come along and put matters right, taking her burden and shouldering it himself. From the moment he arrived, a lot of things changed for Hermina. As Jacob served Laban to win the beautiful Rachel, so Cornet Carl served Baron K*** to lighten Hermina's drudgery. He went hunting and fishing, stocked up the larder, and had to be dissuaded forcibly from doing the cooking too, when he saw how Hermina had to scorch her lovely face and pretty hands over the fire. He did not dare to offer the couple, so proud and haughty in their poverty, any other kind of help.

Until then, Hermina had served her mother almost like a slave, but without the reward of the affection she so much deserved. Baroness K*** seemed accustomed to accepting others' sacrifices without thanks, and showed no inclination to make any herself.

She found it hard to bear the poverty and humble circumstances into which she had been transplanted. She demanded that Hermina should, like herself, be always tastefully and extravagantly dressed, and this was made possible by a quite extensive wardrobe, which they had brought with them from Italy. It was as if she wanted to seek solace from her present fate in these remnants of a lost splendour and greatness, or as if she believed her present situation was not in earnest, but just a temporary enchantment, which could dissolve at any moment, as if she expected some fairy's magic wand to change the little grey house into a palace, and that was why she always held herself at the ready, in a costume worthy of her rank and dignity, to be attended on and congratulated.

By her stepfather, Hermina was treated with indifference and harshness at the same time, and it was plain to see that the things she did for him were done not for his sake but for God's.

From the moment the Cornet came into the house, he assumed a kind of authority there, which grew daily, and this he used to make Hermina's life happier.

Baron K*** was away all day, more often than not, and only returned towards evening; sometimes he was even away for two or three days. During these peaceful interludes, the Cornet saw to it that Hermina enjoyed a freedom which she had never experienced before, and which she now enjoyed with childish delight. He persuaded her mother (who was very susceptible to the beauty of nature) to take long walks in the wild but romantic countryside. Botany had once been her favourite pastime; the Cornet reawakened her interest in it, seeing flowers everywhere (even where I believe there were none) in an effort to convince this Italian, so enthusiastic about the lush vegetation of her native land, that Sweden was as rich in flowers as it was in heroes and iron. It is certainly true (and he admitted it himself later), that he did not hesitate to boast that even cat's foot, lady's finger, flax, wild rosemary, bog-myrtle, sorrel, wormwood, common tansy, yellow rattle, monk's hood and the like were the most unusual and remarkable of nature's products.

He commended as the most beautiful thing in nature the wonderfully pretty flower named after 'the world's greatest natural scientist, Linnæus of Sweden.' He tried to infuse the Baroness and Hermina with the greatest possible desire to find this wonder plant. Every day he would have a new feeling that it would be found in some new place or other. He searched long, long and well, and did not discover it until the moment he discovered his love.

These walks gave the Cornet a chance to be constantly with Hermina. He gave her his arm as they walked; when they rested, he shielded her from the sun's glare; gradually he encouraged her to run around and clamber on the rocks, in a word, to *enjoy* the free and healthy young life of which her hitherto quiet and cloistered days had given her no conception. As she now, cheeks flushed with health and happiness, light and lovely as an Oread, moved so lightly in the fragrant spring air and often turned her angel-like face, shining with gratitude and affection, to the one who had brought such pleasure into her life, then ... then the Cornet felt something strange in his heart ... a warmth, a sweetness, a wholly, especially, hitherto totally unknown feeling.

The Baroness seemed to view the two young friends as two children, whose games she tolerated, because all their joy and all their flowers were brought as tributes to her. The Cornet possessed the admirable gift of keeping people in a good humour with themselves and thus with others.

Yet he meant most to Hermina at those times when the recurrent and unpleasant scenes which took place in the house reduced her to bitter tears, which she usually went into the kitchen to hide. Then he would follow her and comfort her with a brotherly affection, or persuade her to come out with him and then try to divert her attention to happier topics by talking to her and telling her interesting things.

Once, Hermina had been needed in the house and they had called her. She had not been there, and this had led to severe reproaches from her stepfather. The Cornet accepted these as a gauntlet thrown down to him, and his way of answering the challenge led to new freedoms for Hermina. He was now often able to go out alone with her. Her education in the more serious branches of knowledge had been neglected. He became her teacher (particularly of Swedish history); he became like a brother to her. She soon began to call him by that sweet name too, and when they were studying Swedish grammar together one day, they agreed that the familiar form of address sounded so much nicer than the polite form, and that they should start using it between themselves.

Hermina meanwhile became for Cornet Carl, not exactly a teacher, nor precisely a sister, but she imperceptibly became the light of his eyes, the joy of his life, she became his ... It is high time to inform my readers, especially my young lady readers, how things stood with Cornet Carl. He was – in love!

I am sure no one would ever have guessed it. He himself did not believe or suspect or guess it until

The Third Glimpse of the Sun

when he was walking one evening at sunset beside the smooth mirror of the lake. Hermina was on his arm. She was quiet and pale – with the kind of pallor which reveals that the heart is without joy; that one has submitted, but is suffering.

She had just witnessed a scene between her parents, deeply upsetting to her gentle soul. Cornet Carl had taken her away from them almost by force, and was now trying, without success, to distract her and lift her dejected spirits. After they had been walking a while, they sat down beneath the birch trees on a flat, mossy rock and silently watched the last traces of purple painted on the mirror of the water and on the wooded slopes of the opposite shore.

Only then did Hermina turn to Cornet Carl with tears in her eyes and say, 'You are very good, my brother ...' She wanted to say more, but her voice faltered; she fell silent, seemed to be fighting back her emotion, and then went on, her face half turned away from him, 'You are staying here for my sake, and for my sake you have had many unpleasant and difficult moments, and ... yet you could be so happy. After all, you have a father, a mother, both so good and excellent ... brothers and sisters, for whom you care so much; they must miss you ... go back to them – and stay with them ... be happy ... do not come back here!'

The Cornet sat dumbly staring at the lake, and it seemed to reflect his soul, for all at once he could see into his own heart.

'Why should you keep coming here?' Hermina began again in her soft, sweet voice, as if trying to persuade him. 'You are causing yourself a lot of trouble and distress, yet you still cannot alter my fate. Today my father said bitter and threatening things to you ... oh, do leave us! Why hesitate? Do not worry about me, Carl! ... God is sure to give me help and strength.'

'Hermina!' said Cornet Carl, 'I cannot leave you ... but it is as much for my sake, as for yours ...'

Hermina turned her face to his with a questioning gaze, as several big teardrops slowly trickled down her cheeks.

'Because ... because,' the Cornet continued in great agitation, 'Because, Hermina, I love you beyond description, and

have no joy in this world, if I cannot see you and be with you
…'

Hermina's angel face radiated surprise and deep-felt joy. 'So
there is someone who loves me … and it is you, my brother!
How good God is to me!' And she gave the Cornet her hand.

'Do you care for me too?' he asked in secret dread, holding
the little white hand between his own.

'How could I do otherwise?' answered Hermina. 'You know
I have only been happy since I came to know you. You are so
excellent, so good. You are the first to love Hermina.'

'And the first Hermina has loved?,' enquired the Cornet
uncertainly.

'Yes of course! Except my mother.'[1]

A deep feeling of happiness crept over the two young lovers.
As if Amor himself had drifted down in a rosy cloud onto the
heather bank behind them, a perfume came wafting past so
sweet and intoxicating (and certainly Mount Olympus had no
better ambrosia) that Cornet Carl in the midst of his soul's
delight jumped up and cried, 'It is Linnæa! The flower of my
life is found!' It really was growing there, in deep, leafy drifts
along the mossy rocks. A coronet was quickly woven for

---

[1] I am only too aware what a romantic treasure trove I am foregoing at this
point. I see clearly, how everything in this little scrap of a novel could have
been introduced better, with more interest, and carried on in a more
exciting way, how both the opening and the conclusion of this section could
have doubled the sales of my book. But all that would have taken more
words, ergo more lines, ergo more paper, and my publisher is so dreadfully
afraid that my book will be too big and not be able to be sold for one
Swedish crown, that I have felt obliged to compress both my soul and my
ideas in order to squeeze my book into the bookshops at the stated price.
My publisher thinks that the Swedish public is simply not prepared to pay
a lot for such everyday items. I think that he is right, and that I am right to
abide by their judgement.

Hermina's head. Who can describe the scene of pure and utter happiness and innocent joy that followed?

Hermina was no longer pale ... there was no more talk of Cornet Carl going back to his family. For Hermina was *his*. He was Hermina's. They understood each other, they were happy. All would be well – they would be together always. *Nothing* would keep them apart – they belonged together, on Earth – in Heaven.

Nature seemed in sympathy with the happy young pair; mild and loving, she enfolded them in her gentle arms like a tender mother.

Who would not gladly give ten heavy autumn years for a moment of Springtime and Love?

The Fourth Glimpse of the Sun
shines down on the Cornet's anger,
so fearsome.

One warm June day, the Cornet arrived at the house in the forest hot, tired, longing, yearning, thirsting for a kind look from his beloved, a cooling drink from her hand. From outside he could hear the sound of her harp. He ran upstairs and saw Hermina sitting more beautifully and tastefully dressed than ever with her harp on her lily white arm, and beside her ... o horror, thunder and lightning and death! Work of the underworld, hellish invention! Beside her sat – not Cerberus, the three-headed monster, no, worse! Not Polyphemus with one eye, no, worse, worse! Not the Devil, no, worse, still worse! Ah, it was not 'la Bête' sitting there beside 'la Belle', but a strikingly beautiful young man, a second Prince Azor.

The beautiful, haughty, calm, cool, refined and decorous Genserik G*** regarded with surprise the hot and dusty Cornet H***, who was wholly nonplussed at what he saw. The former nonetheless promptly roused his Apollo-like form, came towards

145

the newcomer with a charm born of good breeding, held out his hand with kindly condescension, expressed his delight at seeing the Cornet out here in the country, and reminded him of the last time they had met in Stockholm. The Cornet did not seem in the least delighted, nor did he utter a single polite remark. Genserik went back to Hermina and asked her to sing. The Cornet found some pretext to cross the room, and whispered to her as he passed, 'Do not sing.'

With a commanding voice and look, the Baroness instructed her daughter to sing. Hermina sang, but her voice was trembling. The Cornet went to sit at a window and mopped his brow with his handkerchief. While Genserik's visit lasted, he said scarcely three words, partly because no one spoke to him, partly because young G*** himself was speaking continuously. And he spoke so well, using such choice and polite phrases, about such interesting things – he had such knowledge and insight, that it was a real *pleasure* (for the Cornet, read *mortification*) to hear him. What is more, his consciousness of his own importance coloured others' perceptions.

'I am – I have – I do – I like – I think – I want – I shall – I said,' was the theme on which his rondo of thoughts and words was played and constantly replayed. Sum total: this *I* eventually grew so big, so important, so swollen, that Cornet Carl saw his *I* seem to melt away and be pushed out. He felt close to suffocating in the oppressive atmosphere, and had to go out for fresh air. He paced up and down the garden thinking desperate thoughts.

'What primordial storm wind, doubtless from the sands of the Saharan desert, had blown the young property heir, the fatal Genserik G***, here? The Baroness was openly fawning and fussing over him. What did it all mean? He was rich, he was beautiful, educated, would come into property, he was ... ah, dear God! What wasn't he? He was clearly expressing his

146

admiration for the lovely Hermina – especially (a man could go mad) when she sang.

'And Hermina? Why did she sing, when *I* asked her not to? Why did she allow herself to be paid compliments by a strange man (and heir to property, what is more) ... ? Why had she given her only friend scarcely a kind glance, and not taken a single step to give him so much as a glass of water? But let him stand there desiccated and parched and plagued and tortured in body and soul?'

No-one answered the unhappy lover's questions. The sky darkened above his head, his feet became entangled in the trampled plants in a bed of peas. Suddenly the sound of hooves was heard. It sounded like a drum roll of joy to the Cornet's ears; Genserik was riding away, and the Cornet went swiftly back to the house in search of explanation and redress. He found neither. The Baroness received him coldly and distantly. Her strict and watchful eye remained on Hermina, who sat sewing without daring to look up. It was at that moment of tension and displeasure on both sides that the Cornet was surprised by his family's visit. My reader already knows what ensued.

A time of mortification followed for the Cornet. He could no longer visit his beloved's home without finding Genserik G*** there before him. His rival was openly favoured by Baron K*** and the Baroness. They treated the Cornet with growing indifference. Hermina alone was gentle and kind, but low in spirits, quiet, guarded, and avoided his questions.

To be in a better position to observe the movements of the forest family, the Cornet decided to go on a so-called walking tour, which took the form of installing himself in a hayloft in the immediate vicinity of Hermina's dwelling. Here he spent the nights, whilst devoting his days to circling round Hermina's home like a bee buzzing round a flower. It is possible to be very happy in a hayloft – to think oneself in Heaven lying on a bed

147

of straw or hay! But if indignation and dissatisfaction are pricking your heart, then the hayloft and its bed of thistles will add insult to injury. The Cornet made a mental note of this.

Great changes were gradually taking place in the forest house. There was now an abundance of foods, wines and other luxury goods, more servants were hired, Baron K*** was in sparkling good humour, the Baroness increasingly majestic and haughty – and the Cornet increasingly superfluous and overlooked. Genserik G*** eclipsed him. The greatest antipathy developed between the young men; but the Cornet, vexed, bitter and sarcastic, showed himself more often than not in an unfavourable light, when compared with the polished Genserik, always unruffled and coldly polite. He knew it, read it in everyone's faces, and this put him in an even worse temper. He cut a sorry figure, and so as not to offend the eyes of sensitive readers any longer, I suggest we take a look at

The Fifth Glimpse of the Sun

More displeased than ever with Hermina, her sad kindliness, her uncommunicative manner, with himself, with the world in general, Cornet Carl took a thoughtful stroll one evening through the gently sighing pinewoods. He came to the well where he had first seen Hermina, and stood in melancholy mood, staring into the clear mirror at his sunburnt, discontented, far from handsome face, mentally comparing it with Genserik's beautiful, clear, clever looks. Suddenly he saw in the well another face appear beside his. It was as lovely as an angel's – it was Hermina's. A shiver of joy went through the Cornet, but was instantly quelled by feelings of bitterness.

'Hermina,' he said, 'No doubt it was Genserik you expected to find here'.

Hermina was silent for a moment, then she gently put her hand on his arm and said simply, 'Carl! Have we stopped understanding each other?'

He looked at her, and her gentle, loving, but tearful gaze met his.

You lovers! If the silken skein of your love and happiness has tangled itself up and you want to set it straight – do not speak. Look at each other!

Cornet Carl felt as though a veil was suddenly falling from his eyes – the mist was disappearing from his soul. At once, everything seemed clear, so divinely clear. For a long time the young lovers stood silent, drinking light, peace and happiness from one another's radiant faces.

When scarcely a spark of anxiety was left in them, it was time for the lovers' explanations and assurances.

'Are you not,' Hermina said, among other things, 'Are you not the one who loved me first, who made me realize that it can be a pleasure to be alive? And even if you had not done so – how can you believe that I think as much of a cold egotist like G*** as I do of you?'

'But he is so awfully handsome!' said the Cornet, laughing but still half embarrassed.

'Is he? I had not noticed. He is not to my taste. I know one person, who is – one, whose face it does me good to see – one, I find handsome ... Would you like to see his portrait?'

She led him over to the well. There the Cornet regarded with satisfaction his sunburnt, beaming face.

'But your parents prefer Genserik ...'

'And I prefer you.'

'He loves you.'

'And I love you.'

'Hermina!'

'Carl!'

When a person quits this earthly life for a better one in Heaven, we say with confident hope, 'Peace be with her!' And then we turn our minds to other things. In the same way, when two lovers have emerged from their doubts' vale of tears and reached that clear Heaven where they are reconciled once more, we can say, 'Peace be with them,' and think of other matters.

But as a last 'God grant you peace' over them, we will just catch

The Sixth Glimpse of the Sun

And that shines down on the delights, which streamed over Cornet Carl for a few happy days. He was sure of Hermina, and her silence, her reticence, her politeness to Genserik, his persistent visits, his *I*, his lover's compliments, the coolness of Baron K*** and his wife towards himself – none of this worried him now. The hay loft provided him with a blissful bed. Springtime in nature mirrored the springtime in his soul. The woods, the flowers, the waves, the wind, the birds, everything was singing to him and for him. 'Joy, joy!' Joy? Alas, Rinaldo, Rinaldo! Hark! The sound of trumpets is calling you from Armida, and you must forsake your joy.

The trumpets are calling! Not from the field of Palestine, not from the promised land, but from the Royal Park, or rather from the regimental parade ground next to it. It is all one! Our new knight Rinaldo, Cornet Carl, you must leave one who is more virtuous, more modest, and therefore more beautiful than Armida. You must wrench yourself away from her magic palace (the little grey house). That is the will of the unrelenting General-in-Chief of all life's regiments, *Fate*, which takes so little account of the demands of the heart.

The trumpets are sounding, duties are calling – to camp, to camp. And is washed away by the lovers' tears of farewell.

To prevent ourselves shedding any of our own, we will command our thoughts: 'Right turn, forward march!' back to Torsborg. There, with some old acquaintances, we will meet with some new adventures, such as

Digging through the Earth
(and other projects)

One evening, when we were all assembled round the blind girl's sickbed, Professor L. read aloud to us from a translation of Herder's *Ideen*. The subject was: Humankind's preparation for another world; the revealing glimpses of our transformation which we receive here on Earth by noting the transformations in the lower realms of the natural world, which are all positive refinements.

Professor L. concluded with this reflection on what he had just read: 'A flower shows itself first as a germinating seed, then as the shoot of a plant; this bears the bud, and only then does the flower unfold. Developments and changes like this take place in many creatures, among which the butterfly has become a well-known symbol of mankind's transformation. There we see the ugly caterpillar creeping along, ruled by its basic urge to eat; its moment comes, it is overtaken by a deathly tiredness: it fastens itself firmly, and wraps itself up, having carried within itself the material for weaving its shroud, together with some of the organs for its reincarnation. Now the rings go to work, the inner organic powers exert themselves. At first the transformation goes slowly, seeming more like destruction: ten legs are abandoned in the cast-off skin, and the new creature still has none of its limbs fully developed. Gradually, these form and take up their rightful places, but the creature does not awaken until its transformation is complete. Now it forces its way out to the light, and the final change takes place. Just a few minutes, and the frail wings grow five times larger than they were within the chrysalis. They are endowed with elasticity and with the brilliance of every ray of light under the sun. Its whole nature is transformed; instead of the tough leaves it ate before, it now drinks honeydew from the golden cups of flowers. Who could discern the future butterfly in the caterpillar's form? Who could recognize the same creature in both guises, unless experience had shown it to us? And yet both are part of the life cycle of one and the same creature, on one and the same earth. What wonderful possibilities must lie dormant within nature's womb, where its organic cycle is broader, and the stages of life it develops span more than one world.

'And so nature shows us through these analogies of developing, transitory creatures, why she interwove the sleep of death with the fabric of her kingdom. It is a beneficial trance, which envelops a creature while the organic powers strive towards a new form within it. The creature itself with its greater or lesser consciousness lacks the strength to oversee and direct its struggle; so it falls asleep and only wakes when it is finally transformed. Thus even the sleep of death is a gentle, fatherly means of relief; it is a calming opium, under the influence of which, nature gathers its forces, and the sick get better as they sleep.'

L. fell silent at this point. We all felt deeply and delightfully moved. We sat quietly, with our eyes fixed on our own poor sick one, who had great tears running slowly down her cheeks, and was making soft, involuntary little moaning sounds. Her Ladyship stroked her tenderly; the Colonel laid his hand on her head as if in benediction. A deep, sustained and tuneful snore drew our attention to Lieutenant Arvid, who had fallen asleep sprawled comfortably in one corner of the sofa, with his mouth open and his nose in the air. His trumpeting was a signal for departure, as far as Julie was concerned; she hurried out of the room with burning cheeks. After a while, I went to look for her, and found her standing on the steps outside, leaning on the balustrade with arms folded, her gaze fastened on the light evening sky, where pale stars were beginning to appear. 'Julie!' I said, putting my arm round her waist.

'Oh Beata!' sighed Julie, 'I am unhappy – really unhappy. Will I have to stay like this all my life?'

Before I could answer, Lieutenant Arvid came out onto the steps and called, through a yawn, 'By Jove, what are you doing here Julie? Standing about catching a chill – getting a cold and a bad chest. Come back in, dear girl. And I think they have begun to set the table. Come along!'

'Arvid!' said Julie, '*You* come *here* a moment,' and taking his hand in a friendly way, she said enthusiastically, 'Look how lovely everything is this evening. Let us go down into the park – you know, to the place where we once agreed to ... I want to talk to you there, ask you to do something ... '

'We might just as well talk in the drawing room ...'

'Yes ... but it is such a lovely evening. Just look around! Listen to that bird singing so sweetly, listen to the horn from the meadow over there. Look at the sunset ... what a wonderful red. Oh, it is a lovely evening!'

'*Charmant*, my angel,' replied Lieutenant Arvid, stifling a yawn, 'But – I am mad with hunger, and there was a heavenly smell of beef stew as I went past the kitchen; I am longing to rediscover it in the dining room. What is more, it is getting confoundedly misty. Come along, my angel!'

'Arvid!' said Julie, pulling her hand away, 'We have such different likes, such different tastes I see ...'

'You do not like beef stew?'

'God bless you and your stew – but I am not talking about that. I mean our inclinations, our feelings – they just do not fit in with each other …'

'Well – I cannot help that.'

'No, but I am afraid that we do not suit each other… that we shall be unhappy.'

'Dear girl, it is sure to be all right. Do not worry about things before they happen. It ruins my appetite. Let us eat our supper in peace. Come along, my little wife …'

'But I do not want to … and I am not your wife,' said Julie, turning away from him. 'And,' she added quietly, 'I no longer want to be betrothed to you.'

'No longer want to?' Arvid said calmly, 'But you must see how difficult it will be to call it off. You have my ring, and I have yours … and anyway, I am not taking you seriously … girls have their whims. Now now, it will be all right to-morrow. Farewell, Julie! I shall go and eat my stew, you can swallow your caprices!' And he disappeared into the porch.

Julie took my arm and we went down into the garden; she was crying bitterly. I walked beside her in silence, waiting for her to vent her feelings in reproaches of her betrothed. But she said nothing, kept squeezing my hand, and carried on crying.

As we turned into the walk, a figure swathed in a cloak came walking towards us. Professor L.'s voice was heard, making good-natured jests about Julie's Romanesque taste for evening walks. As he drew near, he saw that her eyes were swollen with crying, and was at once quiet and grave.

'Professor L.,' said Julie, trying to sound comical in spite of the tears in her throat, 'Tell me, what do you do, when you realize you have done a very foolish thing that cannot be undone?'

'In such a case,' said Professor L., 'Wisdom must bear the consequences of folly.'

'So you have to be unhappy all your life?'

'Not unhappy, no – but better and wiser, using your mistake as a stepping stone bringing you nearer to perfection.'

'It sounds lovely, and very edifying – but in the meantime you could grow tired of wisdom and perfection and your whole life – and find each day unbearable.'

Professor L. said gently, 'Only someone very weak would fall so deeply into lethargy and dissatisfaction. Even the grimmest and most joyless position in life has its moments of brightness, if we can just see them. In sorrow and distress, we should all look within ourselves to be most sure of finding the seeds of comfort. When everything around us disturbs and torments us, we should seek a refuge and a deep inner life within ourselves. Then we should say, with Hamlet, "I could be bounded in a nut-shell, and count myself a king of infinite space!" Getting to know this world within us, putting it in order, making it lucid and ready to develop still more, is a pleasure which no station in life can deny us, and a pleasure which will soon be acknowledged as great enough to make us love even the bleakest life here on earth. To learn to think is to learn to live and enjoy.'

'But,' sighed Julie, 'How can I learn to think with a ...'

'With a husband who only thinks about beef stew?' I added silently.

'Good books,' continued L., 'Are gentle comforters, leaders and friends. With their help, if you are serious, you cannot fail to reach inner harmony and stability.'

He fell silent for a moment, then added warmly and with feeling, 'How much I have to thank my books for!'

'So you have been unhappy?' said Julie, her heart full of sympathy.

'I have lost everything that I loved most dearly on this earth, and not only through death. Ever since childhood I have been dogged by this misfortune. Everything to which my heart has become sincerely attached has been wrenched away from me. Much bitter time passed before I was able to resign myself to the will of the eternal Good One, and still ...'

'If only someone could console you,' burst out Julie in childlike and deeply affectionate tone.

L. continued, 'I have tried to harden my heart, to preserve it from such bitter suffering, I have struggled to subdue its sensitivity – I am no longer young – and yet (this said with a rueful smile) I may soon have to go back to my books for consolation once again.'

'I want to be a book,' said Julie with tears in her eyes.

Professor L. looked at her with paternal ... no, not exactly paternal, with a tenderness that is hard to describe.

'Dear, good girl!' he said in his wonderful harmonic voice, and continued after a moment more calmly: 'It is weakness to complain. The strength to endure can only be found in prayer and in doing our duty. We should draw strength from these sources.'

He gave Julie his hand, and she took it tearfully.

Just then we came upon an arbour, where three small black figures seemed to come rising up out of the ground to meet our surprised gaze. And we were hardly less surprised to see that it was the little Puddings and a friend of theirs, standing up to their middles in a hole, absorbed in deep thought. Our repeated enquiries about what they were doing brought at first only silence on their part, then some vague gruntings, and finally the revelation and somewhat incoherent explanation of their big secret. They had in fact decided to dig right through the Earth, to give the family, and especially the Colonel, a surprise.

What was holding them up now was certainly not the difficulty of the venture, bah! but a profound thought which had come into Claes's head, that when they had made a hole right

156

through the Earth, they might themselves immediately fall through it, and where would they end up? That ... that was what Professor L. must now be kind enough to tell them.

We all had to laugh.

Professor L. postponed his explanation until the next day, and with some gentle teasing sent those pygmies with giant plans off home. At that point a servant arrived, having been sent out to look for both them and us, to say we were late for supper. The little triumvirate set off at a gallop. We followed more slowly, but found ourselves enveloped in Lieutenant Arvid's confounded mist, which seemed to form a wall between the garden and the precincts of the house. It was only then that we realized Julie was without a shawl. I was not much better equipped. L. took off his cloak and wanted to wrap it round Julie. She did not in the least want to allow him to, as L.'s health was not the best. They would still have been standing there arguing and protesting, if I had not intervened and suggested a compromise, namely that they share the generously-sized cloak between them. This was accepted, and Julie's slender, zephyr-like form disappeared under one corner of the cloak, which she laughingly wrapped around her. And on went the procession through the night and mist.

Well, perhaps I did lose my head a little there, I thought then. Neither our dear departed Madame Genlis, nor Monsieur Lafontaine, would ever have allowed two lovers to share a cloak in the world of their novels without exploiting the situation and letting a declaration of love slip out, and I do just wonder whether Lady Nature will make something happen here, some sigh, some word ...

I was paying close attention as I followed the occupants of the cloak, but – they kept quiet – not a word, not a sound. But now! ... What was that? Julie sneezing. Now surely L. will say

157

'Bless you!' and that could lead on to something el… , no, he said nothing.

We leave the garden, we cross the courtyard. Won't anyone speak? Now! … no. We go up the steps, we go in through the front door; now, then! … no. The cloak fell from Julie's shoulders, she thanked L. and curtsied, he … bowed.

When we reached the dining room, we found Lieutenant Arvid already eating his beef stew. We were very late. By way of an excuse, I explained about the argument over the cloak.

Throughout the meal, her Ladyship shook her head at Julie every time she looked her way, to reproach her for such unheard-of recklessness as going out so late without a shawl.

When Lieutenant Arvid became aware of his betrothed's swollen eyes, he seemed quite dumbfounded, but I expect he thought, 'She will be all right once she has eaten and slept,' for he did not hurry his supper, nor try to speak to his betrothed afterwards, and rode off at the usual time with his usual nonchalance.

But the discontented Julie was not all right. In fact, on the contrary, her discontent seemed to grow. Arvid would invite her in vain to take 'a little nap' and consider him a pillow. She did not seem able to rest. Arvid's father, old General P***, came with his magnificent coach and horses and invited his little future daughter-in-law to 'ride with the Swans', but all in vain. Every day the couple had numerous *brouilleries*, which in spite of Arvid's peerlessly phlegmatic temperament seemed to grow more and more serious in nature. Her Ladyship, who was now becoming aware of what was happening, began to feel extremely uneasy and always had some kindly quip or conciliatory word at the ready to retie the broken thread of unity. She succeeded quite well at first – but the thread had more knots with every passing day.

Things went on like this for a while. At the end of his time in camp in Stockholm, Cornet Carl went off to Roslagen on the coast. From there he wrote the most desperate letters about dust and heat, and it being dull, boring, unbearable etc. Of botany he said not a single word.

During the summer, Elisabeth's condition remained unchanged, and her Ladyship persisted in the belief that a milk diet was necessary for my chest and my melancholy.

Fate span the life-threads of the rest of the family from ordinary flax, mixed with a little rough tow, but mostly with silk, until the end of August – when she raised her scissors. Let us find out

Why?

After a close, oppressive day, thunderclouds gathered towards evening and by sunset covered the whole sky. A kind of deathlike silence descended on the area. No sound could be heard from the cows hurrying homewards, no birds were singing, the aspen leaves were still, not even the swarms of mosquitos dared to give their usual cheer as the sun set; the whole of nature seemed to be in painful suspense, awaiting some terrible and extraordinary scene.

Later that evening, the terrifying and beautiful spectacle began.

Every few minutes, pale flashes of lightning illuminated the area, which otherwise seemed as black as night, and in the flashes the masses of cloud could be seen growing darker, and gathering in menacing shapes above the house. From time to time a sudden stormy gust of wind went howling across the sky, then all was deathly calm again. The rumbling of thunder in the distance grew to a crescendo as it approached.

Her Ladyship ran from chimney damper to chimney damper and from window to window to see that they were all firmly shut. Julie and Helena stood with their father at one window, hugging him more closely with every flash of lightning and crash of thunder.

I went in to the blind girl. She was sitting on her bed, leaning in a slumped position that seemed to express how tired she was of life, and was singing in a low and dismal voice:

> It is night, it is night!
> My eye is dark, my heart beats faintly;
>   It longs to rest.
>
> Give me peace, give me peace
> And room in the house of the worms,
>   O pale angel of death!
>
> Let me fall asleep gently;
> Night watches and tears have made me so tired,
>   So tired of living!

She let her head, so tired of life, sink down onto the pillows. She was silent for a while; I saw her give a sad smile, and she began to sing once more, but in a clearer voice and a more cheerful tone:

> If morning should come before too long,
> once reach to my grave the resurrection song,
>   a summons unto life ...
>
> If your light I may behold,
> O radiant king, and from earth's stony hold,
>   my brow be raised upward ...

160

At this point she began to cry and sang through her tears in a changed tone and in broken-off verses:

> O mother, o mother!
> In supporting arms
> Enfold your guilty,
> Repentant daughter!
> Teach her to pray,
> Teach her to hope..
>
> . . . .
>
> Give her tenderness,
> Give her rest!
>
> O mother, o mother!
> Enfold me in your arms,
> Press me to your heart,
> Tender and warm!
> Let me feel,
> How, from love,
> Heart against heart
> Can beat so divinely!
>
> Ah, I never knew
> This feeling here on Earth!
>
> . . . .
>
> Alone I have trodden,
> Alone I have loved,
> Alone I have suffered,
> Bitterly, o bitterly!
>
> . . . .

Alone I love
Even in death.

O Mother, o Mother,
Take me, o take me!
Away from the world,
Away from the pain!

. . . .

Glimmering spark
From the dust of night!
Lift me from darkness,
Up to the light!

A sudden large thunderclap which reverberated around the house broke off her song; more and more followed, growing louder and louder; a wild storm began to rage.

'Is there anyone there?' asked the blind girl. I went up to her. She said, 'I can hear music which makes me feel good. Take me to the window.'

There, she crossed her arms on her breast and turned her face up to the sky. The lightning flashes illuminated the beautiful, pale face, and the terrifying thunderclaps seemed to be threatening to destroy the creature who lifted her calm face to the spirits of devastation in a sort of defiant joy.

Elisabeth seemed gradually to be gripped by more violent emotions, and the battle of nature outside was echoed in her soul. Suddenly she cried out, 'I can see something! A hand of fire with glowing fingers passed across my eyes!'

She stood tense for a moment, as if waiting, and then said, in a kind of quiet ecstasy, 'How gloriously, how gloriously it is singing up there in the clouds. Harmonies of kinship are calling you, my heart. Here in my breast is the first part of the harmony; up there now I hear the second part. Now there is unity – now there will be life and joy! Fire of Heaven! motherly bosom! wrap me in your burning embrace! Mother, Mother, is that your voice I can hear – your hand that I saw? ... that I see ... I see again now? Are you beckoning me? Calling me?' – 'Air!' she shrieked wildly, imploringly, 'Take me out into the open air! I want to hear my Mother's voice – I want to fly to her breast and be warm again. There are wings of fire out there, they shall bear me. There is a chariot there ... listen to its rumbling! It will carry me. Quickly, quickly! Can you not see the hand? It is beckoning. Listen to the voice. It is calling! Hah! Can you hear?'

I held her lovingly and asked her to be calm. She interrupted me, saying solemnly, 'God will refuse to hear your last prayer, if you refuse mine. He will bless you, if you obey me. Take me out into the open! It will be the last time I ask anything of you. You do not realize that my fate rests on this moment. Take me out into my kingdom – into the hurricane's kingdom ... there, only there, I shall find peace. Beata, good Beata! See how quiet and composed I am, I am not mad. Hear me ... hear my prayer! I have been in chains all my life ... let me be free just for a moment ... and all my bleeding wounds will be healed.'

I had not the heart to resist that voice, those words. I led her down to a terrace, cut out of the rocky hillside itself, a little way from the house. The young girl who watched over Elisabeth was too frightened of the thunder to follow us.

I soon regretted my compliance. No sooner were we out in nature's wild uproar than Elisabeth pulled away from me, ran a few steps forward and then stopped with loud cries full of defiant and demented joy.

It was a scene of terrible beauty. The red tongues of lightning flickered all around; the storm engulfed us, and the thunder crashed and crackled as it circled overhead. The blind girl stood

on the rocks and threw her arms wildly about, like the spirit of
the hurricane. Sometimes she laughed, and clapped her hands
with frantic delight; sometimes she span round with arms
outstretched, singing in a strong, clear voice:

> Lightning and flames,
> Burning waves of the sea
> That is the world's fire!
> Storms that roar
> And break the chains
> Of the grave of silence!
> Thunder – and all
> You powers that swell
> In the breast of the world,
> See, in a woman,
> Your sovereign,
> Hear my voice!
>
> Ring, o ring,
> Sing, o sing,
> Hail day of freedom!
> . . . .
> The victory song resounds
> And life finds wings!
> . . . .
> It is I who am free!

She gave another wild laugh and cried, 'How glorious, how
glorious! How wonderful! I am so happy, happy, happy! My
day of government is here! A crown ... a crown of fire will
descend from the dark clouds to be placed upon my head. My
day is here, my hour has come!'

At that moment I saw with indescribable relief the Colonel at the unfortunate girl's side.

'You must go back to your room,' he said.

Elisabeth jerked her hand violently out of his grasp, and instead of meekly obeying his wishes as usual, she stood before him, proud and defiant, with the look of a Medusa, and repeated, 'My hour has come! I am free! Must? Who dares to say that to me in this place? Am I not in my own kingdom? Am I not in my Mother's arms? Can you not see how her arms of fire are enfolding me and pushing you away?'

The Colonel, fearing a worse attack of madness, tried to take her in his arms to carry her back to the house, but Elisabeth suddenly put her arms around *his* neck with infinite tenderness, and said, 'If I hold you in my arms like this, and you hold me in yours, my Mother will take us both into her bosom of fire. What clear and heavenly happiness! Today is my day – my hour is here! I am free, and you are captive. I defy you – I defy you, ever to get free!'

Whether it was the word *'defy'* that awoke the man's *defiance*, or whether it was some other feeling, the Colonel disentangled himself quickly from Elisabeth's embrace and moved a few steps away from her.

'Yes, I defy ... I defy you,' she went on. 'You fettered my limbs, you tied my tongue, but still I stand before you now, powerful and strong, and wanting these terrible words to strike you like lightning: 'I love you! I love you!' You can no longer forbid me them, your anger is powerless. The thunder is with me – the storm is with me. Soon I will be up there with them forever. Like a cloud in your sky, I will follow you all your life; like a pale ghost I will hover above your head, and when everything else around you has fallen silent, you will still hear my voice calling: 'I love you! I love you!'

The Colonel seemed strangely and deeply moved; he stood motionless, arms folded, but dark flames flickered in his eyes.

With a quieter ecstasy, Elisabeth went on, 'Oh! Did I not love you dearly? No mortal ever loved more dearly, more warmly! Heaven, as you rage above my head ... Earth, which will soon open my grave – I call you as my eternal witnesses! Hear my words! Feel them, you my life's beloved torment, noble, exalted object of all my thoughts – of my love, of my hatred – yes, *my* hatred ... hear what it says: I love you! With the innermost, holiest life of my being I have loved you – my feelings were as deep as the ocean, but as pure as Heaven. You did not understand ... no-one on Earth will understand ... my Mother knows ... and He who is above us all. If we had lived in a world, where words and deeds can be innocent, like feelings and thoughts ... o then, like a clear, warm flame, I would have engulfed you and shone around you ... filled you with bliss ... burned as a clear sacrificial flame, for you alone. Such was my love. But you did not understand it ... did not love me ... and you rejected me, and you despised me ... and I became a criminal ... but I still loved you ... and still do ... always, and forever, and – *alone*!'

'Alone?!' burst out the Colonel, seeming to forget himself under the influence of some powerful emotion.

'Yes, alone ... ,' repeated the blind girl, astonished and trembling. 'Was it not ever so? There have been times when I have sensed ... but ... my God, my God! Could it be possible? O tell me, is it possible? By the eternal bliss which you deserve – and which can never be mine – by the light you see, which I will never behold – I implore you – tell me, tell me: have you loved me?'

For a moment, complete silence reigned in the natural world around them. It seemed to want to hear the answer, which I too was awaiting with trembling and anxiety. Only the pale, slow flashes of lightning flared around us.

Solemnly, with an emphatic, almost aggressive expression in his voice, the Colonel said:

'Yes!'

The blind girl turned her face upward, radiating an unearthly happiness, as the Colonel, deeply moved, continued, 'Yes, I have loved you Elisabeth, loved you with all the power of my heart ... but God's power in my soul was greater and stopped me from falling. Only my severity saved you and me. My love was not pure like yours. It is not the poison your hand prepared for me which has destroyed my health, but the struggle with passion and desire ... it is the sorrow I feel for you. Elisabeth! You have been infinitely dear to me ... you still are ... Elisabeth ...'

Elisabeth could no longer hear him; she somehow sank down under the weight of the happiness that was descending on her, and the moment I reached her she collapsed, like someone dying, onto the ground, as her lips whispered with an expression of indescribable happiness: 'He has loved me!'

The Colonel and I could barely manage to carry her back to her room. I was trembling – his strength was as if paralysed. Anxiety caused beads of sweat to form on his brow.

Elisabeth did not regain consciousness for a long time ... but when she opened her eyes once again and life flowed in her veins once more, she just whispered, 'He did not despise me! ... He loved me!' and stayed calm and quiet, as if she had settled her account with the world and had nothing more to wish for. The thunderstorm raged on violently for the rest of the night, but the lightning now illuminated the blind girl's face, radiant with inner happiness.

From that hour and for the remaining few days of her life, everything about her changed. All was gentleness and calm. She spoke little, but gave a friendly and grateful squeeze to the hand of whoever came up to the bed, where she lay almost motionless. She was often heard to murmur, 'He loved me!'

One day, her Ladyship was standing beside Elisabeth, who seemed unaware of her presence and continued to repeat in indescribable bliss the words she so treasured. I saw a look of pain come over her Ladyship's gentle, kindly face, saw her lips tremble and a few tears trickle down her cheeks. She quickly turned and went out. I went after her, for she had forgotten her bunch of keys. We went through the drawing room. The Colonel was sitting there with his head resting in his hand, and appeared to be reading. He had his back to us. Her Ladyship crept quietly up behind him, kissed his brow and, stifling a sob, went on into the bedroom. The Colonel looked after her in surprise, then looked at his hand, wet with his wife's tears, kissed them away and resumed his thoughtful pose. After a while I followed her Ladyship into the bedroom, but she was no longer there; her psalter lay open on the couch. The pages bore traces of tears. Finally, after searching all the rooms nearby, I found her in the kitchen, where she was giving the cook a talking to for forgetting to take the cutlets off the breast of lamb already sizzling over the fire, which certainly was an unforgivable offence, as I had already told her twice that we were to have the breast for dinner and the cutlets for supper.

'One can never rely on anybody but oneself,' said her Ladyship, by way of a little dig at me, as I handed over the keys.

From that time I did not leave Elisabeth day or night. Her earthly being seemed to be rushing towards its disintegration at a wondrous speed. It seemed as though the first words of love she had heard had been the key to free her tortured soul.

So it is for many of Earth's children. They fight the fierce sting of pain for many, many years – live, suffer and fight. The sting is gone – and they collapse, exhausted. Happiness offers them its cup. They set their lips to its purple rim – and *die*!

Besides Helena and me, Professor L. was almost constantly with Elisabeth. Sometimes he would read aloud to her, sometimes he would talk to us, in a way which must have awoken her dormant piety and strengthened her belief in those sacred truths which stand like bright angels round the dying person's bed.

On one occasion he asked her a number of questions about her inner state. She answered, 'I lack the strength to think clearly now, I lack the strength to test myself. But I feel ... I have a sense of expectation ... of everything becoming clear! ...'

'The Lord lift up his countenance upon you!' said Professor L. with quiet dignity and trust.

The following day, Elisabeth asked for the whole family to gather round her. Once all of us, including Professor L., were gathered in dreadful silence in her room, Elisabeth named each person she wished to approach her bed – took that person's hand and kissed it, saying, 'Forgive me!' In that way she went round us all. No-one could bring themself to speak, and the sad 'Forgive me, forgive me' was the only sound to rise above our agonized sighs.

Only the Colonel and his wife remained where they were. Elisabeth fell silent for a moment, her breathing heavy and laboured. Finally she said, 'Would my uncle come to me?'

The Colonel went over to her, she stretched up her arms to him, he bent down to her – they kissed. And what a kiss! The first and the last – the kiss of love and of death!

Not a word was heard. Pale as a dying man, the Colonel drew back with faltering steps. In a voice that shook, Elisabeth said, 'Lift me up out of bed, and take me to my aunt.'

We obeyed. She proved to have extraordinary strength and, supported between two of us, she walked the length of the room

169

to where her Ladyship sat crying, seemingly unaware of her intention.

Elisabeth said, 'Help me to get down on my knees!'

Her Ladyship got up quickly, to try to forestall her, but Elisabeth knelt down even more rapidly at her feet, kissing them, as she stammered out through convulsive sighs, 'Forgive me! Forgive me!'

Almost lifeless, she was borne back to bed.

From that moment, the Colonel did not leave her again.

That night and the following day she lay quiet, but seemed to be suffering physical pain. Towards evening, as Professor L., the Colonel and I sat silently at her bedside, she awoke from a quiet sleep and said aloud in a clear voice: 'He did love me! Earth, I thank you!'

Then she sank back into a kind of slumber or torpor, which lasted for about an hour. Her breathing, which had been quite rapid during this time, gradually became irregular. There was a long interval – then a sigh... another long pause, and another sigh. All at once she seemed to stop breathing altogether. It was a dreadful moment ... a slight spasm jerked through her limbs ... another sigh or exhalation, followed by an awful moaning sound ... and all was silent.

'It is over,' said the Colonel in a choking voice, and pressed his lips to the death-pale forehead.

'Now she can *see*,' cried Professor L., his face radiant as his eyes turned heavenward.

The perfume-laden breeze of the summer evening played in at the open window, and the birds sang joyfully in the honey-suckle hedge outside. A gentle pink glow, a reflection of the setting sun, enveloped the room, and lent the departed a sympathetic hue.

She lay there now so quiet, so free from pain, she who had struggled and despaired for so long ... now so calm – so quiet!

Her luxuriant brown hair trailed across the white pillows and down towards the floor. On her lips was a strange smile, filled with an expression of higher knowledge. I have seen that smile on the lips of many who have passed away ... The angel of eternity has pressed her kiss on them.

Peaceful moment, when a heart which has pounded so long in anxiety and pain finds rest. Peaceful moment, which reconciles us with all our enemies, brings us closer to all our friends, which draws a veil over all our failings, puts a bright halo round our virtues, which opens the eyes of the blind and releases the fetters of the soul. Beautiful and peaceful moment, although borne on the wings of an angel of the night, you smile on me like the blush of sunrise, and having seen you dawn on others, I have often yearned for you to come to me too.

The skein becomes tangled

Elisabeth was no longer with us. She had moved among those nearest to her like a dark and overshadowing thundercloud. Now that it had disappeared, everyone felt a sense of peace and security. Many a tear was shed in sad memory of her, but no heart called her back. Poor Elisabeth, you only brought peace, once your own heart had found it in the grave.

We see it all the time. The most insignificant and limited people, if they have only been good and peaceable, depart the world more loved and lamented than the distinguished and richly gifted, who have made poor use of their talents and with all their beauty, genius and warmth not brought happiness to a single being.

The Colonel remained in sombre mood for a long time and was more uncommunicative than usual towards his wife and children. Their tenderness and solicitude were just beginning to lift his spirits, when events occurred within the family circle to shatter his peace once again and arouse his naturally violent emotions.

One day, Arvid's father General P*** came rushing into the Colonel's room in high dudgeon. He first gave vent to his feelings with a salvo of curses and oaths, and when the Colonel coldly asked him the meaning of this he spluttered, quite beside himself, 'The meaning? ... The meaning ... damn it! The meaning is that your – your – your girl is a blessed ... '

'General P***,' said the Colonel in a tone that brought the furious figure abruptly to his senses, so that he repeated, a little more slowly, 'The – the – the ... meaning of it ... is ... that your daughter is playing around with trust and honour, and telling fibs, damn and blast it ... that she wants to break off her engagement to my Arvid ... wants to give back the engagement ring, damn and ... that Arvid is beside himself ... that he will blow his brains out ... violent and wild as he is ... and I will be left a wretched, childless old man!'

At this point, a few tears trickled down the old man's cheeks as he went on, in a voice caught between anger and grief, 'She has been mocking my son's composure ... mocking my grey hair! ... I liked her so well ... like a father, brother ... like a father; I had put all hope of happiness in the evening of my life in her ... it will be the death of me. She has said to Arvid's face that she will not have him ... to my son's face ... damn and blast it! He will be the laughing stock of the parish ... he will blow his brains out, brother; he will blow his brains out, I tell you ... and I will be a childless, wretched old man.' (And so on.)

The Colonel, who had listened to all this in complete silence, rang the bell violently. I was in the adjoining room and answered the Colonel's summons so I could spy out the lie of the land and prepare Julie for what lay in store for her.

The Colonel's expression was one of uncompromising anger. He asked me to send Julie down to him.

I found Julie in a state of great anxiety, but already alerted by the General's presence to what lay ahead.

'I know ... I know...,' she said, going pale at my words, 'It had to come to this ... it cannot be helped.'

'But have you really broken off your engagement?' I asked.

'I have ... sort of ...,' she replied with a dejected and anxious look. 'There is no time to explain ... yesterday evening I let slip a harsh word to Arvid ... he was being so cold and sneering ... I lost my temper, he got angry ... and rode off in a rage ...'

173

The Colonel's bell rang again.

'My God!' said Julie, pressing her hands to her heart. 'I must go now ... and must be brave. Oh, if only it were not for that withering look ... Tell me Beata – did Papa look very grave?' I could not deny it; I begged her not to be hasty – to consider her own promise, solemnly given, and the Colonel's strict principles regarding the sacred nature of a promise.

'Oh, I cannot ... I cannot! ...' was all that Julie could utter as, pale and trembling, she went downstairs to the Colonel's room. At the door she stopped, seemed to find new resolve, and went in.

After about half an hour had passed Julie, looking utterly forlorn, came into Helena's room, where I also was. She threw herself down on the sofa, rested her head on Helena's knee and began to sob loudly and violently. The good Helena sat there quietly, but sympathetic tears fell from her eyes and fell like pearls onto Julie's golden braids. A long time later, once the worst of Julie's distress had abated, Helena said gently, running her fingers through her sister's thick locks, 'I have not done your hair yet today, dear Julie. Sit up for a moment and it will soon be done.'

'Oh, cut off my hair! – I want to be a nun!' answered Julie, but she got up nonetheless, dried her eyes and allowed her hair to be set in order, helped Helena with hers, and calmed down in the process.

It is so true, that the little cares of everyday life possess a quite remarkable power to distract us from sorrow.

In answer to our questions about what had actually happened, Julie replied, 'What has happened is that I have been condemned to pay for a moment's thoughtlessness for the rest of my life – and to be a miserable creature ... that is – if I accept the verdict – but I do not ... better Papa's displeasure ... better ...'

'Oh Julie, Julie!' interrupted Helena, 'Consider what you are saying!'

'Helena! You do not know what I have suffered, how I have been struggling with myself for a long time now. You do not know how clearly I see what a wretched and sorry fate will be mine if I must be Arvid's wife! Oh, I was sleepwalking before and in my sleep I gave him my hand; now I have awoken – and I am not allowed to take it back now that I realize I have given it to a ...'

'Arvid is a good person, Julie!'

'What do you call good, Helena? Someone who is merely not bad? Arvid (I have tried and tested him) seems good, because he has not the energy to be vindictive; calm and steady – because he is not bothered about anything except his easy-going ways; sensible – because he sees no further than the end of his nose ... he is nothing but a concoction of negatives ... why should we be afraid to add to his collection – and give him yet another *no*? Do not think that it will trouble him for long – he does not love me ... he is incapable of love, he has no feelings! Oh, he is a log of damp wood, which my little fire would struggle in vain to light – the flame would gradually be turned into smoke and finally go out altogether!'

'Dear Julie, even if Arvid is not the man you deserve and could not make you happy as his wife – why should not your fire burn brightly even so? Arvid is not vindictive, he would never be your tormentor. There are many wives, joined to men who stand incomparably far beneath them, but who still make themselves noble and excellent creatures, creating happiness and cheer around them and finding happiness in the awareness that they have done their duty. Look at our cousin Mrs M***; is she not admirable and amiable? And what sort of husband has she got? Look at Emma S***, look at Hedda R*** ...'

175

'Yes, and look at Penelope and her sisters *et compagnie* ... Oh Helena, those ladies have my deep admiration, my respect, my esteem; I wish I were like them – but one thing I know for certain – that I cannot do it. That independence of opinion and judgement, that composure, that clear-sightedness, that confidence and clarity of principle, which are all so necessary, if one is to be the leading partner in a marriage – I do not have them ... not at all! *I* am the one who needs to be led – I am a vine, and need an oak to support me. This is a time when my concepts are developing – I feel a better person stirring within me – a new world is opening up to me! If I could go through it hand in hand with a husband I could love and admire, one who in his heart could answer the purifying fire in mine; who with the clear light of his intelligence could enlighten my dusky soul (she means Professor L., I thought), then I might become a better person – and reach a goal, which I can as yet not see, only imagine ... But with Arvid, you see Helena, with Arvid ... my world would be just like a larder – with me like a lump of mouldering cheese.'

'What an image, dearest Julie!'

'It is truer than you think. Oh, marriage really is a dreadful thing. In it, many have found what I may now find ... they have foolishly hoisted the matrimonial sail – believed themselves on course for the Island of Happiness – and have run aground and been stuck for life on a sandbank. They have crept around there like the oyster in its shell, looking for a little sunshine ... until a merciful wave has come ...'

'Julie! Julie!'

'Helena! Helena! It is an everyday picture – each day confirms the truth of it. Have not many nobler natures gone under in that way? And *mine* will do likewise, if I cannot steer round the sandbank in time!'

'Julie! I fear that cannot be. Papa's principles are unalterable. And the first among them is keeping strictly to one's word. And I believe he is quite right. What is more, as regards breaking off a betrothal, taking back a promise of marriage – there is in that something deeply offensive to feminine delicacy – so that I consider ...'

'Delicacy my foot! ... I consider it highly indelicate and more to the point highly unreasonable, to sacrifice a whole life's happiness for mere delicacy.'

'Could you be happy, Julie, knowing that you had lost your family's – your father's – devotion, the world's respect?'

'The world's respect... I do not care two farthings for that ... but the respect of those I love ... oh dear! Helena, Beata – is it possible that I could lose *that*? If so, it would certainly be better to condemn myself to be unhappy ...'

'You will not be unhappy, Julie,' said Helena with tears in her eyes, taking her sister into her arms, 'You will ...'

'You know nothing about it, Helena,' interrupted Julie in impatient irritation. '*I* know that I will be unhappy. It is more than just Arvid's unworthiness that will make me so ... it is the conviction of having failed to fulfil my purpose, the conviction that a noble and happy lot could have been mine, that I could have lived on earth for the happiness of a high-minded and excellent being. Oh, I know it. I could have risen to the heights like a lark in freedom, light and song – and now I shall – as I feared – creep around like an oyster on the sandbank of life, dragging my prison with me.'

At the repetition of this dreadful, but rather inaccurate image, Julie was overcome by renewed and violent distress; she threw herself down on the sofa once more, and stayed there all day, wanting neither to eat nor to be consoled. Her Ladyship was constantly running up and downstairs, or sending me to do so, with drops and scented water.

Julie really did become unwell, although not seriously so, and stayed in her room for two days, during which she did not see her father. There was no word of either Arvid or the General during this time, to Julie's great relief.

Her Ladyship had always had her own little tactic, or domestic policy, for when conflicts arose between her husband and children. When she spoke to the former, she would always speak as if on the latter's side, and with the latter she would always claim and argue, that the former must be in the right. Yet I believe her heart was often a defector to the weaker side, for when in certain cases everything had to bow to the Colonel's will of iron, her Ladyship would always cuddle her children twice as tenderly as usual. This time, too, she had pleaded Julie's case to her husband and advocated dissolving the betrothal, but had found him uncompromising ('unreasonable' said her Ladyship). Now, seeing Julie so unhappy, her attitude to him became imperceptibly – not unfriendly, perish the thought ... but somehow a little less friendly, apparently (and I can vouch for its not being so in actual fact) somewhat less concerned for his sustenance and comfort in many little ways. An uncomfortable sort of feeling, previously unknown in the family, reigned over the house for some days.

'The mountain will not come to Mohammed – so Mohammed must betake himself to the mountain, I suppose!', the Colonel said to me one morning with a genial smile, as he prepared to mount the stairs to Julie's room.

At that moment, a cart stopped in the courtyard and Cornet Carl, looking overheated and one might almost say embarrassed, leapt out and ran up the steps, hugged his parents and sisters hard but wordlessly, and at once requested a moment's interview with his father in private.

The moment had grown and become an hour before the Cornet, his face pale and contorted, emerged alone from his father's room. As if in a trance, he crossed the drawing room and dining room, entered her Ladyship's boudoir without seeming to notice either her or me, sat down with his elbow resting on a table, and hid his eyes in his hand as if the daylight hurt them.

Her Ladyship observed him with a mother's anxiety, and at length got up and stroked his cheek with her hand, saying, 'My dear boy! What is it?'

'Nothing,' replied the Cornet in a quiet, suffocated voice.

'Nothing?' echoed her Ladyship. 'Carl, you are worrying me ... you are so pale ... are you unhappy?'

'Yes,' answered the Cornet in the same quiet voice.

'My child ... my son! What is wrong?'

'Everything!'

'Carl! ... And you have a mother who would willingly give her life for your happiness!'

'Dear Mother!' cried the Cornet, putting his arms around her, 'Forgive me!'

'Dearest child! Tell me what I can do for you ... tell me what is wrong – tell me everything! There must be some way out ... I will not live to see you unhappy.'

'But I *shall* be unhappy, if I cannot find today a sum of, or the guarantee of a sum of, ten thousand crowns. If I do not get it today – then Hermina ... *my* Hermina, will be the wife of another within a few days! Good God! I could buy a whole lifetime's happiness and that of another with that paltry sum ... and it is denied me! I have talked to my father, opened my heart to him – told him everything. He has the money ... I knew it ... and he ...'

'And he has refused you?'

'Definitely, categorically. He says it is the inheritance of the poor and unfortunate ... and for the sake of these needy strangers he ruins his son's happiness!'

Here the Cornet suddenly rose and strode across the floor, crying, 'What low creature has dared to blacken Hermina's name in my father's hearing? That holy God's angel! She is said to be deceiving me! She ... She loves the hateful G***! Only he or his envoy could have ...'

Here the Cornet massacred a coach and horses (property of the little Puddings), and her Ladyship in alarm removed from the vicinity of her son a vase of flowers, whilst acknowledging his complaint with her anxious, 'But why? ... But how?'

'Do not ask me now!' cried the Cornet impatiently. 'Just now I can only say one thing: my future depends on my obtaining the stated sum today. I could be the happiest creature on earth – or the unhappiest – and not alone in my fate ...'

'Carl,' said her Ladyship solemnly, 'Look at me! ... Bless your honest eyes, my son. I – I know you – you would not want to allow me to take a step whose consequences I might regret?'

'Mother! ... Would you regret having engineered my life's happiness?'

'Enough my child! *I* shall now go and talk to your father. Wait for me here.'

The Cornet awaited his mother's return in a state of extreme emotional turmoil. I could see that he was in one of those moments of youthful frenzy when we consider it unthinkable that anyone would oppose our will or our wishes. At times like that, we cannot grasp the word 'impossibility'. We think we can command the sun itself, think we can tear up mountains by their roots or (which amounts to the same thing) tear deep-rooted principles from resolute human breasts.

It took a long time for her Ladyship to return. Julie and Helena accompanied her. She was pale, tears were glistening on her eyelids and her voice was unsteady as she said, 'Your father will not ... he has his reasons, he believes himself to be doing ... quite certainly is doing the right thing. But – my dear child, something can still be done. Take these pearls and jewels, they are mine ... to use as I wish ... take them. In Stockholm you will be able to get a good price for them at once ...'

'And here ... and here, dearest Carl!', said Julie and Helena, each proffering their valuables with one hand and putting the other gently round his shoulders, 'Take this too ... Carl, we beg you ... take it – sell it all – and make yourself happy!'

A deep flush suffused the young man's face and tears flooded down his cheeks. At that moment the Colonel came in, stopped short in the doorway and fixed the group on the far side of the room with a piercing gaze. An expression of anger mixed with contempt came over his face. 'Carl!' he called loudly, 'If you are unworthy enough to exploit your mother's and your sisters' weakness for you – to satisfy your own blind passions, then you have *my* contempt, and I do not recognize you as my son!'

Deeply unhappy and now so deeply misjudged, the young man's heart filled with the gall of bitterest indignation. He went deathly pale, clamped his mouth shut, stamped his feet violently and was out through the door like a flash. A few minutes later he was mounted and galloping away from the house.

————

The Cornet. The Cornet. The Cornet.

'Halloo! In the forest the hounds are out.'

Halloo! The hounds are out. The hunted one flees and the hunters pursue. What is the quarry? An unhappy human being. And the hunters? The furies of indignation, despair and rage. How they drive forward! A matchless hunt! The hunted one flees, but the hunters follow. Halloo! Halloo! They do not lose the scent – they pursue, they pursue, through densest forest,

181

upon dancing waves, over hill and dale, jaws gape and wail ... want to swallow their prey ... and do not stray ... but the chase is now easing ... Halloo! Halloo! It soon will be ceasing!

Onward! Onward! The quarry spurred his panting steed which flew foam-flecked over hedges and fences. Wild confusion raged in his soul. Whirling onward in a cloud of dust, he galloped along the country road through dismal forested stretches, trying to deaden every feeling, every thought in his soul, obeying only the urgent 'onward! onward!' which roared in every beat of his wild, feverish pulse.

The peaceable inhabitants of the cottages past which he whistled like a storm wind ran to their doors in amazement, wondering whose horse had bolted. And one of them (Stina Andersdotter in Rörum) swore that she had seen a dog and a hare come out, the one from the cottage and the other from the forest, and sit down facing each other, watching the wild rider wide-eyed before, timid and disorientated, they changed places, the hare running into the cottage and the dog into the forest.

The wild rider, Cornet Carl, did not stop until he reached the front door of the house in the woods, already familiar to us. He leapt from his horse and ran up the stairs. All the doors up there were locked, all was silent. He ran down the stairs. All the doors down there were locked, all was silent and dead. He ran across the courtyard and into a little outhouse, and wrenched open a door. Inside sat a little, dried-up old woman, humming a psalm and spinning tow on a spinning wheel.

'Where are the Baron and Baroness? Where is Miss Hermina?' cried the overheated Cornet, almost out of breath.

'Eh?' answered the little tow-woman. 'Where are your employers?', yelled the Cornet with a voice and a look that could kill.

'What?' answered the old woman, contentedly sticking her nose into a little box of snuff.

The Cornet stamped. (A mended cup fell off the shelf, three unstable glasses chinked together).

'Are you stone deaf?' he yelled fortissimo, 'I asked whether your employers were out.'

'The way out? To Torsborg manor, you mean Sir? Well, you cross the field, and ...'

'I asked,' screeched the Cornet with all the force of desperation, 'Whether your employers had gone away.'

'The other way? To Wresta? Oh well, then you go ...'

'This is ridiculous,' said the Cornet, at the end of his tether. 'It is enough to drive one mad!'

'Oh well, yes indeed,' sighed the little old woman, disconcerted and alarmed to see the Cornet angry, and went quietly over to pick up the pieces of the broken cup.

A banknote worth two silver crowns came flying and hit her on the nose, and the stranger was gone.

'God preserve me! ... God bless! ...,' stammered the alarmed and contented old woman.

Another door in the same outbuilding burst open with a violent shove from the Cornet.

Inside, by the hearth, beside her piglet (I mean, her child) sat a dear, fat mother, feeding gruel to her little, bristle-haired boy.

Here the Cornet impatiently repeated his question, and received the answer:

'Yes, well, they be gone away.'

'But where? Tell me when ... and where? Was no message left, no letter for me?'

'Letter? Oh yes, I did have one, to deliver to Cornet H***, and I am just going to Torsborg with it, as soon as I have got a drop of gruel into the boy, poor wretch ... eat up, boy!'

'In God's name, bring the letter here at once, hurry, get it immediately I say, go ...'

'Yes, yes ... as soon as I have got this drop of gruel into the boy. He be hungry, poor wretch.'

'I will feed the boy, give me the spoon ... just go, bring the letter here at once!'

At last the woman goes over to her chest. The Cornet stands by the hearth, takes a spoonful of gruel from the pot, blows on it with an anxious expression, and puts it into the little lad's open mouth. The woman rummages around in her chest, searching and searching. Snuff-box and butter-dish, stockings and petticoats, psalm book and bread roll are taken up one by one and laid out on the floor – but of the letter there is no sign.

The Cornet fidgets and stamps in an agony of impatience.

'Hurry up! Well, have you got it? Oh really!'

'Just coming, just coming! Wait a bit, wait – here, no here – no wait a bit ... wait.'

Wait! You can just imagine how inclined the Cornet now felt to 'wait a bit'.

But the letter cannot be found. The woman burbles to herself and mutters through clenched teeth:

'It has gone – it is not there!'

'Not there?' cries the Cornet, and in his dismay pours a spoonful of hot gruel down the throat of the little boy, who responds with shrill cries of complaint.

The letter was not there. 'My boy must have got hold of it, chewed it up or burnt it.' And the dear mother, who is more concerned about her boy's predicament than the Cornet's, says crossly to the latter, 'Go to Lövstaholm, they will be able to tell you. The Baron and Baroness went that way, and Miss Agnes was here with Miss Hermina the other day.'

The Cornet, leaving a crown piece as consolation for the scalded throat, curses under his breath about geese and their young and vaults into the saddle, Blanka having meanwhile been

184

grazing the yellowed autumnal grass which grew here and there in the yard.

Now to Lövstaholm. Over six miles' ride. Blanka feels the spurs and goes off at a full gallop.

A river cuts across the road. The bridge is up for repairs. There is another route – but – it is over a mile's detour. Soon Blanka is snorting boldly through the waves, which wash the foam from her neck and muzzle, and kiss the feet of the rider standing on the saddle.

Two wayfarers were watching the proceedings from a distance.

'Do you know, mother,' said one with a thoughtful expression, 'I believe it is the Water Sprite himself, riding down into the river on a black mare.'

'Do you know father,' said the other, 'I believe it is a young man riding to his beloved.'

'Believe me, dear wife.'

'Believe me, dear husband.'

And 'believe me, dear reader,' is not the rider already on the far bank, and onward, onward he chases through field and forest.

Poor Blanka! By the time Lövstaholm's white walls come into view between the greeny-yellowy-brown trees, you are ready to drop, but at the sight of them the rider slows a little and, having reached the courtyard, Blanka is allowed to rest and catch her breath alongside three other mounts, who bear witness to the presence of guests at Lövstaholm just now.

That foundry-owner and knight Mr D*** was sitting in his room, considering with the look of a satisfied connoisseur a charcoal sketch of a head done by his particularly promising daughter Eleonora, and his wife Mrs Emerentia D***, née J***, was standing at his side, concentrating with great enthusiasm on the reading of a poem about the pleasures of country life and simplicity, penned by her very promising son, Lars Anders (who was known in the family as 'little Lord Byron'), when Cornet Carl rushed into the room, and after a brief apology, not caring what people might think of him, his agitation and his questions, asked to be told what they knew there about the hasty departure of Baron K*** and his family.

'Not much more,' said Mr D***, frowning, 'Than that they came by yesterday afternoon, and that Baron K*** saw fit to come up and hurl abuse at me and repay approximately a quarter of the sum I lent him ages ago out of the goodness of my heart ... A Dido – Cornet H*** – of my Eleonora ...'

Mrs D*** took up the story:

'The Baroness, or whatever we should call her (for I have an idea she is no more a Baroness than I am), did not even deign to greet me from the carriage yesterday. Pretty thanks for showing people some courtesy. No, she sat there fine and upright like a princess in her carriage ... *her* carriage, I say ... charming! It was young G***'s coach and horses, and he was sitting there too, like a captured bird in a cage ... and perhaps that made her so proud ...'

'G***'s carriage? G*** was with them?' shrieked the Cornet. 'And Hermina?'

'Sat there looking down, like a turkey. Yes, I was sorely mistaken about that girl. I felt sorry for her, and let my daughters show her a little *soin* and *encourager* her musical gifts. Thérèse had become especially *engouée* with her. But I soon discovered that I had committed an *imprudence*, and that she and her family were not suitable society for my daughters. There are all sorts of strange rumours circulating about that distinguished family – they have behaved in a manner ...'

A servant came in with some tobacco pipes, which he arranged in one corner of the room. Mr D*** thought it best to put the whole conversation into French.

'Oui, c'est une vraie scandale,' he said, 'Une forgerie de tromperie! Un vrai frippon est la fille, je sais ça, et le plus extrèmement mauvais sujet est sa père.'

'*Son* père,' corrected Mrs D***, 'Et le pire de toute chose c'est son mère. Un conduite, oh! Ecoute, cher Cornèt: dans Italie, le mère et le fille et la père ...'

All at once there came from the next-door room a terrible noise, a shriek, a laugh, a din, an unparalleled jubilation. There was a scraping of fiddles, a clattering of fire-irons, there was singing and whining and squeaking. And amid all this din, the only sound to emerge with any clarity among diverse other cries was:

'Papa, Papa! Now we know which play! Now we can get ready for the spectacle! Hurrah, hurrah!'

The cheering crowd came pouring into the room like a roaring torrent, but when the young people saw Cornet Carl, their joy knew no bounds. Up went a general cry of 'Iphigenia, Iphigenia! Hurrah! Hurrah! Long live Iphigenia the Second, long live Cornet Iphigenia! Long live ...'

'Death and damnation!' thought the Cornet, as the wild crowd fell on him and tried to drag him off, shouting, 'Come on Iphigenia! Come on Cornet Carl, quickly, quickly! We are just going to have a rehearsal. The Cornet can read his part ... come on, do come on!'

'Hocus pocus over Cornet Carl! Kneel down and arise as Iphigenia.'

The last was trumpeted by sweet little Agnes D***, who was standing on tiptoe trying to place a veil on Cornet Carl's head, but could reach no higher than his ears. Lieutenant Ruttelin came to her aid. Eleonora D*** and Mina P*** had already draped a large shawl around his shoulders, and three young gentlemen wound a sheet around him to look like a skirt.

Lieutenant Arvid was also in evidence among the aides of the Misses D***.

The Cornet resisted; to no avail; he raised his voice, even shouted – to no avail – in all the noise, he could not make himself heard, let alone understood. Utter desperation born of pure vexation overwhelmed him, and led him to a desperate decision. Using his strength in a manner that was hardly polite, he elbowed the crowd aside to right and left, tore off the sheet and – ran. Ran through an open door which he spied in front of him, found himself in a long series of rooms, looked neither right nor left, just ran, ran, ran! He knocked over a maidservant, three chairs and two tables, and ran on from room to room, until he emerged in a large dining-room. Beyond it lay the entrance hall. The Cornet knew this – and is about to set off in that direction when to his dismay he hears the cheering troop coming towards him from the hall, blocking his path and uttering loud and reproachful cries of 'Iphigenia, Iphigenia!' Deeply agitated and on the verge of turning back to repeat his grand tour, the Cornet catches sight of a half-open door, leading to a little spiral staircase.

He went down it like an arrow. It was dark and cramped – kept on going round and round. The Cornet's head was going round and round too, by the time his feet touched firm ground. He was standing in a dark little passageway. A shaft of light came from an iron door standing ajar. The Cornet went through this door too. Through a window opposite, protected by heavy iron bars, the dull light of a setting autumn sun fell on the whitish-grey stone walls of the tiny room. The Cornet found himself – in a prison cell? – No, in a larder.

The Cornet searched for a way out. There was indeed a door in the little passageway, facing the door to the vault, but it needed a key to open it, and there was no key. The Cornet searched and searched – in vain. He sat down on a bread bin in the vault, freed himself from shawl and veil, and was comforted to hear the sound of the wild hunters going by up above and moving further off in their efforts to track him down. Yet they still sounded close enough to prevent the Cornet going back upstairs. Miserable, indignant, tired, feeling bitter towards the whole world, he stared vacantly ahead. A plate of pastries, the remains of a pie, of some roast veal and blackcurrant fool, standing in the sunlight on the table, met his eyes in a friendly and beckoning manner.

The Cornet felt a strange sensation; in the midst of his despair, tormented by a thousand agonizing thoughts, he felt – hungry!

Poor human nature! O humanity, pinnacle of creation! Dust-king of the dust! Is it Heaven or Hell which dominates your breast? – Yet you must eat! One minute an angel, the next an animal! Poor human nature!

And conversely: Fortunate human nature! Fortunate dichotomy, which alone maintains the unity of the being. The animal comforts the spirit, the spirit the animal, and only thus can the *human being* exist.

The Cornet existed – was hungry – saw food, and wasted little time in satisfying his hunger with it. The pie had to surrender its forcemeat and poultry filling to that purpose.

Forgive me! Forgive me, my young lady readers! I know ... a lover, and a hero of a novel in particular, should not be so prosaic, so earthy ... and our hero may be in danger of losing all your gracious sympathy. But consider, consider, you sweet creatures who live on feelings and the scent of roses, he was a man, and worse – a Cornet; he had had a long ride and eaten not a bite all day. Consider it!

But is it fitting, to eat from other people's larders like that?

Ah, my most gracious chief mistress of ceremonies! If someone feels really miserable and bitter, really heartily sick of the world – then they think anything is fitting that seems fitting to them, and offends *nothing* other than propriety At such times, we feel such an urge to trample on that like any other weed, and in such a mood we often assume a fine, cosmopolitan air which makes us feel able to tell the whole world to 'get out of my way!'

Cornet Carl had just very reasonably got the pie out of his way, when a rising volume of noise, renewed howls of the accursed 'Iphigenia!' and a din and a racket at the top of the stairs alerted him to the fact that the hunting party had got wind of him, and was hard on his heels. Quite frantic, he ran to the window and grasped one of the iron bars with all his might, intending to wrench it loose and get out at any price. It bent, but held firm. The clamouring mob was closing in. At that frightful moment a ray of sunlight, gleaming in, caught a key, lying right at the back of the window recess.

O ray of salvation! The Cornet seizes the key – it fits the lock – the door flies open, and as if pursued by furies (in this moment of confusion, the Cornet pictured all the charming, educated Misses D*** with Medusa heads) he sprinted down a long passageway out into the front hall, down the steps, across the courtyard and up onto Blanka's back. He was barely in the saddle before the boisterous tribe erupted from the doorway like a swarm of bees from a hive, singing, no howling, in chorus:

> 'Iphigenia, Iphigenia!
> What base poltroonery is this!
> Where are you going, fair young maid?
> Return to us, return!'

The Cornet rode on, and soon disappeared from the choristers' view into the trees. Three young men, who had got so carried away that they still did not realize there was anything more to this than a tremendously good bit of fun, were immediately in the saddle and riding after the fugitive.

Seeing himself pursued once again, the Cornet at once slowed his pace, to the amazement of the triumvirate of hunters, who soon caught up with him and surrounded him with shrill laughs and cries:

'Aha! Aha! Now we have you, Cornet, nothing can save you now! Surrender, Cornet H***, and come back with us at once!' And one of them took hold of the horse's bridle.

But his arm was roughly pushed away, and with a haughty, unswerving eye on his pursuers, the Cornet said vehemently:

'If you, gentlemen, had had the least sense, you would have seen at once that I am not in the least in the mood to play and be played with. You would also see now that I find all these pranks utterly offensive; ... to hell with them, and you! Leave me in peace!'

'That was a damn good scolding,' said one of the triumvirate, bringing his horse into step beside Cornet Carl's, whilst the other two came to a halt, dumbfounded, and then after a moment made up their minds, and galloped back roaring with laughter.

The Cornet rode slowly, with his sharp, angry, inquiring gaze on his uninvited companion, who regarded him with a sort of ironic composure from a pair of clear, light blue eyes.

The two silent riders soon came to a by-road. Then the Cornet turned haughtily to his companion and said:

'I assume we part company here. Good night, Sir!'

'No,' replied the other, scornful and nonchalant, 'I still have a few words to say to you.'

'Name your time and place!' burst out the Cornet.

'Oho! Oho!', said the other in ironic tone, 'You take offence easily. "Name your time and place" is a phrase usually reserved for invitations to name an occasion for killing one

191

another. Well, by all means "name your time and place," but this time I did not intend anything so serious. I only want to stay with you and keep you company, to see if I can cheer you up a bit, buck you up a bit ... have a chat ...'

'I prefer to converse with some people,' said the Cornet, 'with a sword in my hand ... it helps to keep a distance ...'

'Sword,' said his opponent nonchalantly, 'Why particularly a sword, why not pistols? They speak louder, and also serve to keep people at a distance – I do not care to fight with swords.'

'Perhaps you prefer pins?' asked the Cornet contemptuously.

'Yes, pins – or hatpins,' replied his opponent with a smile, taking off his hat, and drawing a long hairpin from the most luxuriant braids that ever graced a female head. With this he (or rather she) speared a little note, which she held out to the Cornet with the words, spoken in quite different tone, 'If you find this more painful than the prick of a sword, please forgive the one who must give it to you against her will!'

And the blue-eyed rider, Thérèse D***, gave the Cornet a friendly, pitying look, turned her horse and was soon out of sight of his wondering gaze.

Another emotion soon coloured that gaze, as he recognized the writing on the outside of the note as Hermina's. With emotions one can easily imagine, the Cornet opened the note and read the following:

'My only friend on Earth! Farewell, farewell! By the time you come – it will be too late. I have had to give in to my mother's desperate entreaties. Today I go to Stockholm. Tomorrow I shall be Genserik's wife ... if I am still alive. My brother, my friend, my everything ... alas, forgive me! Farewell!

>*Hermina.*'

The letter was dated the previous day.

'Now to Stockholm!' said the Cornet, with the desperate but decided intention of winning her – or dying in the attempt! 'Eternal Heaven, be thanked! There is still time!'

The evening was growing dark and stormy. The Cornet, oblivious to this and to everything around him, spurred his horse on at full gallop to the inn.

'Bring me a swift and agile horse this instant!' thundered the Cornet, 'I will pay whatever you ask!' A snorting stallion was soon whinnying with excitement beneath the weight of the wild rider, who was urging his impetuous spirit still further with voice and spurs, and in a blind impatient fury went racing onward, onward over ... but let us catch our breath for a moment.

To-whit! To-wooo!

Tawny owl

It was night. The moon's silver river streamed silently down over Torsborg manor, where everything seemed at rest, for no light gleamed out from the deep windows, betraying a watchful human eye or a heart that could not rest. Ah! – And yet ...

In the Colonel's room, the clear lamp of the night came shining in, illuminating one after another of the gold-framed family portraits, whose subjects seemed to come back to life in the pale, bluish rays, and from the night of the ancient world, whose shadow had long since extinguished their joys and pains, hatred and love, prayers and glances, they now look out with dreaming smiles on their living descendants' battles with life's dark forces; and these choirs of the spirit, which we can merely hear in our thoughts, whisper:

> You will *forget*, and *forgotten* be!
> The battle of day will be hidden by night -
> Spirit – remember – have peace and be free!
> Rest will be sure to come after the fight.

Rest? Quiet ghosts, you wish to console. But there are times, when the thought of these words of the grave and of Heaven cause us to shed bitter tears.

The Colonel stood at his window, looking out at the moonlit night. His high forehead was paler than usual, and dark flames were flashing in his deep-set eyes.

A gusty, stormy wind went rustling to and fro around the precincts of the house, sweeping with it flocks of yellowing leaves, which danced in rings in front of the ancient, solid buildings, like courtiers trying to entertain their prince of the dark looks. On the tops of the towers, the flags creaked as they flapped, and an uneasy, anxious whining, such as one hears in big buildings during a storm, went wailing back and forth around the house. Such sounds deserve to be harbingers of misfortune; they are like mournful premonitions filling us with anxiety.

White clouds chased across the sky in strange and fantastic shapes, looking like fleeing armies rushing past with tattered standards. They draped storm veils over the queen of the night, although she soon broke through them with her victorious rays, and gathered finally in dark grey crowds lower down on the horizon.

The Colonel regarded nature's wild battle in uneasy, sombre mood. He was bitterly aware that the spirit of strife with its poisonous breath had disturbed the tranquillity of his previously happy and united family too. *He*, who loved them so much, and was loved so tenderly in return, had all at once become alienated from them. His wife, his children were drifting away from him – turning their faces from him – and it was his doing; he had refused their entreaties – they were unhappy because of him. At that moment, as his conscience bore witness to his having held to his principles of justice, having acted blamelessly in accordance with their strict but lofty ideals – at that moment, painful emotions stirred in his heart, seeming to accuse him of having been mistaken in the application of those principles – and thus having caused suffering he could have prevented, having embittered the days of those beings he was called upon to protect and bless. A physical sensation of pain, which was peculiar to him and tended to occur whenever he was in severe states of mental agitation – a tightening of the chest, which made it hard to breathe, came on with unusual intensity at these sombre thoughts. He felt alone ... no one sympathized with him at that moment ... no-one's thoughts were hovering around him on the peace-bringing dove's wings of prayer – he was alone! A tear forced its way into his manly eye, and he looked up to the skies with a vague wish that he might soon leave an earth where suffering prevailed.

A white haze in the shape of a human form with outstretched arms seemed to come floating from the arch of stars – seemed to come lower and lower, and the misty outstretched arms seemed to draw close to the Colonel. He thought of Elisabeth – of her love – of her promise to be all around him after her death. Was it not as if her spirit now wanted to enfold him – now everyone else had deserted him? Was it not her ghost which now, all the voices of love around him having fallen silent, came down to be the only one to call to him through the night: I love you! I love you!

The ghostly haze came nearer and nearer; the Colonel's gaze followed it with melancholy yearning, and almost unconsciously he held out his arms to it. Then it was suddenly caught by the stormy wind – the outstretched arms were torn from the ethereal body, and the white cloud was carried away over the tops of the towers in a wild, flaming tangle, as if in a terrible dream. The heavens were empty. The Colonel put his hand to his breast – it was empty there. Several deep sighs forced their way up from its depths. At that bitter moment, someone approached with a gentle tread – an arm tucked itself into his; a hand was placed sympathetically and tenderly on his hand, and he felt a head gently rest on his shoulder. He did not turn round – he did not ask – he knew that *she* was close to him now, the one who had shared joy and pain with him for so many years. Only she could have any notion of his hidden suffering – could come to him in the silence of night with comfort and love. He quietly put his arm around his life's companion, and held her close to his breast, where both the spiritual and the physical pain soon

196

eased. The couple stood there for a long time, watching the storm pass over the earth and chase the clouds. Not one word of explanation was spoken, nor one word of apology. What would have been the need? *Reconciliation* enfolded them in its heavenly bosom. They stood, heart against heart, and were *one*.

The storm, growing fiercer by the minute, beat its raging wings against the bell on the tower, which had just struck twelve. A dull tolling could be heard. The Colonel pressed his wife closer to him as an involuntary shiver ran through her at the sound. She looked up at her husband. His eyes were motionless, fixed on a single point and hers, following them, grew still as she too stared.

On the road, which from this side could be seen stretching away for a considerable distance, a black shape was moving, growing larger and assuming an ever stranger form as it advanced towards the house. In the moonlight one could soon make out that it consisted of a number of individual people, some of them grouped together in a strange formation as if somehow joined, moving forward rather slowly but all together. Several men seemed to be carrying something heavy with great care.

'It is a funeral procession,' whispered her Ladyship.

'At this hour! Impossible!' replied the Colonel. The dismal crowd drew ever nearer. Now they were entering the grounds of the house. The wind tore at them, scattering dead leaves over them and taking with it several hats from the heads of the bearers, but none left the group to retrieve them. The procession made straight for the main house. It mounted the steps ... so slowly, so carefully; there was a hammering at the front door – then all was silent and still again for a moment – the door opened and the procession entered the house. Without saying a word, the Colonel moved from his wife's side, swiftly left the room, locking the door behind him, and ran downstairs. The

197

bearers had put down their burden between the pillars in the entrance hall. It was a stretcher. A dark cloak was draped over it. The bearers stood around looking uncertain and dejected.

'Who is it you have there?' asked the Colonel in a voice he was clearly trying hard to keep steady. No-one answered. The Colonel went closer and lifted the cover. Through the high Gothic windows, the moon's rays came streaming in and down onto the stretcher. A bloody corpse lay there. The Colonel saw that it was his son. A father's pain! Angels of Heaven, cover your smiling faces with your wings; do not look down on a father's suffering! Dazzling lights of the firmament, go out, go out! Come, dark night, use your sacred veils to hide from all eyes this mourning which has no tears, no words. Let no inquisitive look from a human eye ever desecrate a father's suffering! Noble and wretched father! As we saw your eyes fall on your son, we averted ours – but you had all our most fervent prayers.

The arrival of the tragic tidings had brought all the servants, and me, running; we stood silently assembled around the stretcher. At a gesture from the Colonel and the words 'A surgeon', everyone leapt into action. A messenger departed at once for the town to fetch a skilful surgeon known to the family, and the lifeless body was lifted from the stretcher and carried into another room. Those who carried him shed tears over their dear young master's body. The Colonel and I followed the slow, sorry procession. I dared not look up at him, but could hear the deep, almost wheezing sighs, with which he was labouring to breathe.

When the body had been laid on a bed, we began urgently, albeit without much hope, to try all the means normally used to bring round the unconscious and even the apparently dead. His feet were stimulated, his chest, temples and wrists were massaged with alcohol. Blood was still trickling from a wound in his head; this was bandaged. As I busied myself with the feet, I darted an anxious and inquiring look at the Colonel – but looked away quickly with a shiver. His colour was that of death – a spasm had contracted and contorted his features. His lips were compressed, his eyes glazed.

All at once I felt a sort of slight tremor run through the stiff limbs under my hand. I hardly breathed – it happened again – I looked up at the Colonel once more.

He held one hand clamped to his chest, but extended the other to his son's mouth. He took my hand and placed it there – a slight exhalation of air could be felt. A faint pulse could be discerned at the temples, a sigh – the first greeting of reawakened life – made his chest rise, and some slight colour came back into his face. The Colonel looked up to the heavens! With such an expression! Oh joy of a father! You are worthy of being purchased with pain. Angels of Heaven, look down with radiant eyes on a blessed paternal heart! That is a sight for you.

Now the sleeper's eyes opened and were reflected in his father's gaze, resting on him with the clearest expression of agonized joy; the eyes looked for a moment, and gently closed again. In alarm the Colonel put his hand back by his son's mouth to feel whether the breathing had weakened; then the pale lips formed themselves into a kiss on the father's hand, and an expression full of peace and reconciliation spread across the young man's face. He still lay motionless with eyes closed, like someone asleep, his breathing faint but easy, and made no attempt to speak.

Once the sensible and tender Helena was seated at her brother's bedside beside me, the Colonel went to see his wife; he motioned me to follow him, and I ran up the stairs, pinching my cheeks so I would not look like death's messenger. Her Ladyship was sitting quite still, hands clasped, looking by the light of the moon not unlike the pale spirits of ages past, who

199

were staring down at her all around in a silent family circle. When we came in she said, quietly but anxiously, 'Something has happened! What has happened? Tell me ... tell me everything!'

With admirable calm and infinite tenderness, the Colonel prepared her for the sight which awaited her, trying as he did so to offer her a sense of comfort and hope which was certainly greater than his own. Then he took her to the sickroom. Without saying a single word, without uttering a sound, without shedding a tear, the unfortunate mother went over to her son, who was now looking closer to death than shortly before. The Colonel stood at the foot of the bed, still maintaining his strong, manly composure, but when he saw his wife gently lay her head on her son's bloody pillow, and kiss his pale lips with such an indescribable look, expressing a mother's whole love and pain, the unusual similarity of the two faces intensified by the shadow of death – then he bowed his head, hid his face in his hands, and cried like a child. Ah yes, we all cried bitterly. It seemed to us that the spark of hope which had gleamed just now would go out – and no-one believed the mother would outlive the son.

And yet – earthly sorrows, corrosive pain, sharp swords, which penetrate the depths of the soul – you do not kill. The wonderful seed of life can find sustenance in sorrow itself – can, like the polyp, be cut to pieces and grow back together again, and continue to exist – and suffer. Mourning mothers, wives, brides, daughters, sisters – female hearts, always the more deeply affected and wounded by grief – you bear witness to that. You have seen your loved ones die – believed you would die with them – and yet live – and cannot die. But what am I saying? If you live, if you can resign yourself to living – is it not because a breeze from higher realms has sent comfort and strength into your souls? Can I doubt it, remembering you, noble Tilda R***, grieving bride of the noblest of men. You were there to hear his last sigh – with him, you had lost everything on Earth – your future was dark and joyless – yet still you were so resigned, so mild, so kind, so good! You cried – but said consolingly to sympathetic friends, 'Believe me – it is not so hard!' Then we understood that there is comfort beyond what can be given on Earth. And when you said, in an effort to distract yourself from your suffering, 'I do not want to worry him with my grief,' who could doubt that *he* whose happiness you wanted to preserve on the other side of the grave was near you, and surrounding you with his love, comforting and strengthening you:

'And there appeared an angel unto her from Heaven, strengthening her.'

Patient sufferers, I salute you! You reveal to us God's Kingdom on Earth, and show us the way to Heaven. We see everlasting roses sending up shoots from the crowns of thorns on your heads.

But I must return to the inconsolable mother, overpowered by the first, unexpected blow of misfortune. She recovered – but in order to undergo a long period of trial – for her dear one's life hung in the balance for a long time. She herself lacked the strength and resources to give him the proper care. If Helena had not been there, if the Colonel had not been there, and if (though I hate to say it) I had not been there, then ... but we *were* all there, and so (by God's grace) the Cornet stayed – alive.

In times of sorrow and distress, our souls are drawn closer together. When external misfortunes come raining down on us, we unite, and it is usual for a watering with the tears of affliction to produce the finest flowers of friendship and devotion. Within the family, a common misfortune usually obliterates any little conflicts and differences of opinion, focusing everyone's minds and interest on a single point. Particularly when death

201

threater.s a loved family member, all discordant notes in the family circle are silenced; only harmonious feelings, albeit sorrowful ones, move every heart, colour every thought, and form a poppy-wreath of tranquillity, in which the beloved invalid nestles and finds rest.

After Cornet Carl's accident and during his illness, all the unpleasantness and tension in the H*** family disappeared; all the attention, feelings and thoughts were united around him; and once his life was out of danger, once he began to get well – everyone felt so intensely the power of their love for each other – and felt such an indescribable urge to make each other happy – and was afraid to cloud the clearing skies in any way at all.

It was truly touching to see ... but I have no idea what is making me want to be so very emotional today – and make my readers cry over my grief and joy – as if there were not enough unnecessary tears shed into the cup of sentimentality – or as if I had myself become nervous and frightened at the H***'s. So let us pay a flying visit to the D***'s, and see if more fun is to be had there. By the power of my magic wand (the most miserable goose quill on earth), I go now to transport us, that is my reader and I, instantly to

Lövstaholm

It was lunch time. All the seats at table were occupied. There were bowls of punch on the table, and toasts were being proposed.

'By Jove!', said a voice (which the reader may recognize), 'I just have a fancy to drain my glass again by drinking a toast to Miss Eleonora!'

His peony-red, bright-eyed neighbour gave him a friendly warning, 'What will Julie H*** say about that?'

'Julie H***? By Jove, I care very little what Julie H*** says … Miss Julie must take care her caprices do not get her into trouble. One of these days, by Jove, I might decide to send back her engagement ring … oh yes!'

'A toast, Arvid,' shrieked Lieutenant Ruttelin, 'To all free men!'

'And their brethren!' shrieked little Lord Byron. 'I meant girlfriends,' he whispered to Eleonora, 'But it didn't fit – because of the rhyme, you see.'

'Well, it is of little consequence to me,' she answered.

'Lieutenant Arvid! Lieutenant Arvid P***, I have the honour to drink your health!' cried the host, Mr D***.

'And I, and I, and I!' added other voices.

'Refill your neighbour's glass, Eleonora!'

'Gentlemen! I propose a toast to Lieutenant Arvid's betrothed … that she may come to her senses and see what is good for her – and take him back …'

Chorus

'Yes, that she may …'

A voice

'Gentlemen … by Jove … gentlemen – that is something which bothers me very little, by Jove. I have a great fancy not to take *her* back – I … but … but to … well, to send back her ring … by Jove!'

Chorus

'A toast to all free men! To Lieutenant Arvid!'

'And to girls without caprices; a toast to Eleonora and her sisters,' cried Mr D***.

Chorus

'To them! To them!'

203

'And their merry men!' added little Lord Byron with a grimace.

Tea and supper

Just now I had the honour of seeing my readers at a little lunch: I shall now request the pleasure of their company at a little supper. No, no, do not be alarmed! Nothing big or grand, not like paying one's respects to his Excellency *Ennui*, nor will it mean the torment of having to stay awake until gone midnight.

I have set a small, round table in the little blue room at Torsborg. In the middle of the table, Helena has put a large basket of grapes, and wreathed it with asters, stocks and other flowers which still had some colour in the pale rays of the autumn sun. Spread around this brilliant crown of Bacchus are those simple dishes we hear about in the story of Philemon and Baucis, and indeed in every idyll where supper is mentioned. So I will not waste any paper on milk and cream and lists of other pastoral dishes.[1]

But I think her Ladyship would never forgive me if I failed to mention a dish of honeycombs, oozing their aromatic liquid, and a large tart (which she herself helped to make) filled with plums – light and delicious and more delicate than one can ... although the Colonel said he had a heavy feeling in his stomach after trying a little bit – but (as her Ladyship rather disappointedly said): 'You never know what is weighing people down sometimes. Gentlemen have so many strange ideas.'

---

[1] Oh mercy me! I have just remembered that when Baucis had unexpected guests, she ran and sacrificed her only goose for their delectation. And I – having *invited* my supper guests – can offer them neither goose nor calf nor turkey! I could die of shame!

At that moment, for which I ask my gentle readers' attention, her Ladyship finished trying to polish away a blemish on the stopper of a water carafe, deciding after five attempts that it was a defect in the glass itself and therefore, regrettably, immovable. In the room, softly lit by a lamp, Julie (without her engagement ring), Professor L., the tutor and his disciples gradually assembled. Finally, Cornet Carl came in, supported by his father and Helena, this being the first time since his fall from the horse that he had joined the family circle in the evening. Her Ladyship went to him with tears in her eyes, kissed him, and would not rest until she had seated him on the sofa between herself and the Colonel, comfortably resting on soft cushions, which she even tried to pile up round his head, where they could only have stayed with the help of winged cherubs. Thus the Colonel was able to observe with secret satisfaction and a few laconic exclamations of 'Oops!' how the cushions went tumbling right and left. Her Ladyship insisted the Colonel was blowing them down. When she had them more or less as she wanted them, she sat quietly watching her son's pale face, oblivious to the tears running down her cheeks. The Colonel observed her for a long time with a mild and earnest look, until his expression made her aware of herself, and she mastered her emotions so as not to disturb her dear invalid's composure.

It was sweet to see the little Puddings, with hungry looks and open mouths, carrying to their sick brother the tasty things Helena was serving up at the table, and how incredibly hard it was for them to hand over each plate. Julie knelt beside her brother, selecting the largest and choicest grapes from a dish she had placed on the sofa, and giving them to him.

I had a fancy to ask Professor L., 'What is that book you are reading so earnestly and attentively?' He would either have replied, 'Julie', or else been rather embarrassed and turned to the title page, which would have looked extremely suspicious, at least – as far as his reading of the book was concerned.

There was something quite unusual in nearly every look in the little company that evening – a sense of expectation, of animation, something, in short, like the sparkle in children's eyes on Christmas Eve as they await the arrival of the straw Christmas goat with their presents.

Only Cornet Carl was dejected and quiet, the dull, indifferent look in his eyes giving expression to a joyless heart, and although he responded in a kind and friendly way to all the endearments being heaped upon him, there was something so melancholy in his very smile, that it brought fresh tears to her Ladyship's eyes.

The tutor, meanwhile, was trying to catch someone to play chess with him. More than once he had set up and rearranged all the chessmen on the board, and had coughed at least seven times by way of a signal that prospective opponents could report to him. But since no one came forward willing to do battle, he himself went off on a crusade to encourage any challengers. Professor L., the first to see himself under threat of being challenged, buried his nose so deeply in his book that the tutor felt too discouraged even to try him, and turned to Julie – who flew off to the far end of the room. Next he prowled over to Helena – but she was so busy serving the food – then he headed straight for me with a determined expression.

I said, 'I must just go and see whether the moon is shining tonight.' (It was the last night of the waning moon.)

Finally, with a deep sigh, the poor tutor caught sight of the little Puddings, who were just getting to grips with the tart, and exhorted them to 'Eat up!' as he intended to show them the moves of chess.

The Colonel, who was blowing on his tea and watching the comings and goings in the little company with a smile, now raised his voice and, with unusual emphasis on each word, said:

'I heard it mentioned today that our neighbour, Lieutenant Arvid P***, is said to be seeking (and indeed finding) consolation with Miss Eleonora D*** for a certain other young lady's fickleness.'

How Julie blushed! Professor L. dropped his book on the floor.

'I think,' continued the Colonel, 'That it could turn out rather well. I believe Eleonora D*** is a sensible girl who knows what is what and sees the best in other people. Arvid P*** is a good match for her, and she a good match for Arvid. I wish them every happiness!'

'So do I!' said Julie under her breath, and crept up to her father, delighted at finding in his words approval of the breaking off of her own betrothal. She looked at him for a moment with an expression of mingled hope, joy, affection and doubt; but as his face, full of fatherly kindness, continued smiling back at her, she put her arms around him and gave him more kisses than I could count.

Professor L. put his arms around himself (presumably feeling the need to hug someone) and regarded the attractive pair with a look ... oh, a look can sometimes speak volumes!

'Get me a glass of wine, Beata!' called the Colonel – 'I want to drink a joyful and joy-bringing toast. A glass of Swedish wine, of course!'

(Dear reader, it was berry wine he meant – made by me. Forgive my little boast.)

I poured the Colonel some wine.

'To you, my son Carl,' he announced, beaming.

At that moment the marvellous and melodic sound of a chord played on a harp rang out from the next room. It was as if an electric shock ran through everyone on the room, and everyone's eyes somehow lit up. The Cornet wanted to leap to his feet, but was restrained by his father putting an arm round him, while his mother, alarmed by the obvious depth of his emotion, sprinkled him with more eau de cologne than was affordable or pleasant. This chord on the harp was followed by another, and another. And then, like the scents of a spring morning, an enchanting stream of pure and lovely melodies came pouring forth, rising and falling with such sweetness and reaching deep into each heart, with such beneficial effect one felt an angel's fingers were touching its strings. A young female voice, pure, clear and sweet, at first trembling but then ever surer and so delightfully expressive, sang:

> Recall the hour, in which your heart
> Another heart did find,
> Love's flame then burned with all its art
> With happiness entwined.

> It was so sweet, it was so bright;
> The whole world seemed so fair;
> Each thought to Heaven took its flight
> With gratitude and prayer.

> Then came an hour, in which we heard,
> Our souls apart must dwell,
> We spoke that bitter, painful word,
> A trembling '*Farewell*!'

> Farewell – all joy the Earth can store,
> Farewell – that was our plight!
> My friend, you lost. Now grieve no more,
> For all is set aright.

> The one you love is near again,
> And whispering, delighted,
> 'I shall be yours, and we shall then
> Forever be united!'

And what did the Cornet do in the meantime? A whole firework display of joy and delight flashed in his eyes. His feet shifted, he stretched out his arms; but restrained by the arm, the plea and the look of his father, he could not get up from the sofa. His urgency abated a little in the course of the song; a sense of quiet bliss seemed to take possession of his soul, and he looked up to the ceiling as if he could see Heaven open.

Her Ladyship, who had gone out during the song, came back in when it was over, holding by the hand the enchanting singer – the angelically lovely Hermina. The Colonel got to his feet and advanced to meet them. He embraced the captivating creature with a truly paternal affection, and introduced her ceremoniously to the assembled company as his fourth, beloved daughter.

Now no-one must reproach the Cornet for not having jumped up immediately and fallen to his knees before his beloved. He simply could not. The transports of delight which came over him were too much for his weakened powers – and he briefly fainted as he saw the beloved creature, whom he had believed forever lost to him, entering hand in hand with his mother. This time her Ladyship emptied the entire contents of her eau de cologne bottle over him.

When he opened his eyes again, they met Hermina's, which were gazing at him full of tenderness and tears. The Colonel took the hands of the two lovers and brought them together. The family formed a circle around the happy pair. No word was spoken, but the looks, the smiles, full of love and happiness – they are so much better than words!

'But how? But what? But why? But when? But what went ... how did it come about?'

I shall be honoured to present, in a methodical and orderly fashion as befits a family adviser, my

Explanation

When a jelly has almost cooked long enough, you add egg whites, to (as the technical term goes) clear it.[1] In the same way, when a novel, a tale or some other literary concoction of that kind is approaching its culmination, you finish it off with an explanation or interpretation, to clear the cloudiness; and this often has many of the characteristics of egg white in that it is sticky and binding, clear and clarifying and relatively flavourless.

I can already see faces being pulled at my egg white chapter, and I too feel a little uneasy and anxious about it, as I always do about sticky things, and I think it would be best not to write it down in my own words, but to let my readers into a conversation which took place one fine November afternoon between Mrs D*** and Mrs Mellander, who was like a gossip column and advertiser for her, and indeed for the whole district. But to make sure my readers are not misled by the mistakes and speculations of those two ladies, I will (unbeknownst to Mrs M.

---

[1] The reader may be pleased to recall that her rise, or her success, was achieved or cooked up by means of a wine jelly. As a gesture of commemoration gratefully owed to this progeny of the hartshorn, she will now serve it up for dessert.

and Mrs D***) put a prompter on the stage, that is, a breath of the spirit of truth, which whether it blows across the field of world history or through the smallest chink of a door in domestic life, is an important and always dearly bought auxiliary or guide. What is more, unlike those employed by our Royal Theatre, my prompter prompts not the actors, but the audience, to keep on the right lines. But to business:

The scene takes place at Lövstaholm, in Mrs D***'s boudoir.

(Mrs D*** is sitting having her afternoon coffee. Enter Mrs Mellander.)

Mrs D***

Well, my dear Mrs Mellander, well at last – welcome! ... I have been waiting at least half an hour. The coffee is almost cold ... I shall have to ask for it to be heated up ... .

Mrs M.

Heavens no! Your Ladyship my dear ... cold or hot, it will do for me.

Mrs D***

(pouring a cup)
Well, Mrs Mellander, well ... what news?

Mrs M.

Well, your Ladyship my dear, now, thank goodness, I have found it all out ... another lump, if I may ...

Mrs D***

Then tell me, do tell me. I have heard that our little forest bird over there – Hermina – has been taken in by the H***'s like a child of the family ... and that she and Cornet H*** are betrothed, and that there will be a wedding at the earliest opportunity.

Prompter

They must wait three years, Colonel H*** says. The Cornet must travel first and see the world, and Hermina (so her Ladyship says) must learn about rural Swedish domestic economy – and that will surely take her three years.

Mrs M.

I thought I heard someone speak nearby; are we alone?

Mrs D***

No Christian soul can hear us.

Mrs M.

Well in that case I shall tell you, your Ladyship my dear, a dreadful story ... but listen ... I do not want anyone saying that I told you this ...

Mrs D***

No Christian soul shall hear of it.

Prompter
(whistles)

Mrs M.

Well then! It happened like this. In the beginning, the present Baroness K*** was married abroad to a Swedish nobleman, called Stjern- something ... and they had a daughter ... none

212

other than that pretty young thing Hermina. Neither father nor mother cared much about her – for they wanted a son, you see – and the girl apparently had a bad time of it at home. Anyway ... meanwhile, Baron K*** comes to those parts ... Italand ... or whatever the place is called, and sees the beautiful lady – Hermina's mother ... and falls helplessly in love with her, and she falls helplessly in love with him. Her husband finds out ... there is a terrible scene at home, and a fight between the two gentlemen.

Prompter

A duel!

Mrs M.

The sum total of it all was that Baron K*** had to leave the country. He came back to Sweden and for a time lived an ungodly life, gambling and fighting, so that his affairs got in a dreadful state. Then one day he finds out that the beautiful lady's husband has died down there – and promptly sets off, thinking to get himself a beautiful wife, and with the beautiful wife the money to pay his debts. Anyway – he proposes to the widow – she accepts – marries him on the quiet, and thinks she will be forgiven afterwards by her old father – but he (a rich and distinguished gentleman) is furious and disinherits her. So the newly-weds haven't a farthing to live on abroad. Well – then they simply up and come here – and at the same instant, the trading house in which Baron K*** allegedly had all the rest of his fortune invested goes bankrupt – and he had creditors at him from all sides – and had to hide himself well away from them, which was why he lived in the little house over there in the wood and would hardly see even a cat or a dog – and if people happened to come, he was like an angry bull, really nasty – and cross with his wife, thinking she had lured the people there. Yes

213

– it seems to have been an unhappy and miserable state of affairs …

Mrs D***

But how did young H*** come to be there?

Mrs M.

God only knows! I just could not find out … but there he was – and the two youngsters fell in love. And at virtually the same moment, the rich and handsome young property heir G*** comes along and falls in love with Hermina too.

Mrs D***

It is quite incomprehensible! The girl is not even pretty … no *fraîcheur*, no colour.

Mrs M.

Indeed! What is she beside the sweet Misses D***? Like a radish between beetroots.

Mrs D***
(huffily)

I expect … you mean roses.

Prompter

Peonies.

Mrs M.

Yes – that is exactly what I mean … naturally. Where was I? Ah yes! Well … young H*** meanwhile went away and was gone all summer, and our young property heir was constantly at K***s buttering them up. Then one fine day he proposes – and what do you think? Hermina will not have him – flatly refuses. Well, there was apparently a big fuss with her parents.

Mrs D***

The girl always did strike me as ridiculously romantic.

Mrs M.

By the autumn, all Baron K***'s creditors are at him again, wanting to have their money or see him in jail. You see, your Ladyship my dear, the thing is, they say he secretly spent the summer in Stockholm, gambled and won, and managed to maintain his household and keep his creditors at bay for a while. But all at once, his luck changed, and he was in dire straits. Then he swore a solemn oath and told young G***, 'Pay me ten thousand crowns at once – and you shall have Hermina for your wife.' And he answered, 'As soon as she is my wife, I shall pay you the sum on the spot.' First the Baron tried to bully Hermina into saying yes. But failed. Then he went down on his knees and begged her, and the Baroness did the same – and the girl cried and just said, 'Give me three more days!' Her parents were against it, but had to give in; and she used those days to write to Cornet H***, telling him to hurry home ...

Prompter

Not in so many words.

Mrs M.

... pay the money, and take her as his wife.

Prompter

That is *not* what she wrote.

215

Mrs D***

The scheming creature!

Mrs M.

Just so! Anyway ... the Cornet comes home, quite beside himself, tries to get the money from his father, who ... says no ...

Mrs D***

Yes, yes, they always did say the old man was mean. Anyway, I know the rest. Father and son had an argument. The Colonel's wife joined in; ... they said some very silly things to each other ...

Prompter

Wrong!

Mrs M.

Yes, it turned into a real old family row. The Cornet rode off in despair ... reached the house in the woods, found K***s gone, went raving mad, rode around all day, and finally met an acquaintance and threw down a challenge.

Prompter

Wrong!

Mrs D***

Yes ... and was carried home to his parents in the middle of the night, taken for dead. But where had the K***s got to?

Mrs M.

It's like this. Some people came down here, absolutely determined to pin down Baron K***. Then he and the Baroness so besieged Hermina with entreaties – that she was nervous and

216

frightened enough to agree to everything. The young heir spoke to the creditors and promised to pay them within a few days. So then he took Hermina to Stockholm, intending the banns to be read once and for all the following Sunday, with the wedding taking place straight afterwards. Everything had to be done in secret and in a great hurry because everyone, especially G***, was afraid of young H***.

Mrs D***
But why did the wedding never take place?

Mrs M.
Well, because Hermina became ill and went half mad, like that Clamentina in Grandson (a novel, you know, your Ladyship) – she was well on her way to ending her life.

Mrs D***
What godlessness!

Mrs M.
Then her mother was worried and sent for Colonel H***, with whom she was previously very well acquainted, apparently ...

Prompter
Wrong! Wrong! Wrong!

Since of the three speakers it is the prompter who appears to have the best idea what is going on in the play (no doubt because he has the script in his hand), let us allow him to step forward alone on the stage and try to explain things himself, as he has been shouting so capably at other people for getting it all wrong.

My dear Ladies and Gentlemen, it is like this: Hermina's mental anguish, with which she had been struggling for so long, really did induce a kind of quiet delirium during those critical days, and all those around her were frightened. Genserik G*** found out in Stockholm what a desperate state K***'s affairs were in, and became acutely aware of Hermina's aversion to him, so he withdrew from the scene and disappeared rapidly, without anyone knowing where he had gone. Baron K*** soon realized that nothing could save him from ruin, and decided to run away – and his wife decided to go with him. In that hour of hopelessness, a new star rose for the unhappy couple. They came closer to each other – they cried together – the veil of oblivion was spread over the past – they promised to support one another on the difficult path – their former love was reawakened and made them aware that, if they kept its fire alive, they might have some happiness even in the depths of wretchedness. The Baroness's heart, its ice seemingly melted by suffering, bled for Hermina, and shuddered to think of her fate: roaming the world with her unfortunate parents, defenceless, destitute and wretched. One evening she sat watching the girl, who lay sleeping quietly, beautiful, pale, worn out by sorrow and mental suffering; she felt her heart being torn apart and, swallowing her pride, took up a pen and wrote as follows to Colonel H***'s wife:

'A desperate mother appeals for a mother's compassion. Within twenty-four hours I shall be leaving Stockholm and fleeing Sweden. I cannot and will not take my daughter with me. I do not want to see her at the mercy of wretchedness – for it is wretchedness that awaits me. Your admirable character, the goodness I have myself seen in your face, has given me the courage to turn to you with my entreaty ... (If only you heard it spoken by my own trembling lips – saw in my breast the torn and contrite heart of a mother – then you would grant my prayer): take – take my child into your house, into your family! Have compassion and take her! Take my Hermina under your protection – take her as a lady's maid for your daughters – Marchese Azavello's daughter may at least be considered good enough for *that*. She is weak and ill now – weak in body and spirit and cannot do very much ... but be patient with her ... Oh dear! I feel myself becoming bitter – and – I ought to be humble! Forgive me! And if you will deliver me from despair – then hurry – hurry here like a consoling angel, and take my pitiable child in your embracing arms. Then I shall bless you and pray for you; and how I wish that you may never experience a moment as bitter as this.

Eugenia A***. '

The Colonel's wife received this letter a few days after her son's accident. She showed it to the Colonel. The couple immediately travelled to Stockholm – and returned with Hermina, whom they treated with fatherly and motherly affection from that moment on. In the atmosphere of peace and love that surrounded her, Hermina soon bloomed, and became as beautiful as she was happy.

Exit prompter, making way for Beata Workaday, who looks as if she has something to say.

Few people relish the silent roles in the theatre of life. Everyone likes to take a turn in coming forward and saying something, even if it is only, 'My name is Peter', or 'My name is Paul, look at me! Or listen to me!', and as I, Beata Workaday, do not want to do myself the injustice of appearing more modest than I am, I will now step forward and say, 'Listen to me.'

Baron K*** and his wife left Sweden very quickly. They set course for Italy, where the Baroness wanted to make one more attempt to mollify her father. They expected to struggle on their journey with all the disgusting details which want and poverty can cause, but it turned out quite otherwise. At several places on their journey they were aware of a wholly inexplicable courtesy on the part of total strangers. In various towns they found sums of money waiting to be collected in their name – a good angel seemed to be following them and watching over them. The Baroness wrote of these events in her letters to her daughter. 'It is all my husband's doing,' her Ladyship told me one day, beaming with pride, affection and satisfaction. 'K*** was his enemy when they were young – and did him many wrongs. Although they have not seen each other since that time, I know my husband has never forgotten it – for he cannot forget – but this is his form of revenge ... He is a noble person – God bless him!'

And I said 'Amen!'

The final trick

In August 1830

Mrs Bobina Bult, widow of the late Dean, sat in her trap keeping a firm grip on both reins and whip. All around her, well packed in hay, were a quantity of provisions in bags and casks – in the midst of these her good friend C.B. Workaday.

220

The August evening was mild and fine, the road good, the horse in fine fettle, but even so, the prospect of making good progress looked slim – for in front of Mrs Bobina there was a young peasant lad driving an empty cart, and he seemed to have set himself the challenge of trying her patience. This he did by keeping pace with us and preventing us from overtaking, keeping right whenever we moved out to the right, and keeping left whenever we tried to pass on the left, so that he was always directly in front of us. Throughout all this he sang, at the top of his voice, songs that we found most offensive, and often looked round at us with a sneering laugh. I looked up at Mrs Bobina Bult, for I am (God knows!) a small woman, and she is tall and upright and solid as a mast tree, and I noticed how her lower jaw was jutting out in that way which I know means she is angry, saw her chin and the tip of her nose going bright red and the small grey eyes shooting arrows of indignation. We had asked several times, more or less politely, for the boy to let us past – but in vain. Mrs Bobina bit her lip, gave me the reins to hold without a word, jumped down from the trap, strode briskly forward, and in no time was at our tormentor's side, grasping him firmly by the collar and dragging him down from the cart onto the ground before he could even think of offering any resistance. Then with the solid handle of her whip she administered several blows to his back, asking him meanwhile whether he wished to apologize and promise not to do it again, or to test the power of her arm a little further. Apparently he was already quite convinced of its unusual strength, for he quickly became humble and repentant, and promised whatever we wanted. Mrs Bult now permitted him to get up, and delivered a short but powerful sermon on penitence, the conclusion of which was so beautiful that it quite moved me, moved her too, and even the peasant lad, who dried his eyes on the brim of his hat. 'I know you,' added Mrs Bobina finally, 'You are from the parish of

Åminne; your father has been sick for a long time. You may come to me at Lövby tomorrow morning, Sunday, and fetch something for him.'

We could now continue unimpeded, but still had to stop a few times along the way. At one place we helped an old woman who had overturned her cart; in another the widow got down and with great difficulty freed a pig, which had entangled itself in a fence and was uttering shrill squeals of complaint which pierced us to the heart.

As the sun set, we saw its rays greeting Lövby. Small columns of smoke rose like corkscrews from the chimneys of the little houses, dispersed into the clear evening sky and merged into a slight, translucent haze, which hung like a rose-coloured canopy above the village. With its neat cottages, green gardens and clear, chattering stream it made a pretty sight as we slowly drove down a gentle incline, which soon extended two arms, one of which led us to our home, about fifty paces from the village.

The cows were coming home in long lines from their grazing ground to be milked, lowing placidly to the clanging of their bells. Horns were sounded. The peasant girls sang their calling song in clear and strident tones, and these sounds were joined by the 'ding-dong' of the church bells, bidding their Saturday evening goodnight to the week and heralding the day of rest. Mrs Bobina Bult's expression grew glad and solemn. Everyone greeted her with friendly respect, and she had a friendly greeting for everyone. When we reached our little school, the children came swarming out of the house with loud exclamations of delight, and hugged her in a frenzy of enthusiasm and affection. Endearments and ginger biscuits were distributed to them all.

Mrs Bult's time was now taken up with a multitude of tasks. One of the maids had just taken her finished cloth from the loom, the other had just set up hers; the widow must look at both.

A farm-hand had cut his leg; Mrs Bult would have to bandage it up; an ill little boy who lived nearby could not settle (so his mother said) until he had seen Mrs Bult. A devoted couple had fallen out and had a fight – Mrs Bult would have to arbitrate between them, and so on, and so on.

First of all, Mrs Bobina spoke to all her pupils, said prayers with them all, cried with a little one who was very sorry for some serious misdemeanour earlier in the day, gave a warning to another, praised a third, kissed and blessed them all, and then went about her duties outside the house. By the time the clock struck eleven, she had bandaged the cut, first lectured the couple and then made them settle their differences, comforted the little boy, and more. Then she returned, looked at the weaving, gave orders for the work and the household for the following day, quickly ate two potatoes with a little salt, and went off to the other end of the village, where a sick and unhappy mother was waiting, to whom she would be able to give the joyful tidings that her children had been diverted from the paths of vice.

I meanwhile sat in my room. In beds around me, four little girls, all with rosy cheeks, were sleeping peacefully on snow white sheets.

The calm and beautiful August night, so warm that I could leave my window open, the silence and repose around me, the light breathing of the sleeping children had a delightfully peaceful effect, awakening in me that quiet sense of melancholy which spreads calm over the present and often wafts towards us memories of our lost years. The moon, that friend of my childhood and youth, rose and looked down through the birch trees into my room in a pale and friendly way. Its light crept across the children's closed eyelids, stroking them, and then shone quietly on a face faded by life's daylight – on a breast, full of emotions which the years had yet failed to still. How wonderfully all the dear, sad and happy memories of my past life came floating on those kindly rays – how vivid they were as they emerged from the night and penetrated to my heart, how warm and alive! All the people with whom I had come into contact during my life, and who had become dear to me or been important to me, seemed to want to gather round and renew their influence with words and looks. The H*** family, from whom I had now been parted for nearly a year, came so close at that moment that I felt I could talk to each charming member of the family, ask them how things were at home – whether they were happy, whether they still remembered me? Yes – did they? For I had not had the least sign of remembrance from them for a long time, not a line, not a word. A childishly anxious feeling of having been forgotten – of not really belonging to anyone, after all – of in fact meaning so little – so very little – to those one respects and loves – took hold of my heart for a moment. I had to cry – and was still sitting there with my handkerchief over my eyes when Mrs Bult, who had seen me at the window from out in the courtyard, came in. She questioned me gravely, like someone who truly wants to know, and I humbly confessed my weakness. She reproached me emphatically for it, admonished me and kissed me, maternally and affectionately, and told me to go to bed at once, and for her sake preserve my health, which had been failing for some time.

She left me – but I did not obey her straight away; I struck a light, lit my candle, and sat down to write moral memoranda – to myself. As I sat there, I heard the clock strike twelve and half past. Then there was some noise downstairs, and at once someone came running up to my room. My door was opened quietly – and the late Dean's widow Bobina Bult, in nightcap and slippers, stood there with a bedcover round her shoulders, eyes sparkling with satisfaction and a fat letter in her hand, which she gave to me. 'From H***s! From H***s!', she whispered. 'I did not intend waiting up any longer for the messenger from town ... but just as I was going to bed, I heard him coming. I had a feeling! Good night! Good night! God grant you joy!' And Mrs Bobina Bult was gone.

And joy I had. Julie's letter read as follows:

August 13th 1830

It is a little clergyman's wife who is writing to you. For two months I have no longer been Julie H***, but Julie L. I could not bring myself to write before. For some time I have been feeling so nervous and frightened and unable to think clearly. Reasons: first the awful reverence I felt for my dear husband – yes – for a while I really did not know what to do with my admiration for Professor L., my feelings of inferiority, and my precious vanity, which on no account wanted – how shall I put it – to feel I was critical of Julie H***. And then – blessed rural domestic economy! Cows and sheep and eggs and butter and milk etc., and a great flood of little things – and then Mama, who was so worried and wanted to help me, but ... well – gradually everything fell into place quite wonderfully. The Little God with the bow and arrows helped me. My dear L. was even more eager to please me, I think, than I him – and he was and is, praise be to God, very much in love with me. Once I saw that, I had no more worries – I took heart. Cows, calves and hens thrived, there was a new fire burning beneath our household's great pot – and Mama calmed down, thank God. And my husband – well of course he was content – because I was content with him.

Beata, do you know what I pray morning and evening, in fact constantly, from the bottom of my heart? 'O God, make me worthy of my husband's love, give me the power to make him happy!' And I have been given great power – for he is (so he says, and it shows) very happy. If you knew how healthy he looks, how pleased! It is because I keep him in order, you see, he is no longer allowed to mistreat himself as he did before, and also – he no longer sits up at night – he has given that up. Yet even so he thinks and writes (he admits it himself) more freely and powerfully than before. Moreover, I am very careful not to interfere or disturb him when he is in his study writing and reading. Oh! ... When I really want to see him for a moment (for he is handsome Beata, after all) I creep in quietly, do some little thing for him, like putting a flower in his book or kissing him on the forehead or suchlike, and then go out again quite silently, but always, just as I turn to close the door, I catch a glimpse of his eye, which had surreptitiously been following me.

Otherwise I am working on training myself to be a truly admirable pastor's wife. I want people to be able to say that as mistress of her house, L.'s wife is a model for the congregation. Do not think that all this is making me forget or neglect my little appearance, oh no! I often consult the mirror, but do you know which mirror I best like to consult? Yes, the one I see in L.'s eyes. It is such fun to see oneself *en beau*.

Oh Beata! It makes one feel so noble to be united with a person one respects and reveres, and who is also so good! As Arvid's wife, what sort of non-person would I have become, what sort of non-life would I have led? Now I know, with heartfelt joy, that I am rising every day in my own and my husband's estimation. It is a glorious feeling – rising!

Did you know that Arvid has got married – more than three months ago? His wife, Eleonora D***, looks far too wide-awake – and he looks, one might say – only barely cheerful. I am afraid that his peace and quiet have been rather disturbed. Poor Arvid! The young couple give grand parties and the like, however. Old P*** drives past here nearly every day (on

226

purpose, I am sure) with his horses, the Swans, and his daughter-in-law in the fine landau, and goes very slowly, as if he thought it was a funeral procession for my happiness – but I feed my ducks with a glad and carefree heart, nod amiably to Eleonora, and thank the Good Lord for my lot.

It is Saturday evening. I am expecting my husband home. I have laid our little supper table in the bower outside my window. The meal consists of asparagus from our garden, lovely wild strawberries and milk, L.'s favourite dishes. The angelic Hermina Linnæa is just decorating the table with flowers. No one can believe how beautiful, how good, how indescribably charming she is. She has almost ousted the rest of us from our parents' affections – and we are only too willing to forgive her. Ah, brother Carl, you have found a real pearl. He will soon be leaving the shores of the Mediterranean for his beloved North, where he will be reunited with the pearl of his life and enclose her in the shell of matrimony. Ugh! Where did I find that oppressive image? But let it stand. As long as the sun of love shines into that mother-of-pearl dwelling, it will bob along on the river of life like a little Island of Happiness. Carl writes such amusing and interesting letters home. His soul will be like a museum; Hermina will live among its treasures. It really will be like a pearl set in gold. Do you know what happened to my brother before he left us? One evening he went to sleep – a cornet and awoke – a lieutenant. Was that not excellent?

Tomorrow my dear parents, brothers and sisters are coming to dinner. It will be a day of rejoicing.

I have told you how happy I am, and yet there is one more thing I wish quite badly which, if it were granted, would make my happiness brim over. My good friend, here in our house there is a little room, attractive and comfortable, with green wallpaper and white curtains (just how you like it), with a view

227

over meadows where fat cows, who give the most wonderful milk, lazily graze. In the room there is a bookcase, a ... but describing it takes so long! Come and see it, and if you like it, and believe you can put up with your hosts – then – call it yours. My dear friend, come to us, do come ... Now I can hear L. approaching from a distance. He is coming into my room. I shall pretend not to see or hear him. We must not spoil our husbands and let them think that we listen out for their footsteps. Yes ... cough ... put your arms around me, ... I shall not move, not let go of the pen. One need not always give in; one must not spoil one's ...

(*L. writes*)

wife; and for that reason, Julie *must* give me the pen and, seated on my knee, watch me write something that will make her cross: Our good friend Beata, come to us! We await you with open arms. With us you will be sure to feel at home. Come and see how I keep Julie in check. To give you a taste of it right away, she shall not, however eager she is, write another word today.

I *want* to wri...

14th August

I am crying, I am laughing, I am quite beside myself – yet still I must write. Do you know who is here? Who came just now? Guess, guess! Oh, I have no time to let you guess. Emilia is here! Good Emilia, glad Emilia, lovely Emilia – happy Emilia! And Algernon is here, and little Algernon! The most splendid little boy on earth. Mama is dancing with him, Papa is dancing with him, Emilia is dancing, Algernon is dancing, L. is dancing ... wait, wait, I want to come and sing, and cannot write another word, as true as my name is

Julie

P.S. Beata, do come back to us, we beg!

*The H*** family*

You kind and happy family, I thank you – but Beata will not come. I shall write and tell them tomorrow. Innocent children, slumbering around me, I shall stay with you, because I can be useful to you. Foregoing pleasure often brings satisfaction of a higher kind – brings *peace*. Oh, if I may only feel *that*, as the quiet waves of each day roll on, monotonous but calm, carrying me closer to the silent shore – then each day shall be blessed.

The mists of night are rising from the meadows, heralding the dawn and urging me to rest. A chilly vapour is rising up the slopes of my life too – when it draws nearer, I shall write once more, and bid farewell to the H*** family.

Afterword

Those expecting to find in Fredrika Bremer's *The Colonel's Family* (Swedish title *Familjen H****) a pedestrian early-Victorian tale of domestic life are in for some surprises when they read this remarkable hybrid novel. Firstly, it was written in a time of literary transition, when the novel genre was in its infancy and fighting for status. It has often been termed Sweden's first bourgeois novel; its fully-observed psychology, everyday realism and humour were something quite new. Secondly, it is a novel which should not be taken purely at face value, as recent research has shown, not least Birgitta Holm's fascinating and iconoclastic monograph *Fredrika Bremer och den borgerliga romanens födelse* (Fredrika Bremer and the birth of the bourgeois novel), published in 1981 to coincide with a new edition of this classic but underrated work.

However, Birgitta Holm warns us, quite justifiably, against seeing *The Colonel's Family* only as an epoch-making event, a milestone in Swedish literature; for then, she says, the text ceases to communicate. In this context, it is encouraging for a translator to feel that she has a role to play in rediscovering the nuances of that text and making it accessible to the modern

231

reader. The nineteenth-century translations are, in any case, long since out of print.

The Colonel's Family was one of Fredrika Bremer's first published works, and appeared in two parts, along with some shorter pieces, in 1830-31 as parts II and III of what she called *Teckningar utur hvardagslifvet* (Sketches of Everyday Life). Having embarked on her writing career at the age of about thirty, anonymously and diffidently, she was gratified to find that she not only got paid for her writing, but was also awarded a gold medal by the prestigious Swedish Academy for the volume containing the first part of *The Colonel's Family*. The book became, albeit briefly, the talk of the town, and had to be reprinted.

In an autobiographical note written some years later, Fredrika Bremer (somewhat disingenuously perhaps) claims that she wrote the book in the hope of raising a little money for the country people living near her family's country residence, and was pleasantly surprised to find that she had produced something which was successful in its own right, and also even humorous. She wrote: 'The kind of humour which is found in "The H. Family" had been quite alien to me until shortly before that, and it was an unsuspected discovery within me.' There are further clues to how she wanted herself to be seen in relation to the literary establishment of the time in a fascinating passage intended to preface Part 2 of *The Colonel's Family*. It is missing from the published version, and no explanation of this change has been documented, but the text is preserved in a letter to a friend. Like many of the section headings in the book, it bears the name of part of a meal:

First Course

In the great salon of Literature a grand ball was taking place. To the strains of a full Orchestra, they were dancing Minuets, waltzes,

232

anglaises, Quadrilles, as well as solos and ring dances, when along came a little dilettante, and saw the gleaming light and heard the joyful noise — but had no admission ticket, nor did she try to force her way into the party, but remained diffidently outside the door, and executed (with cheerful heart) a few *Assemblées*. A large and splendid Gentleman passed by, smiled encouragingly and said, 'What a nice little thing!' and gave her a coin. The little one cried out in delight, 'Oh, now I see the time has come to get myself an admission ticket!'

The little dilettante, who can be seen as representing women writers in general and Fredrika Bremer in particular, must simultaneously be true to her own creative urge and appeal to the gentlemen of the Establishment. Birgitta Holm concludes that, had it been included in the book, this allegory would have announced to the educated public that henceforward, untrained jumps of joy and freedom dances [women's writing] would have their place alongside the traditional quadrilles [the literary canon].

There are many indications in *The Colonel's Family* that Fredrika Bremer had to duck and weave in order to produce a novel which was acceptable to public taste yet did not compromise her own aims and artistry. The many culinary metaphors, for example, are a public announcement that she is happy to stay within the domestic sphere, but at the same time they are part of the novel's metafictional layer, in which Beata Workaday, the ingenious narrator never surpassed in Bremer's later work, yet whose very name seems designed to reassure that she will make no exceptional or threatening claims on the world, analyses the act of writing in terminology appropriate to her supposed station. Thus making a wine jelly becomes a metaphor for writing a novel, and the novel is at times served up like a dinner, with chapter headings such as 'A little of everything, all stewed together'.

The domestic realism of Fredrika Bremer's early novels was one of the main features to endear her to the reading public. Her depictions of family life were perceived as warm and uncontroversial, and her didactic tendencies were 'forgiven' because they were not overt. Typical of this attitude is a lengthy introduction to a somewhat dubious 1849 English edition of early works, in which the anonymous translator, possibly working from a preface originally in German, seeks to review Fredrika Bremer's *œuvre* and characterizes it as pure, harmless and instructive. The preface continues:

Her labors are directed to the emancipation of women — an emancipation of the most perfect, real and essential kind, namely that of manners; it is not so much the selfishness, the injustice, the tyranny of man or his yoke, which she exerts herself so strenuously to break, but is rather the selfishness, the restraint, the vanity and folly of the female heart, the tyranny of prejudice and conceit, of inherited errors, and of all-powerful habits.

So virtuous and innocuous are Fredrika Bremer's works perceived to be that the preface writer, echoing the general view, considered them suitable for all:

Mothers may offer these writings to their budding daughters, as a gift whose value is not subject to a change of fashion, but which, even after long use, preserves its beauty as well as its intrinsic worth. Not only are these fictions, as appears from their very face, unobjectionable, pure, and bright in morals, but they are so judiciously arranged, and while far from prosaic, are still void of fantasy; on the contrary, are so practically useful, that they may, without the least hesitation, be placed in the hands of a refined young lady.

This kind of critical reception, both in Sweden and abroad, quickly led to a stereotyped view of Fredrika Bremer's work, and the critics were swift to condemn any perceived straying

234

beyond familiar territory. In the case of *The Colonel's Family*, these tensions surfaced particularly in relation to the character of Elisabeth, Colonel H***'s niece. Contemporary critics and subsequent literary historians have found it hard to swallow her rebelliousness, her unrequited (?) love for her uncle, the destructive effect of her thwarted ambition, and her descent into blindness, madness and death. Her part in the novel has repeatedly been dismissed as melodramatic and hysterical. The anonymous preface writer cited above, for example, described Elisabeth as 'certainly a very original character, but one so distorted, that we would much rather suppose her falsely drawn than according to life, we mean, faithfully represented.'

Now, in the light of more recent research, we can appreciate how Fredrika Bremer was attempting through Elisabeth to open a debate on the problems of the frustrated, silenced woman and of repressed passion in an age when self-discipline was a high female virtue. Indeed, a closer reading of the book shows that not only Elisabeth but also Emilia and Julie are in effect anti-heroines, resisting the stereotypes of romantic fiction. Emilia and Julie both marry, but only on their own terms, and after airing their grievances about nineteenth- century marital conventions.

In fact, the thwarting of readers' romantic expectations and the teasing of 'young lady readers' who live on 'feelings and the scent of roses' is an important component of *The Colonel's Family*. The abruptness with which such expectations sometimes founder and the abandonment of the realistic first-person narrative perspective which Fredrika Bremer often employs in the process are doubtless among the factors which have caused uncomprehending critics of various generations to complain about her weakness of composition and wilful shattering of the illusion of reality. This is perhaps most memorably done in the passage in which Beata, trying to write about Cornet Carl falling in love, describes how she has to fight off a horde of rose-tinted cherubs who invade her room and almost confuse her into writing sentimental romantic nonsense. She will have none of it, and also on numerous other occasions undermines the romantic potential of the Carl and Hermina sub-plot, furnishing them with blatantly two-dimensional theatrical scenery for a lakeside encounter, skipping over their sweet nothings because, she claims, her publisher has given her a strict word limit, and causing Carl to become embroiled in a series of farcical delays at Lövstaholm when all he wants to do is pursue his beloved to Stockholm. Fredrika Bremer's critics have often added to their accusations of compositional weakness the claim that she was incapable of writing a love scene because it did not lie within her personal experience, but she stated in various letters and essays that she wanted to escape from the conventional stranglehold of insipid romantic fiction to explore other questions. What she achieves with Carl in *The Colonel's Family* is certainly more interesting, as Marie-Christine Skuncke, expert on the social history and drama of the period, has pointed out. Skuncke and others have also rightly stressed that *variety* is the keyword here, not only in the Carl episodes but in the novel as a whole. The reader cannot fail to be struck by the amazing eclecticism of style, spanning the picaresque, the sentimental idyll, domestic realism, comedy and farce, and a sometimes surprisingly modern experimental prose. The use of everyday language and attempts to imitate the broken patterns of everyday speech are, for example, quite remarkable. In genre terms, it is quite unstable and unnerving, shifting (though sometimes quite seamlessly) from prose to verse to drama and back again. Some critics have viewed the result as a mishmash of styles, incoherent and chaotic, falling apart into a realistic Part 1 and a weak, romantic Part 2, while others have seen the variety as a virtue, the oscillation between high and low life as positively Shakespearean. In Birgitta Holm's words, many traditions are assimilated into *The Colonel's Family* as functional elements of an aesthetic whole. Holm has also pointed out that this blend of the trivial and the sublime was familiar to Fredrika Bremer's contemporaries and so was more acceptable to them than to the modern reader. It was in any case a common trait among those embarking on writing careers at that time to begin by parodying or satirizing the romanesque novel. This is as true of Fredrika Bremer as of Walter Scott or Jane Austen.

It is true that, at times, the book gives the impression of having been put together in rather a hurry. The close reading required by translation reveals, rather endearingly in my view, some rough edges and sloppiness on the author's part. Themes are introduced and not developed, unlikely strategies are adopted to cope with the confines of Beata's narrative perspective, and in places Bremer seems to have settled for weak and implausible links between sections rather than bother to rewrite a paragraph or two. Of course, we must remember that the manuscript was sent to the publisher in instalments, as with many of her works. This method of working is not conducive to consistency or concise writing.

Nevertheless, Fredrika Bremer does set out a clear literary programme in *The Colonel's Family,* usually interpreted as a manifesto for poetic realism. She lets Beata state this directly, once she has banished the rose-tinted cherubs of romanticism. The much-quoted passage in question likens reality to a clear brook, faithfully reflecting any object, and the author (or artist) to a ray of sunlight lending the reflection a more vivid gloss (p.133).

Like many novels of the period, *The Colonel's Family* also finds room for a contribution to the heated debate on novel-reading itself. This occurs at Emilia's wedding party, when the conflicting views of Julie and an elderly uncle on the vices and virtues of allowing young ladies access to novels prompt a lecture from Professor L. in defence of the genre. Provided that such books show virtue getting its true reward, he says, they can act as useful moral and emotional maps to guide young people into adult life. Several guests disapprove, believing women need only read their Bible and their cookery book, but Fredrika Bremer tactfully breaks off the debate at this point by serving the wedding breakfast. As Kate Flint points out in her recent study *The Woman Reader 1837-1914* (1993), it was extremely common in the mid-nineteenth century to assume 'the susceptibility and moral fragility of the woman reader', and Fredrika Bremer gives the impression of being well aware of the folly of alienating the moral guardians of her most important customers, her dear young lady readers. It was only later in her novel-writing career, notably in *Hertha* (1856), that she was confident enough to become more outspoken on issues which today we would term feminist. Even in *The Colonel's Family* we can see that she lets Beata, behind her safe façade of prosaic house-keeper, deviate from the norm of the educator-narrator by encouraging the young female characters to release their pent-up feelings, and by covertly siding with non-conformity.

It is interesting to see how Fredrika Bremer's own literary experiences make themselves felt in her first novel. Her upbringing coincided with the blossoming of romanticism in Sweden, but she also had the heritage of Gustavian literature, Schiller's classical poetry and the work of the Swedish poets Franzén, Tegnér and Anna Maria Lenngren. Some of her greatest literary encounters were with heroic historical dramas and novels such as Schiller's *Don Carlos*. She also devoured Walter Scott, particularly *Ivanhoe,* and Richardson's *Sir Charles Grandison* at this time, and both have left their stamp on *The Colonel's Family*. In the character of Algernon there are clear echoes of Richardson's attempt, stated in his preface, to present in Sir Charles 'the Example of a Man acting uniformly well thro' a Variety of Trying Scenes, because all his Actions are regulated by one steady Principle.' Fredrika Bremer also admired Goldsmith, and there are certainly some parallels between her book and *The Vicar of Wakefield*, not least their status in their respective national literatures as important forerunners of the novel proper.

The first English translation of *The Colonel's Family* did not appear until 1843, but the early novels were not translated in order, and this time lapse was by no means typical. At the height of her popularity abroad, Fredrika Bremer's novels were almost instantaneously translated into English and German, sometimes with the embarrassing consequence that the foreign editions were published first. Initially, English translators adopted the dubious practice of working from German editions, as did Mary Howitt, who eventually became Fredrika Bremer's semi-official translator, having taught herself Swedish. Through their collaboration, *The Colonel's Family* has a place in the history of publishing. Alarmed at the number of cheap, bad translations of the book, including pirate editions, which were flooding the market in Britain and the USA, Fredrika Bremer and Mary Howitt became jointly involved in the campaign which led to a new international copyright law in 1848.

Mary Howitt and her husband William were Quakers, who started a number of literary periodicals and enjoyed introducing new authors, especially from Scandinavia. Hans Christian Andersen and Fredrika Bremer were among their successes, which is perhaps surprising in view of the linguistic errors, misinterpretations and artistic compromises which recent research has found in their translations. Their daughter even wrote of Mary Howitt in a letter some years later: 'It also seemed to me that she could have possessed no adequate Swedish-English dictionary, from the manner in which Fredrika

239

Bremer became a Lexicon'. If one's initial reaction to this is to be appalled, one's second must be to salute her achievement in producing quite readable translations under such conditions. Working on my own translation, I have often felt very close to Mary Howitt, although I always resisted the temptation to consult her version.

Fredrika Bremer remained loyal to her translator despite suspecting in later years that the latter's work was mediocre. Some of their correspondence while collaborating on the translation of the later novels has survived, revealing repeated instances of 'improvements' suggested by Mary Howitt in order to impose her own puritanical moral judgements on Bremer's work. A new, close translation of *The Colonel's Family* is needed for the end of the twentieth century not only because the existing ones by Mary Howitt and others are out of print, and riddled with errors and Germanisms, but also because it will act, in Peter Newmark's words, as 'an instrument to expose the inaccuracies of published translations which have long distorted their originals by consciously or unconsciously burdening them with their translators' prejudices.' I hope that a fresh translation will, like the restoring of an old master, clean away the gloomy Victorian varnish and show this exciting, exasperating novel in its true colours.

I would like to thank Helena Forsås-Scott and Karin Petherick for their invaluable help with many linguistic queries.

S.D.
October 1994